D1736328

MIRACLES

a novel

Sono Ayako

Translated by Kevin Doak

Wiseblood Books

Wiseblood Books
P.O. Box 870
Menomonee Falls, WI 53052

Printed in the United States of America

Set in Baskerville Typesetting
Cover Design by SILK Studio

Fiction / Japanese Literature

ISBN: 978-1-951319-80-9 *(Paperback)*
ISBN: 978-1-951319-81-6 *(Hardcover)*

Wiseblood Books

BENEDICT XVI
+INSTITUTE+
FOR SACRED MUSIC AND DIVINE WORSHIP

CONTENTS

Sono Ayako (b. 1931) is one of postwar Japan's most prolific writers. In spite of her prominence in Japan, only two of her works have been translated into English (*No Reason for Murder* and *Watcher from the Shore*), and both are already out of print. She may well be the most undeservedly overlooked (in the West) of contemporary Japanese writers. My hope is that this translation of her work *Kiseki* ("Miracles") will help to redress that injustice. *Kiseki* was first published in thirteen installments from January 1972 to January 1973 in the *Katorikku Gurafu*, and later published as a single volume by Mainichi Shimbunsha in May 1973. It was published again in 1977 by Bungei Shunjū in the inexpensive paperback series *Bunshun Bunko*, and reprinted at least six times by 1992. It was also included in the hardback collection *Selected Works of Sono Ayako II*, volume 4, published by the Yomiuri Shimbunsha in 1984.

There are several reasons for selecting *Miracles* from Sono's extensive *ouevre* for translation now. First, in his 2006 critical summary of *Miracles*, Philip Gabriel called this work "a minor classic" in Japanese literature. As Gabriel describes it, "*Miracles* is an exploration, from Sono's Catholic viewpoint, of the nature of and possibility for miracles. It is also a meditation on the nature of self-sacrifice . . . [that asks] some basic, yet compelling, spiritual questions: What are the spiritual effects—both on the person involved and on others—of self-sacrifice? Is the miraculous possible in our day and age? And what are the possibilities of faith's being a real part of ordinary, everyday life?"[1] Gabriel's positive assessment of *Miracles* led Roy Peachey, writing in *The Catholic Herald* ("Britain's Leading Catholic Newspaper") to explicitly call for the English translation of Sono's *Miracles* to correct the imbalance in what we know of Catholic literature, which has been mainly limited to the work of Western writers.[2] Finally, interest in miracles, which has never disappeared from mainstreams of intellectual inquiry, is enjoying something of a renaissance today among academics and even in popular culture.[3]

It will come as a surprise to many to learn that Sono became interested in the main subject of this work, Father Maximilian Kolbe, through Rolf Hochhuth's play *The Deputy* (translated into Japanese in 1964 by Morikawa Toshio as *Kami no dairijin*). Hochhuth and his 1963 play *The Deputy* have been largely discredited for unfairly portraying Pope Pius XII as complicit in the Holocaust, for Hochhuth's own anti-semitic remarks, and particularly after the 2007 allegation by Ion Mihai Pacepa that Hochhuth wrote his play based on an outline by General Ivan Agayants, chief of the KGB's disinformation department. Sono would not have known about any KGB link or Hochhuth's later anti-semitic remarks when she read the work in the 1960s. Her inspiration from this unlikely source is, however, a good reminder of how readers can appropriate texts for purposes different from what may have been intended by those who produced them.

Sono has recalled that she was deeply moved by Hochhuth's portrayal of Kolbe as a priest whose life and death were deeply

---

1. Philip Gabriel, *Spirit Matters: The Transcendent in Modern Japanese Literature* (Honolulu: the University of Hawaii Press, 2006), pp. 48-49.

2. Roy Peachey, "Move over Greene, Waugh and Belloc," *The Catholic Herald* (April 30, 2010), p.9, http://archive.catholicherald.co.uk/article/30th-april-2010/9/move-over-gree-newaugh-and-belloc (accessed June 5, 2014).

3. Cf. Steven Justice, "Did the Middle Ages Believe in Their Miracles?," *Representations* 103 (Summer 2008): pp. 1-29; and in American popular culture, the glossy November 15, 2013 issue of *Life* titled *Miracles: The Presence of God in Our Lives* (volume 13, no. 20).

redolent of the modern condition. Drawn to know more, she went to Poland and Italy in 1971 after the conclusion of the PEN meeting in Ireland to research Kolbe's life and the miracles attributed to him after his death. She was thus also able to attend his beatification ceremony at the Vatican on October 17, 1971, and even includes a scene from Kolbe's beatification in *Miracles*. Fact and fiction are hard to distinguish in this work, and Sono takes advantage of the Japanese literary tradition of the "I-novel" (*watakushi shōsetsu*) that effectively blends the genres of fiction and non-fiction. Only in March 1973, months after the work first appeared in print, did Sono identify some of the characters in it as real people: Father S, the man who in the novel inspires the protagonist to undertake the journey to Europe, we find out was Father Sakatani Toyomitsu, OFM Conv (1935–2006), who was at the time editor of the *Katorikku Gurafu* that first published *Miracles* in serial form. She identified Father O as Father Tadeusz K. Oblak, SJ (1922–2006), a priest who helped her during her travels in Poland. She also identified her Italian interpreter, Mr. S, as Suekichi Sakae. And of course, in making these identifications, Sono collapsed *ex post facto* any wall between fact and fiction that the reader may have presumed from the tradition of the I-novel while reading the work.

In the same 1973 postscript, Sono made a personal confession about the effect her travels in search of the miracles attributed to Father Kolbe had on her:

Since returning from my trip to collect materials for this story, I was completely liberated from my earlier feeling that somehow I wanted to avoid making public the fact that I was a rather marginal Christian. I had come to understand in a personal way the rather prosaic point that to have faith is not what the world generally takes it to be (that it makes someone a "good person") but rather that it is only through the concept of God that one can explore without any limitation one's mental state and behavior, whether they be good or bad.[4]

Years later, in 1982, Sono remained strongly enough under the influence of the remarkable story of Father Kolbe to publish an illustrated book, *The Tale of Father Kolbe.*

The second best way to appreciate the significance of *Miracles* is to listen to Sono's own summation of why Kolbe's life lesson moved her so deeply: "If we take up this dangerous aesthetic (that we must come to the aid of others even if it kills us) it will cost us something . . . But if we do not take up this hard and dangerous aesthetic, we may find that we never really lived in this world."[5] The best way, of course, is to read the work itself.

---

4. Sono Ayako, "Atogaki," *Kiseki* (Tokyo: Bungei Shunju, 1977; reprint 1992), p. 252.

5. Sono Ayako, quoted in Maeno Sotokichi, "Kaisetsu," pp. 405-410 in *Sono Ayako senshū II*, vol. 4 (Tokyo: Yomiuri Shimbunsha, 1984), at p. 410.

TRANSLATOR'S ACKNOWLEDGEMENTS

I would like to acknowledge the assistance I received in researching the names and events that appear in this work from the friars, staff, and archivists of Marytown, The National Shrine of St. Maximilian Kolbe in Libertyville, Illinois, and especially from Paul Szerszen, who encouraged me from the beginning to undertake this translation. I owe a debt of gratitude to Kate Weaver and Katy Carl for their excellent work in proof-reading the galleys, to Louis Maltese for his beautiful cover design, and to Joshua Hren and Maggie Gallagher for their support throughout. And I particularly wish to thank Mrs. Ayako Sono, whose gracious support and friendship has truly been one of the many miracles I have experienced throughout this project.

Kevin Doak

MIRACLES

a novel

Sono Ayako

Chapter 1

A Very Personal Preface

Section One

For as long as I can remember, I've thought a saint is like an old tapestry that, beautiful when bathed in a dazzling golden light, in reality is just a dry, tattered thing. From kindergarten on, I was educated in a school that was run by an order of Catholic nuns, and during our hours of recollection (a gathering at a set time and day for prayer and religious readings in silence) I read *The Lives of the Saints*, and that only strengthened my impression of what a saint is. Well, they were really just a bunch of stories, and I could never think of those saints as real, flesh-and-blood human beings.

One day I asked a friend whose entire family are solid Catholics, "What kind of person gets elevated to sainthood?"

"Apparently they require a miracle to have happened in the person's name, and even if there is a miracle, it won't count if it is not scientifically verified. So, it seems a reputable doctor has to say something along the lines of this patient was utterly hopeless but somehow recovered."

"That doctor couldn't be Catholic then, right? If he was Catholic, they'd think he was part of a conspiracy."

It was just two young girls conversing in lowered voices, as if talking about some sublime secret that they were not supposed to go anywhere near.

Even so, I still didn't believe in stuff like miracles. I liked to think I could be scientific—in spite of my bad grades in science class. Before I knew it, the Pacific War was on, and people often said things about the divine wind (*kamikaze*) protecting us and the land of the gods being immortal. But things don't always turn out as you hope, and the divine wind didn't protect us, nor was Japan immortal. Reflecting on it later, it seemed to me that Japan was defeated in an extremely rational way, *as if it had all been pre-arranged.*

Right after the war I was baptized a Catholic. I didn't become a believer after making a thorough study of the essence of faith. I just "surrendered" to the lives of the Catholic nuns who were my teachers. In their lives I witnessed what is called "practice without words." Japan had lost the war, and all our values and morals were overturned. No longer able to believe what they had believed up to then, the Japanese people were running around in utter confusion. At this time, I saw with my own eyes how these nuns had remained steadfast in keeping their lives focused on God.

That was a really unbelievably big turning point in my life.

In a word, that was the time when God came into my life.

Still, I was a fickle, common little thing, and since I lived in Japanese society there were times when I even thought it was shameful to think about such concepts as God. I worried that to believe in God was to be sunk in superstition, and to the extent I fell into it people would think me a fool. I even feared that if people knew I was a believer they would consider me stiff and inflexible. Even though it doesn't really make the slightest difference what others think—whether they take you for a fool or whether they think you stiff-necked—I was just like everyone else, unable to ignore what people thought, keeping my eye on prevailing winds.

Because I was weak, as the years passed I gradually fell into the pleasant habit of thinking that it didn't matter what I did as it was all God's providence anyway. Sometimes I would look back on the various circumstances of my life over the past several decades. What had kept me alive so far? There were several times when I almost died. From illness when I was young, and when I was older, during the war when our homelife was not particularly happy, I felt like joining my mom when she suggested we just commit suicide.

I always made some effort to live. But what kept me alive in the end was certainly not my own effort. At the last moment, I always looked like a mouse caught in a trap. Then, I would pull myself up and threaten God with "do what you want with me! I don't have any control over these things."

I cannot bring myself to utter such proprieties as "leave all things to God." I was always just rotten with infidelity toward God. You want to kill me, then kill me! If you want me to die, that has its advantages, too . . . But if you want me to stay alive and use me for some purpose, I won't fight it. I live only at your pleasure, so it is really all your responsibility. This was my mood at the time, and it really was just like being in a B-grade mobster movie.

In later years, I became acquainted with a Sister Odilia who ran a nursery in Nakano called the Odilia Home. Sister Odilia was a German lady who, with no thought of monetary matters, took in infants up to three years old whose mothers for various reasons were not able to be with them. There were at least two mothers that I knew who had gotten through major life crises by having Sister Odilia look after their babies. One was seriously ill, the other was going through a divorce.

Still a beauty in her later years, Sister Odilia once told me about a time when the babies all came down with the flu and one after another her nurses all suddenly quit, leaving her wondering what morning would bring. Even then, she remained confident that God would provide, and that's just what happened.

This became one of my favorite stories.

"That's right. There is nothing in the world that is not part of His plan."

I encouraged her to continue, all the while thinking how ugly the act of suicide really is. No matter what the particular reasons for it, suicide always contains an element of pride. To give one's own answer. Yes, there is an appearance of decisiveness about it, but I was repulsed by how little thinking was involved in buying into the belief that the conclusion that one—with all one's inherent limitations—

finally arrives at is the absolutely correct thing.

Nonetheless, when all is said and done, I did not believe that God gives us answers in the form of miracles.

There was only one time when I gave some thought to miracles. It was back when I was approaching my mid-thirties.

I had joined the staff of the Tokyo University literary journal *New Currents of Thought*[1] when I was still in my teens. There was a Mr. N among our group who suffered from chronic nephritis. When, at the young age of thirty-five, he announced to us that he was going to die, I first thought that maybe a miracle would save him.

Mr. N was a man from Tosa. With his thoroughly dark complexion, he was very manly, even a bit rough and uncouth, a man who knew a great deal of things from reading books. After graduating from Tokyo University in German literature, he joined the Shōgakkan publishing house where he rose to editor of children's magazines.

Mr. N was a ladies' man. He was actually so slothful that he was called one of the top three dirtiest men at Shōgakkan, but no matter how dirty the collar of his white shirt, no matter how foul his socks smelled, it only stirred up the maternal instincts of the ladies of the night. When he entered a military preparatory school right before the end of the war, he had great pride in his physical strength, but that pride was his undoing later when it was the reason he failed to take care of himself after the outbreak of his chronic nephritis.

Mr. N's face was often dark purple and swollen. On those occasions, he would offer, brightly, "Boy, I'm just beat." I myself didn't know anything about illnesses, just that people said that with chronic attacks the kidneys would be weak for life. But I didn't think at the moment there was any particular reason for concern.

When I was told that Mr. N's death was immanent, I was struck once again by the thought, "how cruel life is." Well, it might be more accurate to say I was scared out of my wits. They say cancer some-

---

1. *Shin shichō.*

times takes a course contrary to what medical science expects and symptoms which should have grown worse gradually improve and then completely disappear. But there are no exceptions for chronic nephritis—the patient just makes a bee-line for death. Here, I want to make it clear that everything I knew about Mr. N's disease was from around 1965. Today, of course, there would be much better methods than what was available then, beginning with the use of artificial kidneys. One night my husband came home and told me that he had heard from Mr. N's primary physician that they can get a very accurate read of when the time of death will be from charting the gradual increase in nitrogen levels in the blood along a draftsman's curve. When I heard this, I instinctively thought I'd ask for a miracle for Mr. N. I had heard stories from my friends about getting water from Lourdes (a Catholic holy site in southern France. They say its waters cure people who bathe in it or drink it) for those seriously ill and having them drink some. But Mr. N would only laugh at the idea if I suggested it to him. Mr. N must have known he would soon die, but given his natural kindness and in order to console us, he behaved as if it were the furthest thing from his mind.

I couldn't very well urge Mr. N to pray for a miracle without causing him to retort, "So, the grim reaper's coming for me, eh?"

In the West it is customary to prepare the patient to face death squarely. There, the relatives, who fear the death of the soul more than the death of the flesh, make sure early on that the patient is prepared for death. They provide all sorts of help so that one can leave this world in peace, offering Confession and the Sacrament of the Anointing of the Sick so that no matter when the end comes, each person can make his own spiritual accounting for his life. They do so because they know that nothing is more certain than death, and the value of all one's acts is determined by how one always faces death even while alive. They do not see death as something that shows up at one's bedside only when one is seriously ill, but as something that is always with us, with an intimacy that makes our everyday lives tedious.

But for Japanese, death is something "inauspicious," as we say. We only remember it when we go to someone's funeral, and when we get home we toss purifying salt at the entrance to our homes with some incantations that we hope will not only keep death itself but even the very thought of death away from our door. Not only that, but if someone's house is in a period of "misfortune," we consider it commonsense to "cut ties" with them until the period is over.

There was no way I could get Mr. N to confront death before he died. While I am a Christian, I am first of all just an ordinary Japanese person. I couldn't find an opportunity to blurt out to Mr. N stuff like "pray for a miracle." I myself couldn't believe in and pray for a miracle for him. And then, one winter afternoon, Mr. N—right on schedule—meekly submitted to human fate and died. He surely left behind much unfinished business in literature and in love. He was thirty-five years old.

Section Two

Ever since, I have considered myself to be someone who has nothing to do with miracles. I was deeply attracted to the miracles in the world of the Bible for literary reasons, but I was able to compartmentalize my thinking, telling myself that things like miracles just don't happen in these tedious, rational modern times. But soon I wasn't able to sweep things under the rug so easily.

It happened during the war at the infamous German concentration camp Auschwitz. The incident itself was not much. A Catholic priest named Kolbe saved a condemned man by taking on his sentence of death by starvation. Father Kolbe was at the time by no means a world-famous clergyman. And the man he saved was just a Polish sergeant. All the players in this drama were just humble commoners. But what took place there confronts us with something of great and profound import. I believe it was around the spring of 1971 when I first heard that the Polish priest who sacrificed himself for another, Father Maximilian Maria Kolbe, was beatified, or elevated to the ranks of Blessed. Blessed is a rank of the holy ones that is bestowed on certain virtuous people after their deaths.

"That means a miracle happened in Father Kolbe's name, right?" I asked Father S who had just told me the story of Father Kolbe, all the while recalling that secretive feeling from long ago when I first spoke to my friend about miracles.

"Indeed, that is what it means. In fact, the report of the investigation has already been sent to Japan. It's currently being translated."

Father S was a precise man who understood the mentality of ordinary people. Father simply looked at me as though he were waiting for me to make the next move, without applying any psychological pressure.

"Oh, how I'd like to know if something like a miracle really happened," I muttered under my breath.

"Why don't you go and see what actually happened? And if you wrote about what you saw there . . ."

"Maybe I should do just that."

I felt caught in the psychological net Father S had thrown.

At the same time, I was disgusted by how truly artless my interest in things was. It was nothing more than the foolish kind of curiosity seeker who goes rushing off to see a place where ghosts are said to haunt. . . .

In order to cover up what I was thinking, I asked, "In any event, who experienced the miracle?"

Father S had already prepared bait for my irresponsible curiosity.

"One was the Marquis Francis Luciani Ranier. This man lives in Rome. The other was a woman named Angelina Testoni, who lives on the island of Sardinia."

According to Father S, there were dozens of eyewitnesses in addition to the doctors for each of the miracles, and the record of their testimony before a kind of Church court had already been sent to Japan.

"Then, that means in addition to those who experienced the

miracles, I could actually meet all those who were there when it happened, too?"

"So it would seem. We know their names and addresses, and we should be able to help with making contact with those people, should you decide to go to Rome."

Father Kolbe was a priest in the Order of the Conventual Franciscans. So, if one goes to the Order's administrative center in Rome, one should be able to get a hold of all the investigations related to Father Kolbe's beatification.

If Father S had known that there was, at that very moment, something in the depths of my mind that for a second didn't trust him, he probably would have been thoroughly disgusted at how incorrigible novelists are. What I was thinking was "I suppose I should let him deceive me into going and having a look." Even if they say there are ten witnesses, one might doubt whether they are all real, existing people. I could imagine, in my cantankerous way, the awkward faces on those in charge when I ask to meet those witnesses.

Long ago, and for no particular reason, I had completely given up simply believing in things as they appear. I took as my excuse the idea that one cannot believe without first doubting.

Not long after, I received a copy of the Catholic Code of Canon Law from Father S. In it, I found the stipulations concerning the detailed processes and procedures for beatification. Article 2116 of the Code of Canon Law is as follows:

> 1. In order to be beatified a servant of God, in addition to heroic virtue or martyrdom, miracles which arise through the person's intercession are required. The term "servant of God" refers to all men. What the Church is saying is that even in our modern era that demands we adopt a scientific posture in all things, beatification still requires miracles.
>
> For proof of miracles, expert opinion from two authorities in the field must be presented at the opening of the deliberations.

If both agree in rejecting the miracles, the proceedings can go no further.

When, as is frequent in the case of discussions over a miracle, it becomes necessary to judge whether a recovery from illness has taken place, the expert witness must be a person of considerable reputation in medicine or surgery. In addition, one must select as far as possible, reputable specialists who have diagnosed and treated illnesses of the same type as that of the miracle in question.

It is not necessary that virtuous acts, martyrdom, or miracles be individually ascertained. A general verification will suffice. That is, it is enough that the rumor arises naturally and not through any artificial strategy or scheme, has its source in a sincere and honest person, and continues down to the present, increasing daily until it is shared by the majority of the people.

This was the first time in my life that I had in my hands a copy of the Code of Canon Law. As I let my eyes pass freely over the solemn provisions of the text, I began to feel that my doubts had run ahead of me a bit too far.

All I knew of Father Kolbe's life came from Maria Winowska's *Our Lady's Fool.*

This book was originally written in French in 1950 under the title, *le Fou de Notre Dame,* and the author Winowska won the annual prize that year from L'Académie française.

Maria Winowska was a Polish woman who seems to have shared much of Kolbe's terrifying experiences, although she has spared us the details. What we do know is that she saw with her own eyes the hunger, fear and death of that place that was designed to display the hideous monstrosity of Man, supposedly made in the image of God, utterly betraying his expectations—that is, the concentration camp. I think there can be no doubt that although she had once become disappointed in Man she was reconnected to a bright hope in the fact that in such a place a priest from her own country was able to die—not only without losing his humanity—but immersed in something we have to call the grace of God.

This was not by any means something that Father Kolbe chose himself. Rather, as Winowska writes, he happened to realize a very modern life and death.

To put it in my own way of speaking—my mode of expression always produces the nasty effect of dragging down nice things to a very commonplace level—this priest's death was, to an unbelievable extent, perfectly equipped with all the elements of our present times. Before he died, this priest flung a tough question like a red-hot iron rod at the dried-up soul of modern Man. The question was, "what does it mean for us to love one another?"

Around then, I had just published a collection of essays. In the preface, I had written something like "The proof of love is whether you are willing to die for that person." So, I was getting quite a few letters about that from my readers. There were some like "I think I love this guy but I don't think I would die for him" and "I don't think death alone is the epitome of love" and there were even some that thought I was darkly promoting love suicide or the notion that widows should follow their husbands to the grave.

The image of "dying for that person" probably belongs exclusively to the one who is perfect. I had simply omitted that person's name. It was Christ, the one who died on the cross for all mankind.

But if I had spoken it, I would hear from people that "I don't believe in any of that crap some legendary figure called 'Christ' did, so give me a break, okay?" If he wasn't a real flesh and blood man to me and if I wasn't sure of the existence of a man who was able to do that, I probably would never have had the courage to write that one line.

I was really thinking about Father Maximilian Kolbe. Father Kolbe confronted every kind of modern evil in the Auschwitz concentration camp, which the Nazis had set up as a horrific psychological laboratory with Man as the object of their experiments. I really think it strange how Father Kolbe, the founder of Catholic mass-communications, was by chance also in his death able to achieve a most journalistic death. When Father Kolbe was beatified, he introduced something new, not the ancient image of a dead servant of God wrapped in a golden, musty glory.

Father Kolbe's question strikes at the core of our being because it is still fresh even today.

"Would you die in place of one of these unfortunate ones?" "Can you wait patiently in the midst of pain and hatred for God's will to come to you on the wings of grace?" Occasionally I give lectures on Father Kolbe, and whenever these things come up I always reply in a low voice:

> To those of you who do not believe in God, I would like to present the death of this priest as a kind of aesthetics. Sometimes you even have to let them kill you if you want to save others. That was, for this man, a kind of pure aesthetics. And under these circumstances, he had to sacrifice his life for his aesthetics. It is only we humans who accept this kind of irrationality. Sometimes I sit back and reflect that when we embrace this kind of dangerous aesthetics it will only cause us harm. And at times it might even actually cost us our life. Father Kolbe was not one of those ten men originally chosen to die, so he could have rejoiced at his good fortune and left it at that. He would have been better off keeping his mouth shut and not stepping forward and dying for some stranger. But Father Kolbe's aesthetics wouldn't permit that. And it just might be that without such an intense, dangerous aesthetics, we would not be able to truly live in this world.

On September 21, 1971, I went to the Bourget Airport in Paris. I had just attended an international conference in Dublin, Ireland, in commemoration of the fiftieth anniversary of the International Pen Club, and I was exhausted after daily immersions in a foreign language that I had not heard for some time. In Paris I had done nothing but sleep for three days straight, and I was now on my way to Warsaw.

Bourget was completely overrun by Japanese tourists. By chance I ran into a certain reporter from the M newspaper. I still had thirty minutes before my departure, so we sat on a bench in the airport and I indulged in a quick and lively conversation in Japanese.

"Have you heard anything about how the Emperor's tour of Europe went down in Ireland or France?"

He was a member of the official press corps, which is to say that he had come to write an article about His Majesty the Emperor's European tour.

"No."

I replied, feeling a bit put out. While I was in Dublin, a Japanese had told me that security officers had died at Narita, but I didn't meet a single non-Japanese who even mentioned the name of His Majesty the Emperor.

"What takes you to Poland and Italy?"

When I had mentioned the countries where I was headed, he had given me a strange look.

"I'm investigating whether or not miracles really happened."

"I see."

It was as though he were fumbling for words in front of an utter stranger. Apparently, believing in miracles was now considered more absurd than all the fairy tales put together. But later on I discovered that a great many intellectuals unexpectedly were interested in this topic, even if they didn't believe in miracles. It only goes to show that in our actual lives we don't live in such perfect conformity with reason that we can drive miracles completely out of our heads. No, it appears that we accept a surprising degree of absurdity in our everyday lives.

But that doesn't tell the whole story. The tendency to believe in miracles stems from the same hope of mankind that longs for the eternal, the infinite, the absolute. Maybe we seek an awareness of those things, not simply as ideas, but as a shared sense of reality that we are not even conscious of. That would explain why even non-Christians did not react negatively to miracles.

Father Maximilian Kolbe was born in 1894 in the Polish town of Zduńska Wola near the industrial city of Łódź. I decided that before undertaking my investigation into miracles I would follow Father Kolbe's footsteps across Poland. This would take me from the village where he was born to the town where he grew up, to Zakopane near the Czechoslovakian border where he convalesced from tuberculosis while suffering from mental anguish, to his religious order's headquarters called Niepokalanów ("the garden of the Immaculate Mother"), and finally to Oświęcism, the place where Father Kolbe spent his final days, more widely known by its German name Auschwitz.

Poland was my first visit to a country in the communist bloc. I noticed there were no other Asians on the plane. And boy, what a strange trip I had gotten myself into! Even after hearing it over and over, I couldn't even correctly pronounce the name of the Polish airline I was flying on. While it is true that Polish is written in Roman script, they add phonetic symbols that mysteriously change the sounds. In short, since I didn't understand the linguistic rules, no matter how much I scrutinized the written words, I couldn't correctly pronounce the name of a single person or place.

How would I surmount these linguistic challenges? At first, Father S and I thought I could seek help from the Japanese embassy there. But that didn't seem possible. Later I found out that there was only one Japanese living in all of Poland (a teacher of Japanese), but that person was also working for some newspaper as a special correspondent so—I might have guessed—he was outside Poland at the time, covering the Emperor's tour of Europe. Poland was linguistically isolated from Japan in ways you just can't imagine. It seemed the only hope was to find someone in Berlin or Vienna who could speak both Polish and English, but we had no concrete way to go about that.

But, through an unbelievable coincidence, I felt I had been given an implicit command to get on with my work. Father O, a Jesuit who had spent fifteen years in Japan, was just then back home in Poland on vacation. But would it be okay to ask a priest on his hard-earned vacation to go to work for me? At first, this caused even me to hesitate.

Those who think in clichés are not always wrong. While there may not be something called "denominations" within Catholicism ("Catholic" means universal), it certainly contains many religious orders with their own different goals in labor, education, etc.

"Can one get the Jesuits to help with a Franciscan task?"

"Is it forbidden for them to help with such things?" Troubled by such thoughts at first, I gradually came to believe it would be no problem. And in fact, the Society of Jesus, in response to a request made by the Franciscan Father S, immediately issued a directive to Father O in Poland to give me all possible help in collecting sources that were in Poland.

On the plane, I pulled out Maria Winowska's book and started underlining all the proper nouns (place names and personal names) that I wanted to confirm in Poland, along with some passages that raised questions for me. And, in the midst of this kind of business reading, I was here and there mysteriously attracted to some words Father Kolbe had left behind.

In March 1938, Father Kolbe said the following words, which were written down by one of the friars. While the Spanish Civil War gives the impression that the Second World War began in 1936, Father Kolbe feared that what was coming was a different kind of battle, a crisis of the soul.

> I want you to know, my Brothers, that an atrocious conflict is brewing. We do not know yet what will develop. In our beloved Poland we must expect the worst.
>
> During the first three centuries, the Church was persecuted. The blood of martyrs watered the seeds of Christianity. Later, when the persecutions ceased, one of the Fathers of the Church deplored the lukewarmness of Christians. He rejoiced when the persecutions resumed. In the same way, we must rejoice in what will happen, for in the midst of trials our zeal will become more ardent.[2]

I wasn't really able to understand the meaning of this passage until some days later. In the plane, I just took these words as if they were Father Kolbe's last words. Had I accurately grasped in these words their prophetic, deeply hidden meaning, I would have trembled with fear. I don't think I could have drowsily tossed and turned with this book dangling from my hand.

I didn't get much sleep. I think I was awakened by that tall, healthy-looking, nonchalant stewardess who was passing out candy.

Warsaw already? I glanced at my watch and realized that Warsaw and Paris were a little over two hours apart. And there was no time difference.

As the airplane began its descent, I could see large, stone houses. Could those be farmers' houses? The houses were all large and well-built, and seemed quite cozy.

It may have been only my imagination, but the Polish horizon, far off in the distance, seemed tinged with a pale indigo color. In the

---

2. Citation is from Therese Plumereau's translation, Maria Winowska, *Our Lady's Fool: Father Maximilian Kolbe, Friar Minor Conventual* (Westminster, MD: The Newman Press, 1952), pp. 138-9. Sono cites the Japanese translation of Winowska by Takeno Keisaku, *Seibo no netsuaisha* (Tokyo: Seibo no Kishi Shūdōin, 1955). There are no significant variations between the two translations, other than the salutation "my Brothers" which in Japanese is rendered "my little children."—K.D.

midst of it, the sepia-colored earth spread out with quiet dignity. And above it, the brilliant colors of fall brushed the tree tops.

Chapter 2

The Blessed Mother in the Wilderness

Section One

I never imagined that the deep, solemn colors of the Polish autumn would be so enchanting.

My first stop in Poland was the monastic headquarters founded by Father Kolbe called Niepokalanów ("the Garden of the Immaculate Mother"), which lies forty kilometers west of Warsaw.

Father O and I rode the train a bit over an hour from Warsaw. The line was well-known as its trains link Moscow and Berlin. But the train we rode seemed to take its time at every station. Along the way, two middle-aged men wearing a mixture of uniforms and civilian clothes who were apparently employees of the railroad joined us in our four person compartment, pulled out a well-worn deck of cards, and started playing a game. Over in another corner of the car there was a young husband and wife. There was a big, round loaf of bread in their handbags above them in the luggage rack, and the soft autumn sun shone pleasantly on their shoulders.

The view from the train window was of a beautiful country landscape. The soil didn't look that fertile. To eyes accustomed to the rich, black soil of a temperate climate, the land in Poland looked gray. Those little bits of green that popped up every now and then were, according to Father O, potato fields—but they didn't look like potatoes to me. I thought to myself, "I wonder if Polish potatoes come in a different shape."

Finally, beyond the forest of trees that lined the tracks, a chapel steeple appeared. That was Niepokalanów.

The station was called Szymanów.

A statue of the Blessed Mother stood in the station plaza. We crossed the tracks and followed a broad tree-lined avenue that was nearly covered in the colorful autumn leaves. It was only a three-or-four minute walk from the station.

A tourist bus stood in front of the impressive sanctuary. There was an endless flow of tourists from all over Poland, especially now that Father Kolbe's beatification was near.

Here I met another unbelievably gifted linguist. It was Friar Henryk, a man who had been in Japan until 1945. Father O and Friar Henryk started chatting amiably in Japanese right in front of me. And then we all took off in the direction of the sanctuary that was built by Father Kolbe back when this entire area was still nothing but wilderness.

It was a small, quiet, simple sanctuary where you could almost hear the soul of the priest who was no longer with us. I guess the room was about sixty square meters in size.

The altar was made of wood, and in the farthest recesses there was the Sacred Heart of Jesus; in front of it, one could see the Immaculate Mother in blue, and in front of her, a crucifix. There were lots of heart-shaped ornaments called votum left at the side of the altar. They included shiny objects in the shape of arms, legs, and service medals. I was told they were presented by people as a sign of gratitude when their prayers were answered.

At six o'clock on the morning of November 19, 1927, Father Kolbe celebrated the first Mass in this sanctuary. It was here that the Franciscan friars, who called themselves "Knights of the Immaculata," first began their true work—proselytizing through publication. In short, Father Kolbe had conceived of the method of proselytizing through mass communications half a century ago. I noticed that there were photographs on the back wall of the sanctuary from when it was established that gave a good sense of what this land was like at the time.

They presented the spectacle of a frozen wilderness that was already half covered with snow. I say "wilderness" but I was told these were actually wheat fields. Judging from the photographs, as far as I could see, the plains were dark and cold and not the kind of place where a person would happily chose to live. Some poplar-like trees stood there silently, in contrast to the piles of lumber to be used in constructing the sanctuary. There was only one farmhouse in the pictures.

The only thing in the pictures that gave off any sense of warmth was the small statue of the Blessed Mother. It still stands at the entrance to the sanctuary.

It was the usual "religious spectacle." To have the Blessed Mother in the midst of the wilderness. We may call that the most decisive mental image of Father Kolbe's faith. If you will forgive my typically awkward way of putting things, what Father Kolbe hauled around with him his whole life was not the faith of ideas. It was based on a more sensuous, intense experience. One might say it was a deeply grounded faith, but more than that it was a predilection for the Blessed Mother who overflowed with warmth. It really was something closer to "love." The Blessed Mother was, for Christ, the perfect, the absolute. If we blindly follow the Blessed Mother, we will thereby perfect our fidelity to God.

How was Father Kolbe able to acquire this land? According to the written accounts, his methods in that matter were forceful and dramatic. He had wanted some new land for a monastery for some time, and when he heard this land would be put up for sale, he secretly placed a statue of the Blessed Mother in the land.

"Please take this land for yourself. It is just right for our work."

Let's review the many things Father Kolbe had been through before he whispered this prayer.

First and foremost, this Father Kolbe was a nuisance to the monastery from the day he returned home to Kraków after taking his final vows and being ordained a priest in Rome in 1919.

At any rate, he does not seem to have been very accommodating. Because his feelings were so pure, the *ordinary* priests found him unbearable. Father Kolbe suffered from tuberculosis, so he always moved slowly because his lungs weren't fully functional and because he wanted to avoid spitting up blood. But his thinking was perhaps a bit too strong.

For example, it was quite normal to be allowed to smoke in the monastery, but this unaccommodating priest stirred up problems by going around saying things he didn't have to—like how much money are you wasting on cigarettes?

Father Kolbe became the leader of the active proselytizing work called the movement of "the Knights of the Immaculata," which he started at Kraków, and while the work enjoyed a huge positive response from people outside the monastery, and membership steadily increased, it was held in low esteem by those within the monastery. "What is the proper monastic life? To quietly pray, preach, and hear confessions. Any other actions are nothing but backsliding!" Here we can see that the reaction against someone who tries to change an existing institutional way of doing things is no different in a monastery than in a regular corporation or bureaucracy.

In January 1922, Father Kolbe was finally able to print a report to communicate with friars who weren't able to attend the regular monthly meetings of the Order. That was the first issue of *The Knights of the Immaculata*. But within the monastery, the thinking was how can we restrain this "frivolous" mass communicating priest?

They had one good method to compel him to stop: don't give him any more money.

From an objective point of view, they had grounds. All of Poland was suffering difficult social conditions. In 1918, after the outbreak of the First World War, the Poles were liberated and Poland became a republic, but at the price of terrible inflation. There was a bad epidemic of the flu, and life was hard. In foreign affairs, they had to confront Soviet power; domestically, proletarian class warfare had begun against the political power that the landowning class monopolized. In such troubled times, wouldn't it be only natural to turn down this priest's "special hobby"?

Nonetheless, Father Kolbe started publishing the second issue. All those around him were cold to his *recklessness*. Really, where does he expect to get the money for that?

That's when the first miracle happened.

One day, Father Kolbe found an envelope on Mary's altar in the monastery. It was addressed to "my dearest Mother, the Immaculata."

Father looked inside and found money. The sum was exactly the amount he needed! He started to dance, he took it to the superior of the monastery and received permission to use it.

Now, even more undeterred, Father Kolbe set to thinking. He realized that his costs were high because he sent the printing out to professionals. If only we had a press, he thought, we could do the printing at practically no cost at all. So, Father Kolbe immediately began planning to buy a press.

Around that time, an American priest came to see Poland after it had been rehabilitated. He heard from everyone that Father Kolbe was a crazy priest who wanted to conquer the whole world with a cheap printing press. Father Maximilian "said not a word in self-defense and showed not the slightest sign of anger. Humiliated, he cast his eyes down and covered his mouth with a silencing hand."[1] But this American priest saw that what Father Kolbe wanted to do was anticipating (to use the language of that time) where the times were a-headed. Right then and there, he wrote out a check for a hundred dollars that he donated to the fund for purchasing Father's press.

With this money, Father Kolbe bought an old printing press from the Sisters of Our Lady of Mercy in Łagiewniki.

That was the final straw for the old friars in Kraków. They considered this fellow Kolbe as someone whose sole purpose in life was to make their lives miserable. He went around always spouting off about "the Blessed Mother." And he never stopped forcing difficulties on others with the excuse that "we must answer her will."

---

1. Winoska, *Our Lady's Fool*, p. 69.

That's it! We'll quiet him down by finding someplace for him where he won't be able to do this work so easily.

Father Kolbe was sent to an old, run-down monastery in Grodno, way out on the eastern end of Poland. The formal reason was that it would be good for his tuberculosis, but they really just wanted to get rid of him.

There were several old, dispirited friars at Grodno. They showed not the slightest interest in Father Kolbe's work.

The old press he had bought for the hundred dollars was a real old monster. It required over sixty thousand turns just to print five thousand copies. Truth be told, it was backbreaking work for anyone forced into it. Friar Albert Olzakowski helped Father Kolbe with this work, and he died from overwork. And Father Fordon, an old priest who was Kolbe's spiritual ally, also soon died from tuberculosis.

One must not assume that Father Kolbe was relieved of any of his regular duties at the monastery. He recited his daily office (the daily prayer of priests based on the Psalms), took the Holy Eucharist to the sick who lived far away, and heard confessions for many hours. It was understood that these things must take precedence over his "hobby."

In a cruel sort of way, the review's circulation just kept increasing. They couldn't keep up with the printing. Those friars who wanted to work under Father Kolbe first had to finish all their day work— cutting firewood, the housework for the monastery—so they had to take time from their sleep for working on the review. Father Kolbe would send copies to anyone who asked without charge, "food for the soul," as it were, along with the note, "We offer free subscriptions very willingly to anyone who is unable to offer anything for the work of the Immaculate, even by depriving himself a little."[2]

Father Kolbe cannot be called an accomplished writer, but he had an amazing ability to read people's hearts. Those who read these lines all felt to some extent psychologically in Father's debt. One by

---

2. Winoska, *Our Lady's Fool*, p. 77.

one people came forth to say that they were sending the money they saved by not buying cigarettes, or a drink, or even a new skirt.

However, Father Kolbe was in one sense upsetting the conservatives.

In the Polish monasteries at that time, there was a clear sense of status distinction between the priests and the laboring friars. The distinction comes out more clearly in English, where the priests are called "father" and the laboring friars are called "brother." Was it healthy to have such distinctions? Father Kolbe felt everyone had to embrace the spirit of equality. Anyone who had received talent from God should be put to work. In fact, Father Kolbe had the idea of publishing reports with photographs of the laboring friars working at the press. The conservatives were upset, questioning whether one can allow this kind of "treatment" of the laboring friars. Was Father Kolbe trying to destroy the tried-and-true rules of the monastery?

What Father Kolbe was trying to do was something that had to be done. It was simply the right position to take in response to the demands of the times. Sweeping away the feudal class-consciousness and adopting a method of connecting people's hearts from a more farsighted perspective were both things that people intensely wanted. This was a key reason for the explosive growth in the appeal of the movement of the "Knights of the Immaculata."

It seemed at first that Father Kolbe had won. By 1925 both the circulation of the journal and the number of friars had doubled. The Provincial came for a visit and saw for himself the great results of Father Kolbe's work. He ordered that the monastery's old dining hall be converted into a printing shop. After the Provincial left, resistance began to spread again among the old friars. Already, thanks to Father Kolbe, the peace of the monastery has been shattered. Now, is there no way to stop this insanity?

Those on Father Kolbe's side also contrived a defensive plan. Their methods were forceful and not very restrained. They got up in the middle of the night, with picks and axes, and tore up the walls and ovens that were no longer needed in order to convert the old dining hall into their exclusive work space. Such an act stemmed from the immaturity of the young friars who couldn't contain their joy at helping Father Kolbe with his work. But in the end, all it did was ensure the complete opposition of the older friars.

Finally, one day Father Kolbe bought a diesel motor that would make the press much more productive. Here again, Father Kolbe used his first-rate methods in buying it. First, before heading out to the home of the landlord who had the motor, he prayed intently to the Blessed Mother along with Brother Zeno Zebrowski, who later became a great help to him after they went to Japan together. When they got to the landlord's house, they found placed above the motor in question, mysteriously, a picture of the Blessed Mother. Father Kolbe whispered to Brother Zeno,

"This motor is ours."

And, he succeeded in buying the machine at a ridiculously cheap price.

Soon after, Father Kolbe was given another period of painful reflection. His tuberculosis flared up again. After promising not to give another thought to the printing, he was sent to Zakopane near the Slovak border.

There he was in the pits of despair. Those around him continued to look askance at his project, as they had from the get-go. His sole source of support was his sense that the work was making progress, and now that had been taken from him.

Zakopane was famous throughout Poland as a most refreshing place near the mountains. There, the houses were known for their deep, overhanging eaves, the air was clear and all nature was tinged in vibrant colors. But Father Kolbe's spirits seemed beyond help. His heart was filled with the sense that he had been abandoned.

"I suppose everyone would be happy if I just died here."

In fact, Father Kolbe's thoughts turned to death from time to time. It was easy for him to think that what lies beyond death would be a better place than the world he found himself in. But during those days, Father Kolbe squarely faced up to disappointment, and from within it he discovered that he was not able to keep living with the consolations of the Blessed Mother. Father Kolbe came to see his own self as completely *lost*. All was dependent on the will of the Blessed Mother. He understood that if the Blessed Mother still had use for a person in this world, then she would pick that person up from however base a condition he had fallen into and use him for her work.

Father Kolbe returned to Grodno.

There, he got some welcome news. The land that later became the site of Niepokalanów was being put up for sale. When Father Kolbe went to have a look at the site, he fell in love with it. So, he put an image of the Blessed Mother right in the middle of those fields.

But Father Kolbe's hopes suffered a setback on the issue of price. The Provincial felt the asking price was too high. Father Kolbe had no choice but to back out of the deal since obedience was just as important to this priest as prayer.

Father Kolbe went to the landlord, Prince Jan Maria Drucki-Lubecki, to tell him that, unfortunately, he wouldn't be able to buy the land after all. The Prince asked him,

"Then what shall we do with that image of the Blessed Mother?"

Sadness filled Father Kolbe's heart.

"Please, just leave it where it is," Father Kolbe replied, with a sad look. Prince Lubecki fell into a deep silence. Then he said in a slow, deliberate manner, "In that case, just take the land. I don't need the money."

Once again, it was back in Father Kolbe's hands. Yes, it seemed like chicanery. But if so, it was the kind of chicanery that one rarely sees in the world, conducted with extraordinary purity and innocence and leaving its victim filled with joy.

Guided by Friar Henryk, Father O and I went to Father Kolbe's quarters, which were right next to the sanctuary.

It was a plank-boarded room of about ten square meters in size. There was an iron bed and a wooden crucifix on the wall.

There was a wooden desk, and the only decorations were the golden pull rings on the drawers. The lamp had an enamel shade, and next to the door there was a statue of St. Therese of the Infant Jesus holding a bouquet of roses.

This is the room where Father Kolbe spent the years from 1927 to 1930, during the time when he developed Niepokalanów.

I read somewhere that during the time at Grodno the priests were so poor that they shared overcoats and boots. Since Father Kolbe wore the same size boots as Brother Zeno, he shared boots almost exclusively with Brother Zeno. But Father Kolbe always used his own overcoat. The reason was that they had no sleepwear, so Father Kolbe wore the coat when sleeping.

Instinctively, I looked around for the heater.

Just outside the plank-boarded room, I found a single stove. Apparently, it was supposed to warm the incensory (the room for storing articles used in Mass), the sanctuary, and Father Kolbe's room. Fortunately enough, there were knotholes in the plank walls. Quite a bit of humid air would enter through them, I thought, while shivering. Suddenly, I heard something like rain falling. I went to the window and looked out over the monastery's courtyard.

There were light clouds, but the sound wasn't rain. Leaves were falling on the plank roof, and it sounded like falling rain. Outside was so yellow from the changing colors of the leaves that it seemed as if the color were painted on my eyes. A solitary friar walked slowly through this forest of colored leaves.

"How many people are here now?" "Three hundred," Friar Henryk replied. "The publication work?"

"We aren't doing any now. Not just here, but all presses

throughout Poland are now under the authority of the government. In addition, there hasn't been a press in a monastery since around 1950."

Instinctively, I refrained from asking him any further questions about that.

"Then, what do these three hundred persons do now?" "Oh, they have plenty to do. There are tailors and carpenters and other skilled workmen among the friars, and they always have work to do."

I had heard back in Japan that you can't even get business cards printed in Poland. It seems that even if you wanted to print a few words from the Bible beneath a religious picture, you first had to submit it to the censors. The only means of copying permitted were printing photographs and the typewriter. Under these conditions, eventually as the manuscripts for the monastery's publications were all forbidden, they ran out of manuscripts and it became impossible to publish the review. And that meant that the press they held onto for so long was no longer needed.

The area right next to the sanctuary had been converted into something like a Kolbe Memorial Hall. They exhibited all sorts of photos and documents related to Father Kolbe. I asked Friar Henryk for copies of some of the materials. They even had things like Father Kolbe's grade reports from his minor seminary in Lwów. With Father O interpreting, it seems they showed that his German was słaby [weak], his Greek was fair, his Latin started off bad but later got better, and he excelled in mathematics.

As we were leaving the archives, Friar Henryk told us that Friar Hieronim Maria Wierzba who had been in the concentration camp with Father Kolbe was free and asked if we would like to hear his story. Friar Wierzba had a gentle look about him, and his head was shaped like a peanut. He came out wearing a small round brown cap on his head and we sat down on a bench in the courtyard where the sunlight on this rather gray day was all the more welcome.

When he said the concentration camp, he did not mean Auschwitz. He meant the three concentration camps of Lamsdorf,

Amtitz and Ostrzeszów [Schildberg] where, after 1939, Father Kolbe and his colleagues spent time before arriving at Auschwitz.

In 1939, at the outset of World War II, the German airforce attacked Poland. Niepokalanów suffered a deadly air raid. Winowska writes:

> Squadrons of Junkers flashed through the sky like gigantic vultures. Bombardments followed endlessly one after another, night and day. Villages, hamlets, whole cities flared like torches at the four points of the horizon. The sky, streaked with purple and scarlet, resembled a racetrack where the horsemen of the Apocalypse galloped their steeds.[3]

According to Friar Wierzba's recollection, around eleven o'clock on the morning of September 19, a man wearing a Red Cross armband came to see Father Kolbe. He said he was a member of the Benedictines who planned to go into hiding, and he asked Father Kolbe to lend him Franciscan robes for that purpose.

Father Kolbe knew immediately that he was a spy. If he lent the robes to this man, Father Kolbe would suffer severe retribution for what would be considered an illegal act.

Some time later, the Gestapo came.

Two priests, thirty-four friars, and one Japanese seminarian were taken to a bus stop, where the Japanese seminarian was sent home.

For the next three months, until December 8, the priests and their company were sent around to the three concentration camps of Lamsdorf, Amtitz and finally Ostrzeszów [Schildberg].

By the time they arrived at Amtitz it was already winter, and cold. The food there was horrible. In the morning, all they got was coffee and a hundred fifty grams of bread. Sometimes there was a tiny bit of margarine. Lunch was cabbage soup. Dinner was also just soup. All they had to fight off the cold with were the plank boards

---

3. Winowska, p. 140.

and light jackets. At night, when they crawled into the straw bedding, they found rats. Nobody had a change of clothes, because they had no time to grab any when they left. Most difficult was that for three months they had not once been allowed to wash their underwear.

I asked Friar Wierzba whether there was a time when, under these harsh conditions, he encountered the worst side of humanity.

At that point, the friar seemed to take my question in the opposite direction.

He said that, through Father Kolbe's leadership, they came to feel quite strongly that suffering is God's providence, and that by bearing with it, they were able to establish proof of their humanity. Even as victims of the horrible passions of war, they had found meaning in life. Other than this, there could be no true salvation, even in a more narrow, psychological sense. They felt that all suffering could be transformed into joy, in equal measure, by offering it up to the Blessed Mother.

That was not the end of the matter. The priests and friars went on to plan a more positive recovery, too.

At Amtitz, it was not permitted to celebrate the Mass. However, one of the friars made an image of the Immaculata out of clay. Since the Mass was forbidden, they prayed the rosary before the clay Immaculata. Before you knew it, even the Germans liked this image of the Blessed Mother. And, even though it was forbidden to move from one barrack to another, this image became an opportunity for allowing people to move around more freely.

The friars already had come to understand that they would never go home. Father Kolbe suggested they make a contract with the Blessed Mother. He said that others may want to go home. But we will stay behind. That will somewhere, somehow (in short, as a form of silent resistance) be something we will do for others.

It was no mistake. Nothing causes someone who hurts other people a greater sense of displeasure than when he sees that his efforts are to no avail.

Father Kolbe raised the stakes another notch. We must have love for our "enemy." So, even if we are really suffering terribly, we must not show any sign of our suffering to our "enemy." Although one might not expect it, this sternness spiritually saved the friars. They begin to burn with a sense of mission. For all I know, this may be very much a Polish style of resistance.

When they were released on December 8, the feast of the Assumption of the Immaculata, Father Kolbe gave a medal of the Blessed Mother to the commandant of the Ostrzeszów [Schildberg] concentration camp. The commandant happily accepted it, and in return gave them a bit of butter. Friar Wierzba told us that they only found out in April of this year that the commandant always kept the medal with him until his car exploded and the medal, which he had left in the car, was destroyed instead of him.

It was getting on to lunchtime. Friar Wierzba urged Father O and me to go get something to eat. Later I realized that every church and monastery in Poland always served me a hot meal.

At lunch, there were several men in the television business who had come to record for a program on Father Kolbe since his beat-ification was quickly approaching. And they were getting quite an earful about Japanese television from Father O.

Apparently they had just come from filming at the home of Franciszek Gajowniczek, the man who survived because Father Kolbe had taken his place. They said that Mr. Gajowniczek's health had suffered a bit but recently he made a recovery.

The next day I was scheduled to make a tour with Father O of several places such as Zduńska Wola where Father Kolbe was born and Pabianice where he moved with his parents when he was two years old. Then, I wanted to go to the town of Brzeg, where Mr. Gajowniczek lives, and see for myself the "joy of life" that had been purchased at the cost of Father Kolbe's life. Much to my relief, Mr. Gajowniczek seemed willing to grant me an interview.

Before we sat down at table, I remembered to give Friar Henryk the bottle of cognac I had bought for him at the airport in Paris. I had bought it because a Japanese in Paris recommended it, telling me that "They don't have things like French cognac in Poland. And the Poles really like to drink, you see. If you take them a bottle, they'll be very happy."

Friar Henryk looked a bit perplexed. He said, "We don't usually drink alcohol."

And then he added, as if to put me at ease:

"Of course, feast days are a different matter. We'll all drink some on Father Kolbe's beatification day."

There wasn't enough for everyone to have some. I had wanted him to drink some for medicinal purposes on cold nights and nights when he had trouble sleeping.

"But why don't you drink alcohol?" I asked Friar Henryk. "Well, it's because too many Poles drink a lot. So, the least we could do is refrain from drinking to compensate for them."

I was dumbfounded, and thought maybe I should do better myself.

Chapter 3

Images of the Holy Family

Section One

We got off the bus at the central plaza in Zduńska Wola and Father O approached some old people, who were lined up like sparrows on two benches, to ask for directions to the Church of the Assumption of the Blessed Virgin Mary. They all pointed in the direction of the Church and told us how to get there. It seemed they had nothing to do at home so they came here to spend hour after hour sitting on these benches just watching the cars and people going by without ever tiring of it.

The sun was starting to set. I was in a hurry. We had to leave this town early the next morning and, if possible, I wanted to see the house where Father Kolbe was born and take some pictures while it was still light.

The pastor of the Church of the Assumption of the Blessed Virgin Mary should know where the house is. But what if Father Kolbe's house was this side of the Church and we passed by it on our way? That would be a problem because my camera was a basic model—kind of like a toy—and the color film in it was not very light sensitive.

Father O sensed my impatience, and he called over to a girl who had paused for a moment on her way home from school and asked if she knew the location of the house where Father Kolbe was born. She was quite a plump little girl. She had long hair, and her cheeks were a bit rosy. When she talked, she slightly pursed her lips. But she didn't seem to know a thing. Zduńska Wola is not a large town. What a sign of the times that here in this town with at best a population of maybe twenty or thirty thousand people one didn't know anything about this famous priest who was born here—not even his name!

Father O decided that we would have to go to the church straightway. We could already see the steeple above the line of houses. The rectory was on the opposite side, set back a bit from the street.

Here, once again, I was warmly received by the pastor, Father Katarzyński. When we told him we were in a hurry, he immediately understood and said in that case we'd better go see the house quickly while there was still sunlight. We just dropped our bags there and took off again without a moment's respite. We cut though a small park and went down a winding lane with loose cobblestones. There, on the left, was a solitary wooden house.

I was about to write, "a small wooden house." But that house was not in the least bit small. To describe it as a small house would imply that even if many large families shared the house, each family would have its own space. But the house where Father Kolbe was born was like a Japanese row house.[1] One can't deny there is something charming about living in a row house. Catching sight of Father O, two or three women and men appeared suddenly in the entrance with a wistful look about them.

Father Kolbe was born on the second floor, about where the three windows were. All three windows were shut. The ceilings in these old wooden houses are terribly low. To look in the windows of the second floor, you hardly have to look up at all. There was a woman in the room where the Kolbe family used to live. In using the generic noun "woman" I mean that she does not appear to be the kind of person who regularly goes to church. But I wouldn't rule out the possibility that she might be an upstanding member of the communist party.

It was now so dark that the automatic exposure setting on my camera controlled the shutter. I put my camera down and took

---

1. *nagaya*

another look at that house. It was truly a miserable house. Not surprising for a house built in the late nineteenth century, its roof and walls were just in shambles. The exterior walls were even lacking weatherboards. They just casually placed knotted boards along the side. It seemed to me as if people walking around on the second floor would make those living below think the whole house was shaking.

Maximilian Maria Kolbe was born in this house on January 8, 1894, at one o'clock in the morning.

It was in the cold of winter. But it wasn't just the weather that was bad. Father Maximilian Kolbe certainly came into this world in this very house as a Polish man, but in those days there was no state called "Poland."

Ever since 1772, Poland had to endure the fate of having its territory divided between Empress Catherine of Russia, Frederick the Great, King of Prussia, and Joseph II of Austria. The Polish King Stanisław II, August Poniatowski, headed a puppet administration under Catherine and had no power.

The Poles did not just throw up their hands and abandon themselves to this fate. A patriotic group was formed and rose up in opposition. It seemed to them that the French Revolution, which has just begun, promised them great possibilities.

But Russia's oppression continued anew. At Grodno in 1795, Stanisław II signed over all Polish territory.

Poland as a state no longer existed, but even after that, thanks to the influence of political thought Poland was able to stay alive as a nation—albeit barely. After his victory over Prussia, Napoleon established the Duchy of Warsaw, and in 1815 Emperor Alexander I of Russia recognized the Kingdom of Poland. When Nicolas I succeeded Alexander I in 1825, Russia's policy toward Poland suddenly became harsh. At the same time, with the revision of the constitution, the Polish independence movement found an opportunity to take a strong stand. The resistance accepted projections of a great number of dead. In 1831, when the revolutionary movement was suppressed, Poland now really had everything taken from it.

Of course, the Polish spirit did not die out. By coincidence, it was also in 1831 when Frederick Chopin went to Paris. Here, I'd like to add a little joke. There is a pun that goes like this: "Chopin doesn't know who Chopin is." In English pronunciation, Chopin sounds like "Show-pin." But in Polish, his name is pronounced "Show-pen." So, the pun really means "Show-pen" doesn't recognize the name "Show-pin." Another unforgettable person was born in Poland at this time. That was Joseph Conrad, who never ceased showing an interest in the sea and the Orient (his Polish name was Józef Konrad Korzeniowski).

Poland was partitioned into three different countries, and each section faced a slightly different situation.

The Poles under Russian rule were in a slightly better position economically, since they were able to market the projects produced in their industrial zone in Russia and the language was comparatively closer to their own as well. But those under Prussian rule suffered greatly. A good many of their Catholic priests were executed. Policies were implemented that completely ignored their human rights, including of course policies that forbade the use of the Polish language as well as those that restricted the use of land by Poles. This was the spark that ignited fires of resentment against Germans by the Polish people. Landlords, peasants, and even the priests united in the resistance movement.

So, when Father Kolbe was born, it was not only an unseasonably cold winter, but it was also historically a dark age for the Poles. His father Juliusz was a poor mechanic. More important to him and his wife Maria Dąbrowska than how poor their family was or how dark the times were was their faith. That light shone powerfully on all the darkness around them in a way that reason alone cannot explain.

They named their baby Rajmund. Actually, even earlier, on the afternoon of the day they named him Rajmund, he was baptized by their pastor, Father Franciszek Kapałczyński. Zduńska Wola was in Russian territory. So, Rajmund's baptismal certificate was written in Russia. The infant Rajmund, only a few hours old, had already tasted the bitterness of life.

Returning to the Church of the Assumption of the Blessed Virgin Mary, I cut across the yard in front of the Church that was already growing dim in the evening light and went in to the sanctuary in order to pay a visit to the Holy Eucharist.

There, much to my surprise, I found they were celebrating an evening Mass.

It was a rather large sanctuary, typical of nineteenth century churches, but there were only about twenty or thirty people there participating in the Mass. Most of them were what you'd call typical Polish women. The town's mothers and grandmothers from the nearby farmhouses. That was my impression anyway. They all were dressed alike, as though they were in uniform. Maybe it was still a bit early in the season for heavy overcoats, but at any rate they were all wearing plain, moss green or dark brown synthetic raincoats. On their backs, they had removable yokes so they wouldn't get too sweaty. Most of them were wearing rubber boots. Maybe the roads near their homes were muddy. It seems they were achieving two purposes at once—both to do their duty to come to church and to get shelter from the cold wind that was already starting to penetrate their skin. They all wore kerchiefs on their heads as if it were prearranged. Some were made of transparent nylon, and others were heavy black wool dyed with the rich, local red flower pattern.

Suddenly I thought of Father Kolbe's mother, Maria Dąbrowska. Little Rajmund didn't live here except for the first two years of his life, so he probably had no memory of the Church of the Assumption of the Blessed Virgin Mary. But Maria Dąbrowska must have come here often, with little Rajmund in her arms.

This was when Maria Dąbrowska was young and she must have experienced her share of life's troubles. There is no other way to read the historical records. Maria wasn't to enter the convent. But, be that as it may, this was not the time when such hopes could easily be realized. Back then, the convents were closed, and the nuns had to leave their habits behind and disperse all over the place. That was when Maria met Juliusz. He was a kind and upright man.

What kind of woman was Maria? Winowska writes that she was "energetic, pious, a little gossipy, a hard worker, very quick at getting out of a fix."[2] I was relieved to find out she was "a little gossipy." I get very annoyed when, in the midst of my research, all I find are upstanding people. The mother of the house should always be chattering a bit warmly, so long as she doesn't do it to excess. When you could hear Maria's voice in it, that wooden row house must have been a bright and happy home.

Gradually, more and more people started coming for Mass. You could tell some of the men had just decided at the last minute to drop in on their way home from work. And among those women in their raincoats, many clutched large handbags.

Suddenly, I felt something tug at my heart. I didn't find either the infant Rajmund or the adult Father Kolbe there. But there was no mistaking my encounter there with the image of Father Kolbe's mother. Surely Maria Dąbrowska would also have worn a simple overcoat, boots, and a kerchief. Surely she often came here to talk to God and to ask for his help. I recalled once again the purity of the Blessed Mother in the Wilderness that I had seen in Niepokalanów.

For Maria Dąbrowska, coming here to pray was a *necessity* in order to get through her days. Praying wasn't an obligation, it wasn't a rule. She came in order to offer up to the Lord all the thoughts and feelings that overflowed from within her.

And the women who were praying here now were not very different from Maria Dąbrowska.

Even today, Poland's sufferings are far from over. Ever since the general election of January 1947, when the Communist Party seized power under the name of the United Labor Party, the people have kept fighting for their faith. The reason the government wasn't able to destroy the Church is because the faith was not an abstract idea but something that burned passionately in the people's hearts.

---

2. Winowska, p. 2.

The Poles don't go to church on Sundays to fulfill a "duty." Once again, I was impressed by the fact that they enjoy going because that is where their "love" of God is.

The Mass ended and I went outside. The trees that lined the streets were decked out in the beautiful yellow colors of fall and were becoming enfolded in the night. There was an announcement board right in front of the rectory, and on it were posted in black several names of those recently deceased. A sixty-ish man with a red nose came along pushing his bike and stopped in front of the board and silently stared at the names of the dead. Some children ran past him.

One of the notices was for a person who had been a member of a group that prayed incessantly from June 2 to 4 in 1967 for the beatification of Father Kolbe. What really struck me was how many people came to this small town's church. They seemed like peas in a pod, as though people's heads were piled on top each other as far as the eye could see. Next to me was just a wall of children.

"In this church alone, about five thousand children come to learn the catechism."

Father O translated for me what Father Katarzyński had said.

"Five thousand!" I stammered. Could this be the reality of Poland, a country that everyone calls a socialist state?

Soon it was time for dinner in the rectory. I'd like to record here a rather humorous incident that happened then.

Before dinner, I got a small package out of my suitcase and took it to the kitchen. It was the uncured ham that I had bought at the airport in Paris. When I bought it I asked how many days it would stay fresh and whether it was from France.

"It's German. But it's very good," the sales lady told me.

I'd never had the opportunity before then to eat uncured ham. Because I hadn't done things like visit friends' homes, I had had no one to give a ham to. Two women were preparing dinner in the spacious and clean kitchen. One was a plump forty-something woman who, I found out later, was the wife of the pastor's younger brother. She could speak a little German, but I didn't know more than fifty words of German, so we didn't have much hope for communicating. The other was a slender, pert young thing with a cute laugh.

Using gestures, I asked them to cut the meat for us. When the pastor and another priest from the parish sat down to dinner with Father O and me, the German uncured ham was presented on a serving dish, beautifully sliced like sashimi. The creases in the table-cloth were perfectly done and the dining room was quite elegantly prepared. In a small dish, the butter was sculpted in the shape of a rose. There was cheese, sardines in oil, honey, pickles, and even fruit.

It was the first time I ever saw someone eat a cheese and honey sandwich. Following the pastor's bidding, I took the first serving of the uncured ham. I thought I should try it first just in case something was wrong with it. Tasting it, I found nothing wrong and said to Father O without much thought, "They told me it's a German ham. I bought it in Paris."

Father O passed on my comment in Polish to those at the table. Everyone appeared quite amicable. But from then on, nobody touched the ham.

I wondered what was the matter.

Somewhat ill at ease, I tried to figure things out. Was it wrong of me to bring them a German ham? Do you suppose they hate everything German so much they won't even eat this ham?

When dinner was over, I suddenly remembered. It was Friday. In Poland, everyone still observed the custom called "minor penance," which meant they abstained from meat on Fridays. I chuckled to myself. The Japanese woman who insisted on eating meat on Friday must have struck them as a very easy-going person.

That night, I was assigned a freshly cleaned bedroom right next to the kitchen. And I was told that Father O would be celebrating Mass in the morning at six o'clock. I wanted to try to get up for it, but I was afraid I'd sleep in, so I asked Father Katarzyński to come knock on my door in time for me to make it to Mass.

I realized I'd better get to sleep early. But not being very used to early risings, I wasn't able to sleep even after retiring to my bedroom.

Then, I heard those two women in the kitchen. I took a package of cookies and went looking to have some fun in the kitchen with them (it seems I always have some kind of food with me!).

Well, after that, things didn't go so smoothly. It would have helped had I been a bit better at German. All I could get out of my mouth was a line from the first lesson in my old textbook, "Eine König hat eine Tochter" (a king has a daughter). But Poland didn't even have a king anymore. In no time at all, a man appeared, the husband of the fat lady (and thus the younger brother of the pastor) who spoke to me in very easy to understand German. He told me that his daughter had married somebody in New York. I told him I had a son. I was grateful I could remember the word for "son." And somehow I remembered the words for "sixteen-year-old."

The younger woman was getting restless since she couldn't say anything to me. Then suddenly, off on a mission, she went somewhere. Presently, she returned, with something wrapped up in her apron.

They were little ducklings desperately trying to get back to their mother. Five of them. She spread newspaper over the countertop and set the five ducklings down on it. The little ducklings were not happy, having been kidnapped from their mother's warm, dark bosom. There was one troublemaker among them who kept plucking out his siblings' tail feathers. Another, desperately trying to get away, started to poop.

I couldn't help but laugh. The young girl also squealed with laughter. I poked the tip of my nose at the duckling and even got the missus to laugh.

It didn't take long for both the pastor and Father O to come see what was going on in the kitchen. The two of them had been having a quiet chat. Father O laughed and said that when they heard all the hullabaloo in the kitchen, they decided they had better come take a look. They seemed to think it strange and wondered what on earth we could be up to since we didn't have any common language between us. At any rate, these ducklings had us falling all over the place in laughter like a bunch of kids.

Not long after, I went back to my bedroom. Nights are short in all rectories. And there's not a lot of noise. I turned out the lights, and looked at the sliver of evening sky in the space above the makeshift curtain. I could only see one star.

The trip to Pabianice was again a smooth one. After alighting from the train in the industrial town of Łódź, Father O and I transferred to a suburban train, but it appeared that after having spent so long in Japan, Father O had lost a bit of the knack for riding trains in Poland. And on top of it all, as we headed out into the country I increasingly found myself stared at by people who had never seen an Oriental person before. They certainly didn't mean to offend. But at any rate, I was stared at by people who looked at me as if I were a giraffe or a hippopotamus. We missed our tram, not because the stares distracted me, but because our tram was completely full and we couldn't get on it. In the end, we were told which tram to take by two kindly grandmothers who said they were also going in the direction of Pabianice, so finally we were able to get on the tram we needed to take.

In response to questions by the two grandmothers, Father O seemed to be giving them a long talk on Japanese color televisions. He told me later than one of the grandmothers had said it sure would be nice to be able to buy one of those color televisions.

We found out from the grandmothers that we should get off at the stop in front of Pabianice's Church of St. Matthew.

The Kolbe family moved here to Pabianice from Zduńska Wola when Rajmund was two years old. That means that Rajmund's life as far as he could remember it probably started right here. All one could see around here were the gently sloping plains of Poland. Who could ever imagine the extraordinary things that would happen to a young boy growing up here? For it was in this church that young Rajmund saw the Blessed Virgin Mary.

The Church of St. Matthew was built in the sixteenth century.

When Rajmund was around ten years old, he was a mischievous little guy. His mother Maria Dąbrowska found she was always having to scold him.

"What do you think would happen to you if I didn't scold you? You'd always be getting into the same trouble over and over again."

One day, his mother's words hit home. Rajmund had gone to the Church of St. Matthew and was facing the altar, giving a full account of his troubles. Just when he started to open his soul to God, the Blessed Mother appeared to him, holding out two crowns. One crown was red, the other white.

"Which one do you want?"

Hearing the Blessed Mother's gentle question, the young boy replied, "I want them both."

Somehow, the young boy understood what the two crowns represented. He knew that the red crown meant martyrdom and the white crown signified holy chastity.

Ever after, Rajmund struggled to understand the great significance of what had happened to him that day. Of course, to have seen the Blessed Mother gave him unbelievable joy, but the responsibility that he had been given terrified him. He seemed like a different person. He would now pray with eyes swollen and red from crying, as he knelt before the Black Madonna of Częstochowa that they had enshrined in their home.

Finally, Maria Dąbrowska made Rajmund *confess* the reasons for this behavior. He replied that ever since that day whenever he went to church, he no longer thought he was going to church with his mother and father.

"It seems to me that I am going with Mary and Joseph." After that, young Rajmund would speak to Maria Dąbrowska from time to time about martyrdom. The reality in Poland was harsh. But still, who would have thought that martyrdom was a real possibility in this young boy's future?

Even Maria Dąbrowska was not convinced that young Rajmund had strong enough a spirit for martyrdom. But in any case, it may well be true that from that day on young Rajmund began to take an intense, daily interest in "dying for the Truth." And that's not something ten-year-old children normally think about.

Father Kolbe kept this apparition of the Blessed Mother deep down in his heart thereafter. Only on two occasions did he talk about it. The first time was to Maria Dąbrowska; the other time was at the "last supper" at Niepokalanów when, unprompted, he told his fellow friars about his experience of seeing the Blessed Mother in Nagasaki.

While in Pabianice, the Kolbe family rented a house on the corner of Kilińskiego and Złota streets. The family was not rich, but they were basically happy. The father Juliusz went to work as a laborer in a factory in Łódź. The mother ran a shop out of their home while working as a midwife. The first thing in the morning, the parents went with their children to Mass. It is said that since they both were Third Order Franciscans (an organization of lay people who live according to the spirit of St. Francis), they even dressed their children in outfits that resembled the Franciscan habit. In any event, it was here that young Rajmund received his First Communion (the ceremony where, after the age of reason, one receives for the first time the bread that is a symbol of Christ) and served as an altar boy for the priest during Mass. Every year they would go on a pilgrimage to Częstochowa, about a hundred fifty kilometers away.

Father O and I went to the rectory where we met Father Stanisław Świerczek, who immediately gave us a tour of the church. The main altar was from the seventeenth century, done in the Gothic style with gold and white setting the tone. In front, one could make out a dark image of our Lord on the cross. But what left an even deeper impression on me was what I saw on the left side altar—a copy of the Częstochowa Madonna, famous as the Mary of Poland. It shows a slit-eyed Black Madonna embracing her Son. She is adorned in silver garments and wears a silver crown with stars on top.

Here, at this altar, it is said, young Rajmund saw the Blessed Mother. It seemed believable to me. The lad was not the kind to wear God on his sleeve, but kneeling in front of this icon, his heart was already turned ardently toward the Blessed Mother! The Blessed Mother was, for him, the mother with whom he had already kept up a constant conversation in his heart. No, she gave him a more certain place for his heart to rest than even his own mother could.

There was certainly a beauty to this altar that is not of this world. No matter how harsh the reality outside was, some part connected to the soul had to shine—indeed was always shining. Kneeling before the altar of the Church of St. Matthew, I was struck by the thought that a church, whenever possible, must be decorated in a beautiful way that raises the mind to God. Those who think of God only as an abstract idea often say they don't need church buildings. They tend to despise the heavily decorated parts as an inclination toward worldliness. But those who try to come to terms with faith from their senses might think that a bit too harsh. One wonders how consoling it must have been for the Polish people when, in their cruel everyday world of foreign oppression, they saw that only the churches (the places where Truth is made manifest) were gorgeously preserved— with a beauty that belonged to another world.

Soon it was time for Father Świerczek to take us by car to the house where the Kolbe family had lived.

It was another dreary apartment building. This dilapidated, ugly old brick building had an open ground in the center that looked like a depressing, unkempt exercise yard; the section facing it was where what remained of the Kolbe house was. The external walls were cracked and stained, and the current residents who gathered to watch their pastor approach seemed rather casual, even a bit slovenly. Only the children showed any liveliness, with their red cheeks and energetic voices. Even the sunlight that fell on the large belly of a pregnant young wife was dim.

I was secretly grateful that Father Kolbe was not born into some important Polish aristocratic family. Since Christ was born in a stable, none of us need anything more than that. And why was it that whether it was the life of the Kolbe family in Pabianice or the circumstances surrounding Maria Dąbrowska's marriage, I could not sweep away an image of the Holy Family that was superimposed on them. What did it mean?

It was here in Pabianice that Rajmund finally showed his exceptional ability to the pharmacist Kotowski. One day, Rajmund's mother, a midwife, sent him to Kotowski's shop for medicine for her patients. Rajmund had memorized perfectly the technical terms for the medicine. Kotowski made some inquiries into the situation at Rajmund's home, and he found out that the lad was too poor to be able to go to school.

It was thanks to Mr. Kotowski that Rajmund was able to go to the trade school that his older brother attended. It is reported that Rajmund got very good grades at the trade school, but this was because, from the very depths of his soul, he was hungry for learning.

Four years later, a Franciscan priest came to Pabianice on retreat. He was also looking for recruits for the Franciscan Order. That was when Rajmund and his older brother Franciszek confirmed their desire to go into minor seminary. In 1907, when Rajmund was ten, his father Juliusz Kolbe took his two sons Franciszek and Rajmund quietly over the Russian border to Kraków, which at that time was in Austrian territory. From there, the two boys went on alone to Lwów where they would join the Order of Friars Minor Conventual.

Pabianice, then, can be seen as that part of Father Kolbe's life before his "public life" commenced.

Father O and I soon left that run-down neighborhood, as Father Świerczek had to get to a funeral. As expected, with fourteen thousand Catholics to look after, this pastor had to be constantly running all over the place. Even Japan's largest parish, Nagasaki's Urakami Cathedral, only has six thousand parishioners.

Father O and I took the bus to our next destination.

There was no schedule posted at the bus stop. When we asked people, they didn't even seem to know whether a bus might come or not, so Father O was getting a bit impatient. Rather boldly, I said to him, "Father, when you were in Japan you picked up some bad habits from the impatient Japanese." This came from my lack of sympathy for others, since I myself never feel rushed to do anything. I sat down on a sunny bench and mulled over the words I had just seen below the holy pictures that I was told were handed out at the Church of St. Matthew in commemoration of Father Kolbe's April 29, 1918, ordination[3] (the formal ceremony that makes one a priest) in Rome. "Holy chastity, permit me to glorify you. Give me strength to resist your enemies." Was Father Kolbe a man of reconciliation, or a fighter? I kept mulling this over in the warm sunlight. In either case, Father Kolbe's long journey began from this quiet little town.

---

3. Most sources say Kolbe was ordained on April 28, 1918. Is Sono giving the Japanese date (one day ahead of Europe)?

Chapter 4

The Bugle Call of the Blessed Mother Mary

Section One

I finally made it to Kraków.

It was night when I arrived. Wandering along the twisted walled roads that reminded me of castle walls in Japan, I saw beneath the red house lights addresses written in old-fashioned lettering. I wouldn't have been surprised to see a horse cart with men in black capes passing by in this narrow lane that seemed right at home in the Middle Ages. I had no idea where the Wisła (Vistula) River was. The hotel, at least, was at the end of this winding road. It was a graceful town, full of ancient history and culture, much like Kyoto. But I didn't find that out until the next day. One must say that the market square in the center of the town still preserved all the atmosphere of fourteenth-century Kraków, when it was at the height of its brilliant, dazzling culture. The roots of the Catholic faith were planted here in 1320 when King Władysław Łokietek was crowned King of Poland in both name and reality by the archbishop of Kraków, thus planting the seeds that would later grow into the flowers of medieval culture.

Right in the center of the square was the old Cloth Hall erected in the fourteenth century. The tower next to it was, I'm told, the Town Hall.

The soft, yet chilly, heavy morning air filled the plaza that was enveloped by all this rich history. Here and there were shops selling flowers, and a flock of pigeons playing. And some rosy-cheeked children chasing after the pigeons. An old couple sat on a bench intently watching this young life.

This square is the kind of place that might be known more commonly as a "church square." The one that stood out most was the Gothic church of St. Mary's that achieves a mysterious harmony with its two uneven towers. Across from it is St. Adalbert's Church, which people say is from the eleventh century. And only a few minutes from there is St. Andrew's Church, the Church of St. Peter and St. Paul, and two monasteries—one Dominican and the other Franciscan. You'll get the picture if you think of Tokyo's Marunouchi financial district and just replace all the bank buildings with churches.

Just my luck, it was Sunday morning.

This Franciscan monastery was where Fr. Kolbe stayed several times back in those days. In 1910, when Rajmund Kolbe was sixteen years and eight months old, he took his temporary vows to follow the rules and constitution of the Order of St. Francis of Assisi in Lwów and then returned the following year, 1911, to Kraków. He came here to enter the "middle seminary." He spent the next year in this monastery. After that, Fr. Kolbe went to Rome for major seminary.

Then, in fall of 1919, Father Kolbe returned to Kraków. His first job in the monastery was to teach church history in the seminary's philosophy department.

I entered the chapel of the Franciscan monastery. It was over-flowing with people, even at the side altars. It was so packed that you had to choose your spot carefully when you went to kneel down. It seems to me that the whole town had assembled here. Young men, but also middle-aged men whose mien revealed that they were seriously ill. Fat housewives. Attractive young couples with their children. Young girls in miniskirts.

Just like waiting for the next show at a movie theater, I stepped outside to make a quick tour of the nearby St. Adalbert's Church. I had some time, since I was planning to attend the next Mass at the Franciscan monastery. St. Adalbert's was also filled with people. They say Kraków has a population of five hundred and fifty thousand.

I don't think all five hundred and fifty were there, but the number of people was just unbelievable. I was struck by the thought that there must have been as many people in the church as turn out for a general election, and I headed back to the Franciscan monastery. People poured out the doors, as if a play had just ended. And this time, I was able to take a seat with a good view of the main altar. Every place to pray was already filled, and people were starting to stand in the side altars and in the aisles. My eyes naturally fell on a seat where two girls were. One was a thin, freckled-faced thing, the other a plump little girl who looked just like a freshly baked loaf of bread. Both were exhibiting their own understanding of proper church behavior. They looked all over the church, giggling, whispering between themselves, and intentionally singing the hymns in an off-key manner. These two struck me as the typical kind of troublesome student whose grades are mediocre and who have little interest in anything other than putting frogs on their teacher's chair.

Still, these girls came to church on their own, without their parents dragging them in.

Suddenly, I recalled those words, "Man does not live by bread alone."

Yes, this expression of an amazing, feverish faith that springs forth from the everyday life of ordinary people may be a kind of answer to socialism.

Two thousand years ago, Christ predicted the battle between liberalism and communism. He was a great psychologist. "Man does not live by bread alone," he said—after fasting forty days in the desert. Communists aim at "giving only bread to people." And it seems that as soon as people have only bread, they once again recall those words, "Man does not live by bread alone." I had never imagined that I would see in the socialist state of Poland such masses of people fervently praying here in this Polish church.

Something like a chill ran down my back. Once again, I recalled the words of Father Kolbe when he had a premonition of death.

"For the first three centuries, the Church was persecuted. The blood of the martyrs became the seeds of Christianity. When the persecutions had stopped, one of the Church Fathers lamented the mediocre state of Christianity. When he saw that the persecutions had started up again, he rejoiced."

That seems about right. For what was providing strong support for the very roots of the faith of Poland today was none other than communism itself. It was quite fascinating how it was lending a helping hand in ways that I, with my simple brain, could not believe.

Section Two

When Mass was over, I went with Father O to the reception desk of the monastery. We went to see Father Anselmo, who had attended minor seminary with Father Kolbe.[1]

It started to rain. When Father Anselmo let us into the semi-underground reception room, the smell of dank air began to seep into the room.

The image of Father Kolbe that Father Anselmo presented was a man of quiet bearing. But certainly not brooding. He was someone who liked math and could also be quite passionate.

"Back in those days, there was a revolution in Warsaw and Łódź. It made a deep impression on Father Kolbe, even in terms of his faith. For a while, he thought about becoming a soldier and fighting for Poland's freedom."

At that point, Father Anselmo had touched on an important point that I think got to the heart of the matter.

How had Father Kolbe, unlike all the other friars, come to possess a faith that burned like fire? Why had Father Kolbe come to show such ferocious tenacity in conveying the truth of Christ to the whole world through proselytizing?

One could simply say that it was because God had given this priest a particular mission and an unusual virtue to carry it out. But for a cynic like me, that wouldn't be persuasive. If God considered

---

1. This "Father Anselmo" appears to be Fr. Anselm Kubit.

this priest as separate from the ordinary kind of man, then I knew I wouldn't have had any interest in this Father Kolbe. Because the greater a man, the less I can relate to him.

For the faint-hearted like me, it is both a guiding principle of behavior and a sense of reality to recognize that all people live not by abstract ideals but by very personal reasons. One's personal sense of reality is God's revelation. So, it seemed to me that the key to unlocking the mystery of Father Kolbe's life had to be somewhere in the history of this priest's everyday life.

It is reported that in 1910, when he was sixteen years old, Father Kolbe had second thoughts about continuing in the monastic life. Partitioned by three countries, Poland seemed hopeless. In 1906 a strike broke out in the elementary schools because Poles were forced to use the German language, along with all schools in Prussian territory. In 1908, the Compulsory Purchase of Land Act went into effect against the Poles. Sienkiewicz's *Quo Vadis Domine* ("Lord, Where Are You Going?") that depicts Nero's atrocities was completed in 1895, but when you consider the historical context, it is clear that Nero was not simply a historical character. Nero was a symbol of the actual, violent force that stood athwart Poland at that time.

Would it not have been normal for the young Kolbe, burning with a sense of justice, to have plotted some form of revenge out of love of his fatherland, whose very existence had been violated in name and in reality? Would it not have been natural for Rajmund Kolbe to have abandoned the monastic life and become a soldier in the revolution in order to throw off the tyranny of Prussia or Russia?

But that was not what God had planned. Fate brought things to a very dramatic conclusion.

It happened while Rajmund Kolbe was on his way to tell the Father Provincial that he was leaving the monastery because he did not feel he had a vocation (God's call to the monastic life).

Maria Winowska tells the story in her biography of Kolbe:

[Rajmund] was called to the visiting parlor. It was his mother glowing with excitement over the news she had for him. Following the example of the two older sons, the third one, Joseph, had decided to become a religious also. Furthermore, she and Mr. Kolbe had decided to enter the service of religion and follow their life-long attraction. The father had already gone to Cracow, to the Franciscan Friars. She was going to Lwow to join the Benedictine Sisters. Now the whole family would belong to God![2]

Instantaneously, Rajmund Kolbe felt that his ambition to be a revolutionary was mistaken. He would never forget that day. In 1919, as soon as he heard that his older brother Franciszek had left the monastery, Father Kolbe wrote to his mother:

"I read your letter of February 23 with a mixture of joy and sadness. I am sure, Mother, that you understand how I felt.

"Poor Franciszek . . . He is not able to understand God's mercy toward us. It was he who first applied to the Franciscans. Together we received our First Communion and our Confirmation (the ceremony when a Catholic takes responsibility for his faith). Together we went through the novitiate and we took our provisional vows.

"Before entering the novitiate, I did not want to receive the habit and I also wanted the same for Franciszek. But how can I ever forget that time when, at the very moment that Franciszek and I were about to go tell the Father Provincial that we did not want to join the Franciscans, we heard the parlor bell? The hand of Providence, working with infinite mercy through the Immaculata, sent you, dear Mother, to us at that critical juncture.

"Nine years have already come and gone since then . . . I recall those events with fear and gratitude. What might have happened, had the Blessed Mother not reached out to me then? . . .

"Franciszek led me to this safe harbor with his example, but

2. Winowska, *Our Lady's Fool,* p. 12.

I was inclined to leave the novitiate and take him with me. And now, I make a daily memento (a prayer offered during Mass) to the Immaculata for him, and I hope that you too, dear Mother, will ask God's mercy for him."[3]

As this letter makes clear, both brothers had decided on the path of revolutionary fighter rather than monastic life, but they had second thoughts because of their mother. Only Franciszek was later able to carry out their original intention. Franciszek's fate is succinctly recorded in Father Antonio Ricciardi's *St. Maximilian Maria Kolbe.* In short, Franciszek joined the volunteer forces during the Great War from 1914 to 1918 and was wounded. When his wounds were healed, he applied once again to enter the monastery but was turned down on grounds of poor health. (It appears Father Kolbe's letter to his mother was written around this time.) Franciszek again joined the resistance movement against the Germans during World War II, but was captured in 1943 and sent to Auschwitz where it is thought he died. However, this last fact has never been confirmed.

In a singular, decisive scene, Father Kolbe understood that God's plans for him did not include the so-called "revenge or resistance through force." But is it likely that this much passion would simply disappear without a trace? It seems more likely to me that it would simply change its mode of expression and continue on in a different direction.

I think it is important not to forget that Father Kolbe was, more than anything else, a patriot. Living in Poland under foreign oppression, he wanted to directly attack the enemy, if at all possible. But once that kind of revenge was not permitted, what would be the best way to subdue the foreign enemy—no, the entire world? Only one way was permitted. Merely to conquer by casting God's truth, like a net, over all the people in the world.

One can find supporting evidence in the many instances of

---

3. I have consulted the English translation of this letter in Ricciardi, *St. Maximilian Kolbe* (p. 28), but changed the translation to more closely align with Sono's Japanese version.

militant language in the various expressions Father Kolbe used around the time he founded the Knights of the Immaculata.

During World War I, Poles who belonged to Austria were not allowed to leave Italy, but those who according to the maps were "Russian" like Father Kolbe were only temporarily detained in San Marino with its castle that looks like a toy (San Marino is a small, independent country that was neutral in the war). Shortly thereafter, he was allowed to return to Rome.

Maria Winowska writes about the atmosphere in Rome at the time:

> At the San Teodoro International Academy they read the daily communiqués. The Rector of the Seminary, Father Stephen Ignudi, did not fail to relate after each of his visits to the Vatican the great sorrow of the Pope, of whom he was a confidant and friend. The Christian family of nations was torn to pieces by fratricidal war. Could there be greater anguish for a Pope's heart? . . .

> Friar Maximilian had no taste for empty ideas. He was not satisfied with words. The Church was suffering. The Pope was suffering. The powers of evil were unchained, and the infernal offensive battered in positions which had seemed invincible. Christian charity stopped short and yielded before the barbed lines. Even the priests no longer dared to talk of love for the enemy. Still, was this a time to sit in the corner, to watch from the sidelines? Was it not necessary, rather, to prepare an attempt at counterattack, to weigh well the methods, and to choose effective weapons and impregnable positions? . . .

> Friar Maximilian meditated upon this and prayed. As a child he had amused himself by setting up a strategic defense of Lwow, "the city of eaglets." The task he now proposed to himself was in a very different way overwhelming. All Christendom was in

danger. Souls were being led astray. It was necessary to save *all* these souls! The blood of a soldier coursed through Friar Maximilian. And the "Lady" of his heart was a Warrior Queen (this very Western mode of expression refers to the Blessed Mother Mary). In Poland, devotion to the Blessed Mother Mary is born at the bugles' blast![4]

By chance, a clearer motivation appeared right before Father Kolbe's eyes. In 1917, a rally was held in Rome to commemorate the two hundredth anniversary of the founding of the Freemasons. Father Kolbe saw banners displayed right in front of the Vatican that said, "Satan must reign in the Vatican! The Pope will be his slave!"

When asked about the circumstances surrounding the foundation of the Knights of the Immaculata, Father Kolbe replied,

"The Freemasons began to spark their demonstrations with more and more effrontery, even raising their banners under the windows of the Vatican, banners which depicted on a background of black earth Lucifer trampling underfoot the Archangel Michael. When they started to distribute vicious tracts against the Holy Father, the idea to establish a company to fight the Freemasons and other agents of Lucifer was born."[5] So, here again we clearly see Father Kolbe's interest in fighting.

What set Father Kolbe's mind on a life-long, vigorous, unceas-

---

4. My translation follows closely that of Plumereau in Winowska, *Our Lady's Fool,* pp. 22-23. Only a few changes were necessary to keep it faithful to Sono's Japanese version. However, one change is telling: although Sono calls "Warrior Queen" (*ikusa no joō*) a "very Western mode of expression," it is actually her own term. Plumereau uses the words "Warrior Virgin" here, and what she renders "Virgin Mary," Sono calls the "Blessed Mother Mary" (*seibo maria*). The concept of virginity is absent from Sono's representations of the Immaculata.

5. This translation of the quote from Kolbe is taken from Plumereau's English translation in Winowska, *Our Lady's Fool,* p. 29, with one minor change: Plumereau's "black background" doesn't catch the key Masonry symbol of "black earth" that Sono makes explicit (*kokuchi*).

ing, propagation of love probably was something that became his own "personal grievance." In that case, those thoughts must have remained with him his whole life, like a scar after a bad burn.

Winowska says, "For it is of a truth that for those who love God, all things work together unto good—even war."[6]

Section Three

Back to my conversation with Father Anselmo that I interrupted.

Father Anselmo told me,

"When I saw what Father Kolbe was doing, I felt it really wasn't the right thing for him. It was just eating him up. Even though I had entered the novitiate a bit before Father Kolbe, I . . ."

"So, when you came to that conclusion, what did you do?" Father smiled softly.

"Well, there wasn't much I could do but watch a little longer how things went."

Such humane words overflowing with gentle, good will! Filled with their warmth, I just listened to the sound of the rain.

"I was at Niepokalanów as one of the elders, and I also knew him during the Kraków years. At times, Father Kolbe could be a bit too impulsive and needed to be stopped, made to think things through."

It suddenly occurred to me that Father Anselmo might be one of the conservative elders who were his "tormentors." Nonetheless, all his difficulties ended up working for his fight and his victory. And certainly nobody knew that better than Father Kolbe.

I asked:

"So far no matter where I've gone to hear about Father Kolbe, all I've heard are kind words of praise. Might you tell me something a bit different?"

"I see. Well, he was generally a cheerful person, but once, when

6. Winowska, *Our Lady's Fool,* p. 21.

he was at Grodno and was being tormented by another friar, he exclaimed, 'Had I known there were people like you, I would never had entered the monastery!' But it was only that one time."

Grodno, it seems, was the time when Father Kolbe was most abandoned by Hope. From the documents, Grodno seems like an old folks' home for aged, dispirited friars. And now, here comes a man who works too much. The powerful elders wanted to keep the monastery quiet, just as things had always been. Everything Father Kolbe did—installing a printing machine, creating such a din it seemed like a war was going on, and essentially undermining the sharp class distinction that had been established between brothers (laboring friars) and fathers (priest-friars)—upset the older friars.

On top of it all, since Father Kolbe and his group considered printing and distributing what they printed as nothing less that the first strike in a true war, there was no ground for compromise.

This was the only time that Father Anselmo dropped his guard and showed some affection for Father Kolbe, whom he generally thought to be a spoiled child who picked fights with "innocent incompetents."

The conversation turned quite naturally to the topic of Father Kolbe's parents.

It is well known that both Father Kolbe's parents had desired to enter monastic life before they were married, but did they both really abandon the secular life as planned on the occasion of their third son Józef's entering the monastery?

According to Father Anselmo's account, Juliusz Kolbe lived in the Franciscan monastery of Lwów from 1910 to 1914 and did housework and such there. He said Juliusz also lived at the same time at a branch of the monastery in a village called Cheshki where he did the same kind of work. As 1910 is the year when Father Kolbe was formally admitted to the Franciscan Order, it does appear that Juliusz Kolbe really did make sure his children were taken care of before he entered the monastery.

"In 1914, his father joined Piłsudski's Polish Legion and was captured in Russia early in the war. I heard he was hanged just south of the village of Lwów. But others say he was captured by the Russians at Częstochowa and killed."

According to a completely different account, Juliusz Kolbe entered the Franciscan monastery of Kraków, but on account of his age he couldn't handle the monastic life very well. He was encouraged to leave the monastery and went to Częstochowa, where he opened a shop selling religious goods and joined the independence movement. With the outbreak of World War I, Juliusz applied to the Polish Legion and was on his way to the Russian border when he was captured in the vicinity of Orsk and hanged.

Father Anselmo said:

> Father Kolbe's mother was in Kraków, in the convent of the Felician Sisters of the Third Order of St. Francis. I should clarify that she wasn't a nun but did various things for the sisters, like their shopping and bill paying. When Archbishop Sapieha of Kraków returned from Rome where he had been made a cardinal in 1946, a large crowd gathered around the station to greet him. Father Kolbe's mother was one of those who went to welcome him, but she collapsed right there in the street and died. I went to her funeral.

His mother received one letter, written in German, when he was in Auschwitz. "I am well. Don't worry. God is always with us." This was written by a son who, confronting his own imminent death, sought to console his mother. When his mother received the news that Father Kolbe had died, she never lost her composure. This could only have been because she was able to see how it was all part of God's plan.

I made a visit to the motherhouse of the Felician convent on Smoleńsk Street. The road passed through a quiet residential district, linking the center of the town and the town's external walls. The feeling of autumn was everywhere, from the ivy-covered brick walls and houses to the brightly colored leaves that had fallen in the streets.

Father O and I entered the chapel. There we found a good number of people praying in the soft darkness.

When I thought about this mother's heart, I wondered who, besides God, could really understand what she felt. She had certainly traveled a long way from that poor, but warm, row house in Zduńska Wola. From 1913 to 1946 (except for those first two years or so when she was in the Benedictine convent in Lwów), she spent thirty years bearing her sufferings and entrusting her hopes to God in front of this altar. I thought about why she moved from the Benedictines in Lwów to the Felician convent in Kraków. The official explanation is that it wasn't possible to remain with the Benedictines while being a Third Order Franciscan, but I think the real reason was something else entirely. Even while in the convent, she deeply desired always to be near her sons. She moved from Lwów to Kraków because her sons had moved to Kraków. But after 1912, when Father Kolbe entered the International Seraphic College in Rome,[7] this mother was not able to spend any time with her Rajmund. Life in Grodno, building Niepokalanów, missionary work in Japan, and then Auschwitz. This mother has precious little time to talk with her son. All she could do was tell God her worries about her son and hope that He would convey them to him.

I took one last look at the courtyard and then went out the gate into the beautiful fall colors. As soon as I did, an old woman came up to Father O and said something to him in Polish.

"What did she say?" I asked Father O.

"She said praise be to the Lord Jesus Christ. In the old days, everyone greeted priests with those words," Father replied.

That night, I was about to be homeless. Because we hadn't

---

7. While Kolbe was originally scheduled to study at his order's International Seraphic College (The Pontifical University of St. Bonaventure), he demurred and eventually enrolled instead at the Jesuit Pontifical Gregorian University, and then at the Pontifical Theological Faculty, where he earned his doctorate in 1919. Ricciardi, *St. Maximilian Kolbe*, 29-30.

followed the schedule I had set in Japan, I didn't have a hotel reservation. Thanks to the kindness of the Society of Jesus, I was able to stay in the large reception room just outside the front desk of the convent.

"Mass will be celebrated at 6:30 tomorrow morning," Father O told me.

"But don't get up if you are tired."

I'm an early riser, but I wasn't too sure I'd be able to get up in time for Mass. This was my first experience staying in a convent. I could just imagine, if I went home and reported to my close friends that I went to Mass "day and night" while I was over here, how they'd take me for some kind of wonder. I decided, in part to protect my reputation, I'd beg off Mass tomorrow morning (after all, it wasn't even Sunday!).

But, just my luck—I woke up early. I looked at the clock and saw it was four in the morning. I had been awakened by the sound of a distant bugle. Shut up!—but I kept the words to myself. At this early hour, it must be a reveille bugle from some nearby barracks.

I tried to get back to sleep, but you guessed it—I woke up at 5:30 and that was that. There was nothing else to do at that time, so I went to Mass. Honestly, I was starting to feel that going to Mass here for several days would be nothing but a welcome pleasure. But I also knew that such thinking just wasn't like me. When Mass was over, Fr. O said something to me to the effect that he appreciated how hard it was for me to get up so early. I asked him, "Where do they blow that bugle? Is there a barracks in this town?"

I was still smarting from being awakened by that bugle. "Oh no. They blow it over at St. Mary's Church."

"At St. Mary's?! But why at four in the morning of all times do they blow a bugle?"

"They blow it on the hour." I was taken aback.

"But I didn't hear it once during the day, nor did I hear it at five or six."

The commotion in the town must have covered it up during the day. And when the five o'clock bugle rang out, there is no question but that I was sound asleep.

"That bugle call stops half-way though. In 1259, when the Tatars attacked Kraków, they came right into the town square and shot the bugler through the heart. The bugler, right in the midst of his song, did a somersault and dropped dead. Ever since the fourteenth century, they have played the bugle like that at St. Mary's Church, on the hour, day and night, facing all four directions. And they still play it just like that, breaking off right at the point in the song where the bugler was shot."

"Father, is that a recording?" I asked a typical Japanese question.

"No, every time a real person blows it."

For the first time, I was able to really understand through the customs of Kraków what Winowska meant when she wrote, "The faith Poland has in the Blessed Mother Mary was born in the echoes of a bugle."

Chapter 5

Extermination Center

Section One

I felt something like a singular, dark premonition. There was nothing rational about it. I just thought that the day I visited Auschwitz it would rain.

And it was just as I had thought. A cold rain fell, as if it were trying to drag the heavy, damp Polish autumn one step closer to winter.

I got in the car that the Jesuits had sent for me with three others—Father O, another priest, and Brother B—and we all set off for Auschwitz early in the day. The car followed along a river until it arrived at a place that seemed to be the Jesuits' villa. There we found a close friend of Fr. O who had not seen him during the fifteen years he was gone from his homeland, and while I didn't understand a word they said, the generous back-and-forth of their conversation dispelled a bit of my apprehension that I was about to have a gloomy experience.

We took a commemorative photograph on the roof of a new building in the villa, and then off we went again. We rode on for more than an hour though quiet farm villages and several small towns. Suddenly, I realized we had just passed the plaza in front of the unbelievably bright and modern Oświęcim station.

Before I took this trip, I thought—as most Japanese do—that Auschwitz was in Germany. But the town where this world-famous concentration camp is located is clearly in Poland and has been known by the name Oświęcim for centuries. According to Antoni

Ricciardi's biography, *St. Maximilian Maria Kolbe,* before the war Oświęcim was a town filled with barracks and factories, but thanks (?) to their destruction in air raids, later the concentration camp was built here.

The road crossed over the railroad tracks and the next minute we found ourselves facing a building that looked like a warehouse with an observation tower. We were at the entrance to Birkenau, the concentration camp paired as they say in "Auschwitz-Birkenau," and this was the building known as "the Gate of Death." The railroad that comes in here links Vienna and Kraków, and all the prisoners who arrived at this "City of the Dead" came under this gate.

"Where is Auschwitz?" I earnestly asked Father O, since I still didn't understand the relationship between the two concentration camps. Auschwitz is only a mere two kilometers removed from Birkenau, and one cannot understand how these two concentration camps functioned without considering them together. They were designed so that Birkenau would be the extermination center and Auschwitz, the industrial center.

Why was this place chosen to be the extermination center? I pondered the question as I shuddered in the cold, passing through "the Gate of Death," and following on foot the railroad lines into the heart of the camp. The rain had let up, but the sand-colored soil at my feet was thoroughly drenched. All around were many groups of people walking along with us, as though they were on a picnic with their children. The children were raising their voices in carefree laughter, frolicking, running on ahead. The scenery around us seemed in keeping with their mood. While the barbed-wire fence continued on as far as the eye could see—marking a line of contrast with the gray sky—the interior of the concentration camp was good, flat ground and the dried grass might remind one of a winter lawn. The concentration camp that long ago held prisoners consisted of large, roofed, brick buildings with small windows. Parts were already in ruins (perhaps the ruined sections had been made of wood), and only sections of the furnace and a tall chimney stood suggestively like grave markers placed in a special section of the overgrown fields.

"Well, at least one can see there was a furnace," I muttered to myself with a sense of relief.

Of course there was. The Polish winters are said to get as cold as twenty-five to thirty degrees below zero. No matter that the prisoners were under a sentence of death, without a furnace they wouldn't have lasted a day. And the camp administrators would be greatly inconvenienced if they all died at once. Still, in spite of all that, I didn't sense any clear sign of homicide there. It wasn't until I entered one of the buildings that I understood what was so horrific about it. Inside the dark barracks the concrete floor was so cold I felt just like I was in a barn. What reminded me that I wasn't was that the interior was fenced off into sections that looked a lot like Japanese closets.[1] And those closets were divided into units about the height of a large closet, which were sectioned width-wise into three.

It appeared that Brother B often guided groups on their visits here, and through Father O he told me that ten people would sleep in one of those units. The length of the units was about the same as an average man's height and I guess they were about seventy or eighty centimeters high. The problem was the width. Each unit had a floor made of boards about twenty centimeters wide. Counting those boards, I could see that the space each person occupied was no more than twenty or so centimeters. Did they take turns sleeping? Or were they able to fit into such an unbelievably tight space, like thin cuts of toast packed into a box, by cramming in sideways people who, through starvation, were merely skin and bones?

This was the first time I had ever stood in the actual spot where Man systematically eradicated his fellow Man. I thought it strange that I could not hear the voices of the dead. Surely it is not right that the resentments and lamentations of every one of those who were crammed into these boxes could later simply disappear without a trace.

---

1. "Japanese closets" = *oshiire*.

Walking across the wet grassy area, we finally encountered an unforgettable ruin. Part of the building—was it the roof or the wall?—was crumbled around us, and ugly, rusted iron support beams poked out where the concrete had been torn off. This was what remained of the human ovens. Sure enough, several of the tourists who had been left speechless just silently climbed up on the mountain of brick rubble that lay around us. Some young birds were playing on the grass now wet from the rain. Wild chrysanthemums were in bloom. Truly, this is a place of silence, I thought. Just the gentle falling rain, the sound of the wind, and the freezing cold that penetrated our hearts, and here people—in keeping with the name of this Center—were extinguished without a sound.

Section Two

The entrance to Auschwitz was packed with people and automobiles. Nothing around suggested the dark atmosphere of intrigue; rather, it all seemed like the entrance to a zoo or a museum. How can people come here with such a carefree attitude as if the "death" of other human beings was a mere spectacle? Just as I was thinking that I would never come to such a place if I didn't have to, I was pushed through the gates by the crowd.

The prisoners' barracks were not what we Japanese think of as "barracks." They were depressing, two-story brick houses with a row of poplar trees soaring above the roofs. If it weren't for the scaffold with railway tracks leading to it standing right there in the open or the steeple-roofed guard houses and such, I would have believed it had someone told me these were dormitories for some school. We went into one of the most typical of the barracks. The walls were lined with photographs of the people who had been interned there. They said that, except for the Jews, prisoners who came here from the winter of 1940 to about 1943 all had their photographs taken. When one thinks of those people who didn't even have a photo taken of them, could we say that these were better off because at least there was some evidence that they had existed? Most of them stared right at us as we walked past them, with their eyes bulging from their sockets, wearing their prisoner uniforms that looked like striped pajamas. You could see the fear in their deep-set eyes and swollen Adam's apples. I couldn't shake the impression that they were just like the eyes of fish about to die. As I was thinking these were the eyes of despair, the expressionless eyes of dying fish, I suddenly decided to walk down the middle of the hallway.

I then realized they were anything but expressionless. It was as though they were silently calling out to me.

"Wait a minute!" one of them said to me.

"Listen to me. Hear what happened to each and every one of us!"

I kept walking with downcast eyes. The people in the photos were depicted only from the shoulders up, but I was trembling with fear that they were about to grab me from behind. So, I walked down the center of the hallway. It was because I had this childish thought that maybe they couldn't get me there.

The dead in the photographs knew I had come to write about Father Kolbe—or so it seemed to me. But they also seemed to know that a writer should write about the many unknown people rather than those who are already famous in history. But in the end, Brother B told me he had found Father Kolbe's picture, and once again I was standing before the face of this dead priest. It was a picture of him in his Franciscan robes with round wire-rimmed glasses. His beard was gone and he was slightly furrowing his brow. "Hello," I said silently to the priest in the picture. "I've finally come. Under your spell."

Block 14 where Father Kolbe was assigned was closed to the public, so Brother B took us to Block 11 where the starvation bunker is. It was the very last block of buildings that were all in a neat row and, while the building itself wasn't any different from the others, in between it and the block next to it was a sight that struck one right in the heart. The space was about the size of a tennis court, and people were milling about, unable to leave even as the cold evening air was already descending on us. Facing us was a wall of bricks piled up to the height of about the second story of the buildings. In front of it were two rows of thick railway ties set on end, six in each row, black as if they had been painted with tar. Here and there, gold and silver papers were stuck on them. There were flowers placed at the base of the black wooden wall, and the candles that were lit along the ground flickered like will-o'-the-wisp.

This was where death sentences by firing squad were carried out. The blood of 200,000 people seeped into the ground under that wall. Were those tinfoil stars stuck on the black boards to mark the spot where victims stood until they fell under the report of the guns?

In the midst of it all, Brother B walked along, inspecting the half-above ground half-underground windows of Block 11 that faced along the right side of the execution ground. It was clear from the thick concrete blinds over the windows that from the beginning they knew what would happen here in the courtyard and wanted to prevent the residents of the underground room from seeing it. Also, they had fixed thick iron bars deep in the windows.

In one of the opened windows to the underground room there was a bouquet of red carnations. That's how we knew that it was under that window that Father Kolbe met his end. I went back through the courtyard, entered Block 11 and went down the stairs to the underground room along with the other sightseers. I stopped on the landing for a moment and thought to myself, "I wonder if the priest and his companions knew this was their road to death?" I felt it was a little hard to breathe. In the underground corridor several office doors were open. Going through one, I entered an even smaller passageway and found several rooms, each about ten square meters in size. These were the starvation bunkers.

My first thought was—what if there is no window in the starvation bunker? My fear was all about me. I'm a bit of a hopeless claustrophobic, and when I get into an enclosed space, I become so terrified that I can't breathe. But fortunately, there was a small, open skylight in the starvation bunker facing the courtyard with that execution ground. Even though it didn't let in a ray of sunshine, at least Father Kolbe and the nine men put to death with him in here didn't suffer from shortness of breath. At the entrance to the bunker there was a wire screen put up to keep people from randomly wandering in. And there were red carnations and bouquets of red roses stuck in the netting, upside down.

"They consider Father's death to be a martyr's death, so people keep bringing red flowers as offerings," Father O explained to me. I fixed my eyes on those flowers, and then I gazed up at the skylight. No sooner had I done so when the silhouette of the flowers turned into the faces of Father Kolbe and the nine men who died with him, and I saw them floating in the pale, yellow light of the skylight.

There was something about the events that led to Father Kolbe meeting his end in this room that was deeply suggestive of the stories in the New Testament.

It just so happens that around 1940 there was a friar named Rembisz[2] at Niepokalanów. The immediate cause of Father Kolbe's arrest was a letter of indictment that alleged he had conspired against the German occupation, and it was Rembisz who had signed the indictment. At the time, Poland was behind the German-Soviet front, so Germany was more nervous about traitors behind the lines than about the enemy they could see. But Rembisz's letter of indictment was a complete fabrication based on a German trap. One day Rembisz was called to the police station and interrogated about whether Father Kolbe hadn't committed any act of treason against Germany. When Rembisz replied that he couldn't think of any, he was told, "in that case sign here"—and a document written in German was placed before him.

"I don't know any German, so not being able to examine the contents, I just shut my eyes and signed."

Rembisz was just another victim.

---

2. Gorganio Rembisz.

It was said that another reason Father Kolbe was arrested was that he was publishing a newspaper, and that the newspaper had "attacked Germany's policy of invading its neighboring countries and had criticized the Nazi's oppression of the Catholic Church and the Catholic faithful." But what seems more accurate are the suspicions that it was the work of a certain Ratajczak who was the administrator for the region that covered Niepokalanów. He was in every sense a man skilled at the art of making dirty profits. Ratajczak was a Bosnian-born Pole, but he got along well with the German army and shamelessly would go and take foodstuff and materials from Niepokalanów. In short, it was in Ratajczak's interest to get Father Kolbe and the other friars out of the way so he could take the monastery's resources whenever and as much as he wished.

Father Kolbe's final journey, so similar to the Way of the Cross, began on May 29, 1941. On the evening of that day, Father Maximilian Kolbe and three hundred and twenty companions were disgorged from a freight car that had arrived at Oświęcim. The Friar Ladislaus Swies who arrived at Oświęcim with Father Kolbe tells us:

"While we were riding in that freight train from Pawiak to Oświęcim, someone starting singing hymns and Polish songs. Lots of people joined in the singing. I wanted to know who had started it, and I saw it was Father Kolbe. Since I like to sing and joined in singing in harmony with Father Kolbe, he took an interest in me.

"The mood was a heavy one. But nonetheless, thanks to Father Kolbe's songs and words of encouragement, after a bit we recovered our good cheer."[3]

Father's new name was prisoner number 16670, and his house was penal servitude Block 17. Three days after arrival, Father was rounded up for work digging a wall for the crematorium. Of course, this work was finished within a few days, and Father was sent to work in the fields of Babice, about four kilometers from Oświęcim. There his work was to carry out lumber for filling the swamps and wetlands.

---

3. There is a longer and slightly different translation of Swies's testimony in Ricciardi, pp. 278-9.

Already Father's own passion was being prepared for him at a place of which he was completely unaware. On April 23, about a month before Father had arrived at Auschwitz, a prisoner had escaped from Block 2 and the camp commandant Höss[4] had come up with a new method of punishment—to seal up ten prisoners in the underground bunker of Block 11. They would be given no water or food until the escapee returned.

Just as when on Calvary Christ gave everything he had to the criminals crucified next to him down to his final moment, so too did Father Maximilian Kolbe become a source of strength for the souls of those imprisoned with him. Mieczysław Kościelniak tells us that Father Kolbe would talk of how the great and all-powerful God gave Man the trial of suffering to prepare him for a better life, and he encouraged them all to endure this suffering as it would all end soon enough.

Once, Dr. Joseph Stemler was told to take corpses to the crematorium. He found himself face to face with the dead bodies of two prisoners. They were completely naked, and the expressions on their faces showed they had suffered torture. Joseph Stemler was a war veteran, but when he looked at those horrible dead bodies, he simply froze up.

"Come on, let's move them."

Stemler picked up one of the blood-smeared corpses and put it in a box and then carried it over to the crematorium. Then, once again he heard the voice behind him.

"Holy Mary, pray for us."

Stemler felt as though the words poured strength back into his body. He had to wait by the foul-smelling crematorium until the bodies were burned. Finally, their job finished, they started to leave and again he heard the voice behind him.

"Eternal rest grant unto them, O Lord."

That was when Stemler first knew it was Father Kolbe. Father

---

4. Rudolf Höss.

had a history of tuberculosis and wasn't able to maintain even a minimum standard of health in the concentration camp. His fever wouldn't come down, so he was sent to the quarantined Block of the Invalids for suspected typhus patients. In the three weeks he was in the Block of the Invalids, Father Kolbe heard confessions from the other patients and offered prayers and blessings for the dying.

Dr. Stemler, who was in the Block of the Invalids with him, testified that Father Kolbe firmly believed that good always triumphed in the end.

"Suffering does not have the power to produce anything. Only love has the power to produce everything. Suffering cannot conquer us but will only help make us stronger. So that those who come after us will find happiness."

Father Kolbe firmly grasped Stemler's hand to press his point. But while Stemler was overwhelmed by these words, he remained unconvinced, as his heart was still full of anger.

Released from the sick quarters, Father Kolbe was assigned to Block 12 with others who were unable to work. Those people in this Block were facing a certain death in the near future. Since they only received half of the already insufficient food rations, it was inconceivable that anyone would recover from his illness. But Father Kolbe made good progress, so a few weeks later he was moved to Block 14 with those assigned to agricultural work.

Section Three

Someone escaped. It was July 31. The guard dogs returned from the swamps looking dejected. The prisoners had already been standing at attention for over three hours. Gino Lubich writes that they no longer looked human, but seemed like grotesque puppets. But they were not puppets. They were shackled with fear, for they knew only too well what would happen after a prisoner escapes.

After 9:00 in the evening they finally heard the order to dismiss. Prisoners brought out a large pot of soup but they were not allowed to take any. It was only to allow the aroma of the soup to cut right through their stomachs. Then, the pot of soup was taken to the edge of the ground and poured out right in front of them to taunt them.

The prisoners of Block 14 were allowed to go to bed, but not one of them was able to sleep. They suffered from hunger and anxiety. If one person escapes, ten will die. Would it be me? And to be killed by this most slow, anguishing method. They say that with death by starvation, one's intestines dry up, one's veins burn like fire, and after going mad, one's brain suffers multiple explosions. For Officer Fritzsch, simple starvation was not punishment enough. His sadistic pleasures could only be satisfied by adding on the extra suffering of dehydration . . .

The next morning, the prisoners were called to assemble. The escapee had not been found. The prisoners, who had not had sufficient food for several months and now had had nothing at all to eat for the last twenty-four hours, were once again forced to stand at attention.

One hour seemed like a century. The sun roasted their heads like chestnuts. Their throats had dried up from lack of nourishment, and their muscles were wrenched from terrible cramping. One after another, the prisoners began to pass out. The S.S. would kick them with their field boots. And if that didn't bring them back to consciousness, they were dragged over to a corner of the grounds and left there. After a few hours, those bodies formed a mountain. At 6:00 pm, the prisoners who had been out on work detail returned. Fritzsch approached the prisoners from Block 14 who were still standing in rows.

"The escapee has not been found. So, ten of you will die in the starvation bunker. Understand? After that, it will be twenty of you."

He began walking in front of these people who had broken out in a cold sweat.

His calm pace seemed like a funeral march. Fritzsch was a very dramatic person. I have no doubt that while he walked like the angel of death among these living corpses, his ears were tuned to the magnificent power of Wagner's works.

He would suddenly stop and, in what was likely very poor Polish, order them:

"Open your mouth and show us your teeth! Stick out your tongue!"

Wasn't that more like how one judges the quality of a horse than how one treats a human being? After this oral cavity inspection, he would suddenly point to his left and cry out:

"This one!"

Thus, one by one, the victims were chosen.

"Farewell! We'll meet again in heaven. Long live Poland!"

Among such cries, one could make out a whimpering voice.

"How cruel. Farewell to my wife, and to my children."

It was the voice of Sergeant Franciszek Gajowniczek. He held his head in his hands and was crying.

Suddenly, a man walked confidently up to the Commandant. His soft voice carried over the men like a gentle breeze.

"Who is that? What does he think he's doing? Is he crazy?" Someone said it was Father Kolbe.

"Polish pig. What do you want?" Fritzsch demanded.

"I'd like to take the place of one of these men."

It seemed as if a spell had come over everyone there. They were too startled to move.

"In whose place do you want to die?"

"For this one. He has a wife and children."

He said it as only a priest who has renounced marriage for life could.

"Who the hell are you?"

"A Catholic priest."

"Accepted."

The S.S. officer at his side erased 5659, which was Gajowniczek's prisoner number and instead wrote Father Kolbe's number, 16670. The ten men selected were ordered to strip. Now all they had on was tattered underwear. And then they walked toward Block 11—of course, in their bare feet. Father turned his head a bit to the left and recited a prayer.

At that precise moment, beyond the high-voltage electrified barbed-wire fence, the sun was giving off its last rays. And then the huge, burning disc sank into the distant marshlands and was seen no more. The sky turned the color of the blood of the martyrs.

"That evening I saw the most beautiful sunset in my life." So said an Auschwitz survivor about a setting sun he recalled in late July 1941.

The starvation bunker was pitch black. There, the prisoners had their remaining possessions taken from them. When the S.S. officers left, they spit out the lines, "You're gonna wilt away like tulips." From then on, everyday one could hear the sound of voices in prayer coming from the starvation bunker. Bruno Borgowiec, who served as interpreter and waste disposer, said, "every time I went down there, I felt as if I was going into the basement of a church. I'd never seen anything like it." Of course, what he found was not just people completely saved by the power of prayer. Every time Borgowiec opened the door and went into the bunker to remove human waste, some of the prisoners would cling to him like madmen, begging for water. When anyone showed enough physical strength to put up some resistance, the guards would kick him in the stomach until he was laid out flat on the concrete floor. If that didn't finish him off, they'd settle it with a single gunshot. Borgowiec thought it was an easy job since he didn't have much waste to remove. The reason was that the prisoners who were suffering from thirst would drink up everything in the lavatory buckets. Like the ebbing of the tide, one by one the people would die off. And with every day, the voices singing and praying would become fewer and fewer.

"Every time we looked in on them, others would be lying on the floor, but Father Kolbe would be standing or kneeling with a serene expression on his face, and he would greet us. Even the other guards respected Father Kolbe, as they knew how he came to be in here. I heard one of them say the following, 'I'm telling you, this priest is a real man. You don't see many like him.'"

It was on August 14 when the phone call came to the clinic and Dr. Boch took it. He just stood there petrified with the color gone from his face, listening. In the end, he merely replied,

"Jawohl" (certainly).

He put down the receiver and entered the room with the glass door cabinet. He prepared four intravenous injections. After attaching sterilized needles, he took a large beaker with *phenol* written on it and filled the four syringes with it. Taking the syringes with him, he then went to the underground starvation bunker. Some days earlier, the other six survivors had fallen silent. Borgowiec secretly observed all this in the shadows. And he knew that they had to hurry up and empty the bunker as other condemned prisoners were waiting. The doctor entered the starvation bunker in his white coat and after a second or two Borgowiec heard him say,

"This will end it all."

When the doctor had left the room, Borgowiec saw the priest motionless, leaning against the wall with his eyes wide open and a clear expression on his face, as if he were still alive. Standing outside the starvation bunker, I thought to myself that maybe Father Kolbe had conducted a certain experiment without ever having intended to. He proved that humans somehow can survive for fourteen full days without a drop of water. During that period, cruel temptations must have occurred to him. He had no water or food. At some point during those fourteen days, they must have carried out executions by firing squad just outside the gloomy underground bunker. How Father Kolbe must have envied those whose sufferings were ended quickly by a bullet.

Pushed along by the wave of people, I exited the building. I felt completely numb to the bottom of my heart and merely followed wherever Friar B led me. When I regained my senses, I noticed a small plaza. I was told it was where Rudolf Höss, the designer and commandant of Auschwitz, was hung. Right behind it there was a crematorium positioned as if it were half-hidden. I followed the crowd down the steps. When I stood in this space that was like a huge, underground cavern, I found I no longer had even the strength to feel afraid—this in spite of the fact that with my phobia, the gas room was what I had greatly dreaded. I simply stood there in the middle of that room. What I was afraid of was touching that wall that so many people, deceived into believing that they would be showering and then locked into the room, gassed with Zyklon B, and just before they died of asphyxiation, clawed at in their last moments of anguish.

But much to my surprise when I saw the two ovens next door, I felt relieved. This came from my recognition that by the time they were brought here, those people had already been released from their sufferings. I had already made up my mind not to feel sad over such things as how Father Kolbe's ashes were scattered all over the place. But when I saw the flowers placed in front of an open cauldron that looked kind of like a strongbox, I said to myself, yes—this is actually a happy place . . .

At that moment, I was sure of only one thing. I didn't want to say another word. I realized that something deep within me, something I had long cherished and believed in, had been smashed to pieces. Could it be true that everything I had believed about mankind until now was all an illusion?

Crestfallen, I left the crematorium. I saw a light in the distance, but around me all was night.

Chapter 6

Survivors

Section One

When Father Kolbe was being passed around among the concentration camps, something happened that deserves our attention. It happened when he was in the Pawiak Prison. Winowska sets the scene as follows:

> One morning, inspection was carried out. At the sight of the priest's Franciscan habit, the S.S. group leader was seized with rage. With bloodshot eyes and foam at the mouth, he seized the rosary that Father Maximilian wore on his cord and pulled it violently.
>
> "Imbecile, idiot, filthy priest! Do you really still believe in that crap? Answer up! . . ."
>
> "Yes, I believe," the priest replied in a calm yet strong voice.
>
> No sooner had he spoken than he was sent flying across the room. Then another violent blow. He doubled up with pain and felt the salty taste of blood in his mouth.[1]
>
> Even after all that, every time the S.S. officer asked, "and now do you believe?" he kept replying, "I do believe." And every time he answered, the S.S. officer would only pound him the harder.

---

1. In translating this quote from Winowska, I have followed Therese Plumereau's English translation where Sono's text permits, but where there are slight differences in the texts I have rendered Sono's Japanese directly into English. Cf. Winowska, *Our Lady's Fool*, p. 152.

One mustn't forget that when I finally was able to visit Auschwitz, it was in the midst of the Polish spiritual climate where ordinary life was inconceivable without the existence of God (whether one affirmed or negated it) and that was where suddenly I clearly felt that I had been able to sense something of the essence of "sadism."

Now I could understand why Geoffrey Gorer wrote that sadism is "the pleasure felt from the observed modifications on the external world produced by the observer."[2] For Sade, God was indispensable. Hence, Gorer said that "all his life de Sade was obsessed by God"[3] and that "he attacks God and the Church with reason, with ridicule, with imprecations, with blasphemy."[4]

I think the S.S. officer who tore off Father Kolbe's rosary clearly was seized by a mixture of terror and pleasure. Certainly it was true of him—and of all mankind—whether we are conscious of it or not—that this is how we think we can succeed in negating the existence of this God who must always remain hidden.

Did he believe that rejecting God would liberate him from God, that this was the way that Man could conquer God, could raise himself up to a position equal with God? Did he really think that by yanking off the rosary and abusing this priest he was able to spit in the face of God?

That sadism is inconceivable without the existence of God is demonstrated by the fact that sadistic acts are premised on the need to violate God's law. If God's law didn't exist, there would be no "pleasure" in trampling on it. For example, if Man burned down all the cities in the world and butchered all the people but didn't feel through those acts he could trample on God, he would not take any

---

2. Geoffrey Gorer, The *Marquis de Sade: A Short Account of His Life and Work* (New York: Liveright Publishing Corporation, 1934), p. 220.

3. Gorer, p. 118.

4. Cf. Gorer, pp. 119-120. Sono made a minor revision to Gorer's actual language by inserting "God and the Church," which Gorer had just stated, for the pronoun "them" in the original quote.

wicked pleasure in such things. Many people have what we might call "strange childhood memories" of finding a kind of pleasure in killing dragonflies or butterflies. But few people still feel good about that after they've grown up. God's existence can never be denied by rising up against Him, no matter how far one indulges in the dark passion of Man just killing and killing his fellow man.

What the Nazis did was tied up with "pleasure"—that is what I learned at Auschwitz. Of course, there were exceptions. In his book *Man's Search for Meaning,* Frankl[5] wrote about how the Commandant at his last concentration camp, who was a member of the S.S., secretly bought medicine from his pocket money and circulated it among the prisoners.

But for the vast majority of those in the concentration camps, there had to be some kind of pleasure in disposing of so many people for so many years or it wouldn't have continued for so long. In contrast, Japan's wartime atrocities were more a matter of fits and spasms. They'd just lose their tempers and kill somebody.

At Auschwitz, however, it was physically impossible to just lose your temper and kill somebody. There, nothing could be done without first having a coldly analytical, detailed plan. According to Roger Manvell's book *S.S. and Gestapo*, between 1943 and 1944, more than twelve thousand prisoners were killed and cremated every day at Auschwitz. That number is way beyond the number of people you can kill on sudden outbursts of hatred.

Twelve thousand people. Where did they get them? How did they control them? How did they kill them? And because dead people cannot just get up and walk away, how did they dispose of them all? It would seem that to work out such a scheme a good many people would have to have had many meetings, make plans, draw up a blueprint, put together an organization, follow up to see if they get

5. Viktor Emil Frankl, author of *Ein Psycholog Erlebt Das Konzentrationslager*, 1947 (translated into Japanese by Shimoyama Tokuji as *Yoru to kiri* [Night and Fog] (Misuzu Shobo, 1961). English translation by Ilse Lasch, *Man's Search for Meaning: An Introduction to Logotheraphy*, second revised edition (Boston: Beacon Press, 1963).

the kind of results they had hoped for, then make further improvements, and do it all over again several times.

It's just not the kind of thing that happens in a fit of rage. And it is hard to imagine that such a continuous stream of murders like that could happen without some kind of underlying passion for it. Leaving aside for the moment the individual guards at the concentration camps, one element of S.S. and Gestapo ideology was surely the pleasure of sadism. And sadism—even recognizing that I can't be expected to completely define the essence of it right here—it has to have something to it beyond the mere tormenting of Man by Man.

What I mean is that precisely because of the pleasure derived from the thought that by tormenting other men one is wounding God sadism is linked to a pleasure that lies deep inside Man. Putting it this way might invite misunderstanding, but it is true that without the existence of God a dark passion like sadism would never exist. In other words, without first accepting God, one can neither understand nor write about sadism.

After visiting Auschwitz, I began to experience some annoying trifles. The most obvious one was my loss of appetite. Nothing I ate had any flavor.

Up to that point, I never had a reaction like this to anything. I'm just one of those typical, happy-go-lucky people who aren't very imaginative, and I was never bothered by any national, social, or individual guilt for something unless I was responsible for directly participating in it. I guess what I'm trying to say is that for Japanese who don't have a sense of God, true sadism cannot be understood except through certain mores that bear some resemblance to it. I certainly should not have been expected to feel any connection to this affair that happened in a distant, foreign country. Nonetheless, I was shocked. That night, when I got back to my hotel, I took two tranquilizer pills—even though, a scant ten years ago, I had almost become addicted to them.

Since then, because of that experience, I was now healthier than I had a right to be and was loath to take any medicine. But that night,

I couldn't sleep without the pills. I took the pamphlets I had bought at Auschwitz and shoved them deep in the bottom of my suitcase, and in their stead pulled out a book of poetry. It was a collection of Rabindranath Tagore's poems. You can't imagine how grateful I was to have a volume of Tagore's poems with me that day. I started reading Katayama Toshihiko's beautiful translation of the poem "Kani" from the collection *Syamali*. "Syamali" means the beauty of pale green color, and Kani is the name of a girl. The protagonist "I" and Kani live next door to each other. Kani is a noble girl who likes to play tricks. "I" is a first-rate student who had memorized all the rules of Sanskrit grammar. Once when he was bragging about that, Kani pounded on his back with her clenched fists.

Eventually, Kani grows up. "I" is a frequent visitor to Kani's house, and one day, Kani's father tests his English ability. "I" doesn't understand the question and is greatly shamed. Kani's father, Shivaramu, did it because he harbored an unbelievable antipathy toward this young man who has been hanging around his daughter.

A day came for both our families
  To move house.
Sivarām, the engineer, would go westwards
  To join an electric lighting firm in some town.
We were for Calcutta,
  The village school was not to father's liking.
Two days before going away
  Kani came and said, "Come into our orchard."
I asked, "Why?"
  Kani said, "We will steal together.
For we shall never again have a day like this."

The two stole a Muzāffarpur lychee from Mr. Sivarām's cherished fruit orchard. I climbed a tree and picked the lychee, Kani waited below to put the fruit in her basket. But they were caught in the act.

He said, "I see what it is that you study best.
　　Keep it up for you are a promising thief."

Many years passed. When I returned from England, I found Kani had married. Kani looked just like a new bride, with the red border of sāri hanging from her head and the red dot of a Hindu on her forehead.

I worked making drugs in a pharmaceutical factory in Calcutta. It was a monotonous life. One day a letter came from Kani. She had returned to the home village to represent her husband at her niece's wedding. Her father Sivarām was opposed to the marriage and left for Hoshiārpur in a fit. Kani said she came back hoping to see me.

I returned to that house next to Kani's house
　　in the old village that I had not seen for so long.
On the side of the reservoir by the stone steps,
　　the Hijal tree still leaned toward the water, as it used to.
From the reservoir came,
　　the same old sweet smell of moss.
And from the bough of the Sisu tree hung
　　that swing even today.

Bending down before me in salute Kani said,

"Amal-dādā, I live far away;

Of meeting you on Brothers' Day (the day before the new

moon in November, when Indian girls paint a white

dot on the foreheads of their brothers and male

cousins as a blessing)

I have no hope.

Today is not a special day to meet you but

I wanted to see you anyway

so I sent you that letter."

There was a good spot with a great view

in the shade of an Ashwattha (Banyan) tree in the

orchard where a small square carpet was spread out.

The rites were performed there.

Kani laid a basket at my feet.

It was filled with lychees.

She said, "It's those lychees."

I said, "It's probably not exactly the same ones."

She said, "Who knows?"

and quickly walked away.[6]

The reason I quoted at length from this poem from Tagore's later period is because that night I found in its poetic world a certain hope in life.

"Kani" is a small fragment of youth that one could find anywhere on this earth. It comes in the hues of a quiet suffering and a natural sadness. Rather, I should say that because it has this kind of shadow

---

6. I have consulted Sheila Chatterjee's excellent translation of "Kani" in *Syamali* (Calcutta: Visva-Bharati Publishing Department, 1955), but adjusted it to follow Katayama Toshihiko's Japanese translation as cited by Sono.

it touches our hearts and we are able to believe that such people really existed.

I felt after returning from Auschwitz that I wanted to believe in it again—that a human life, if it is normal, is not so terribly good or bad. If I had to sum up Auschwitz in a word, I would say "it was not normal." Thanks to "Kani," the outer edges of my heart, which had frozen up at Auschwitz, were starting to thaw. "Kani" was the "ordinary" world, which can be gentle and sad, tediously boring yet also refreshing. It was an excellent antidote to Auschwitz.

Yet, as I turned out the lights, it occurred to me that we are not left without hope. Through his death, Father Kolbe certainly saved one person's life. In the morning, I was to meet Mr. Franciszek Gajowniczek who was alive today because Father Kolbe had taken his place.

How old was Mr. Gajowniczek? I wasn't really sure. And it seemed too much a hassle to go digging through my bags to look it up in my papers. At least I knew he was old enough to have children. Clearly, Mr. Gajowniczek had "children" already in 1941 when he was saved by Father Kolbe. I knew so because when he was chosen for the death penalty, he cried out, "What will become of my poor wife and children!" It was merely from hearing this cry that Father Kolbe asked if he could take his place.

I reckoned that if his children were already born by 1941 they had to be at least in their thirties. The older child might even be nearly thirty-five. Whether they were sons or daughters, I didn't know, but in either case, they were probably married, which means Mr. Gajowniczek was actually old enough to be a grandfather.

I hoped that I wouldn't have any problem hearing him during the interview, with grandchildren running around the place making noise. There were rare occasions when, during interviews, I was annoyed by the sounds of music, construction, or roosters crowing and such. But I also wanted to see Mr. Gajowniczek sitting there, surrounded by his grandchildren. "Kani" is a poem about youth, but we might say that Mr. Gajowniczek was probably enjoying the ordinary life that is the latter half of "Kani." I don't know if Mr. Gajowniczek was strict or indulgent with his grandchildren, but in either case, I could imagine him sitting around the dinner table with his family, in the midst of all the noise that kids make, forgetting all he suffered at Auschwitz and thinking to himself, "after all I've been through, what a great thing it is to be alive." I'm sure that's what he was doing. I was beginning to have something close to a conviction. The impressions of what I had actually seen in the world so far also left me with an uncertain feeling about those kinds of ambiguities or unclear results. Not once had I encountered a heroic story that went just as I had hoped, nor had I ever found the exact opposite. Am I just an unlucky person? What I had found were human beings who mixed together a balance of some good points and some weaknesses. Of course, in hindsight I noticed that in most cases the good points gradually appeared to predominate, and I found that interesting. No, I'm not unlucky. I'm actually a small-minded person with plenty of attitude, and because of that I always go around with my mind made up not to be bested easily by anyone else. That was the real reason that I never met a great or heroic person, but conversely couldn't help sensing something very human even in those people whom the world calls evil.

Finally, the drugs took their effect and I was soon asleep. Yet, even with the pills, for some reason I woke up four or five times in the middle of the night.

Section Two

The next morning, as Father O and I went to the town of Brzeg to see the Gajowniczek family, it occurred to me that the joy of traveling for research is the ability to insert oneself into the local scenery. For several hours, we were tossed about on the train, but when we got to our connecting station we missed our next train because our first train was late in arriving. There was no choice but to grab a taxi, but we got a young driver who had just been given a brand new taxi. He only seemed interested in showing what the car could do, so we just flew out of there. Father O started praying a Hail Mary for our safety, as he does whenever he gets into a car.

So, Father O started praying, and I quickly joined in. We'd already been traveling together now for many days, so I had gotten used to Father O's ways. Still, since I don't wear my faith on my sleeve, I am more the type who forgets about prayer at such moments and only thinks about how to give the reckless driver a piece of my mind. But now, as we sped across the open Polish countryside, I decided that when I got back to Japan and my family or friends drove too fast, I would not get upset or angry and just sit quietly next to them, chanting "Hail Mary, full of grace." I was sure this would "tick off" most of my friends and they would have to slow down.

Brzeg was a quiet little town. So quiet, I suppose one might call it a ghost town. The taxi stopped right in the middle of the residential district, and I just gazed out the window at the neighborhood, while Father O went off to confirm the location of the house. Every house had a large, mansard roof. And it seemed that most of the houses were large enough to have dormer rooms above the second floor. The houses had gardens with space enough for a hen house, a flower garden, or a bit of shrubbery. Flowers that looked like dahlias, rose petals on the black earth—everything looked well-tended and quiet. The children must be off playing somewhere, but even so I found it strangely quiet.

I gathered from watching Father O ask several people where the Gajowniczek house is that it wasn't very famous. If this were Japan, Mr. Gajowniczek would have been chased by the mass media and the tempo of his life would have been turned upside down. But here in Poland, is it possible—perhaps due to the influence of socialism— that the journalists do not have much interest in the rest of a man's life that was saved by a priest, even if someone like me comes from faraway Japan asking about it?

The Gajowniczek house was a large one. But it wasn't until I heard that only the second floor belonged to the Gajowniczeks that I finally understood that all these houses were really what we Japanese would call a kind of apartment building.

Climbing the dark stairway, we ran into a late middle-aged man wearing a smart jacket coming downstairs. He took in Father O's words as if they were music and from that I discerned that this was our Mr. Gajowniczek. It was a strange meeting.

Mr. Gajowniczek retreated back up the stairs and opened the second floor door. I couldn't take my eyes of the shoe box on the stair landing. There were shoes in the lower part and above them, a large round loaf of bread, about thirty or forty centimeters in diameter, was set there with care.

We were greeted at the door by Mrs. Gajowniczek, who appeared simple and modest, and we were led to the living room. They seemed amply provided for with four rooms. There in the living room among a miscellany of flower vases and other decorations was Father Kolbe's photograph, just as I had expected. Saying that the Franciscans had told her to expect our arrival tomorrow, Mrs. Gajowniczek offered us the sofa. Presently, Mr. Gajowniczek re-appeared, having changed into a nice suit, as though he wanted to show respect for Father O and me, or else he was intending to take a commemorative photograph. He was wearing a badge on his chest. When I duly asked him what it was for, I was told it was a kind of "Auschwitz Friends Society" badge.

Through Father O, I asked him whether it was true that at Auschwitz they tattooed prisoners' numbers on them. No sooner were the words out than Mr. Gajowniczek nodded and rolled up the sleeve of his suit a bit. When he did, I saw Mr. Gajowniczek's prisoner number tattooed in blue, at a slight angle, on the outside of his arm.

For a while, I just looked at that tattoo. It's no surprise, but it seems as though that number was carved into the material of human skin from an angle convenient for the one who was doing the tattooing. That is to say, from Mr. Gajowniczek's view, the numbers are upside down but even now, after a quarter of a century has passed,

I felt they showed clearly that there was a human life with those experiences carved into it.

In a quiet voice, Mr. Gajowniczek started talking about what he had experienced.

Before the war, Mr. Gajowniczek was what is called a professional soldier. During the war, he had fought in the offensive and defense battles of Warsaw and Modlin (about thirty kilometers northwest of Warsaw). Afterward he was taken prisoner, but escaped and went to Poronin with several friends. They got as far as the Slovak border, where his friends betrayed him and he was taken prisoner by the Gestapo. It was on January 17, 1940.

He spent seven months in the Zakopane prison. He was given the death penalty, but it was immediately commuted to life in prison.

On October 8, 1940, he was sent to Auschwitz with seventeen hundred others. Only forty-three of them made it to Christmas. And of that group, only two survived until they were liberated in 1945.

The prisoner philosophy that Manvell has written about is supported by these events. According to Manvell, prisoners see their survival as a matter of taking it three months at a time.

"If you despaired you would be finished inside three months; if you showed signs of knowing how to look after yourself, you might well survive through your second three months; if you managed to survive for nine months, you might well survive altogether because you must by then have shown yourself too useful to destroy."[7]

Mr. Gajowniczek did not have that many memories of Father Kolbe. That itself is evidence against the argument that Father Kolbe saved Mr. Gajowniczek because they had become close friends. The priest did not know Mr. Gajowniczek well. It was simply that Father Kolbe laid down his own life for the happiness of a wife and children he had never seen.

---

7. Roger Manvell, *SS and Gestapo: Rule by Terror* (New York: Ballantine Books, 1969), p. 123.

Mr. Gajowniczek knew that Father Kolbe heard confessions from time to time in the concentration camp. With no fear of the S.S., Father Kolbe gave his advice on various matters, and for that he was beaten every now and then.

The day of the incident went just as I've already described. Yet, I never heard from Mr. Gajowniczek any form of self-blame that he was responsible for Father Kolbe's death. This is because the only way to mourn the death of a man who has died for you is to live an "ordinary" life. It should suffice to recall a passage from Frankl's *Man's Search for Meaning* that depicts the inmates of the concentration camps several days after they had been liberated to see how far they had surrendered their humanity:

> In the evening when we all met again in our hut, one said secretly to the other, "Tell me, were you pleased today?"
>
> And the other replied, feeling ashamed as he did not know that we all felt similarly, "Truthfully, no!" We had literally lost the ability to feel pleased and had to relearn it slowly.[8]

My interest turned toward how Mr. Gajowniczek lived after Father Kolbe saved his life. I wanted to know how he, one of only two of seventeen hundred, was able to survive in the camp.

In fall of 1942, Mr. Gajowniczek had a second near encounter with death. He came down with a case of typhus. As soon as he became sick, he was sent to Block 28. The doctors there selected three hundred of the most hopeless cases and sent them to the gas chamber. Of course, Mr. Gajowniczek was one of them.

There was a Polish man named Dering[9] among the doctors. That night, he secretly moved Mr. Gajowniczek to another room and

8. Viktor Emil Frankl, *Man's Search for Meaning: An Introduction to Logotherapy*. Trans. by Ilse Lasch (Boston: Beacon Press, 1963), p. 88.

9. Władysław Dering. On Dering's work in Auschwitz, see Robert J. Lifton, *The Nazi Doctors: Medical Killing and the Psychology of Genocide* (New York: Basic Books, 1986).

put a *freshly* dead corpse in his place.

On October 16, 1944, Mr. Gajowniczek was transferred to the Sachsenhausen concentration camp near Berlin—in retrospect, it seemed as if to ensure he would live and be a witness to history. Sachsenhausen was liberated by the Soviet army on April 25, 1945.

At that time, Mr. Gajowniczek weighed no more than forty kilograms. He spent some time in the hospital, and did not return home until November 10 of that year.

"How quiet!" I thought to myself, as I listened to Mr. Gajowniczek speak. Mr. Gajowniczek would speak for a bit, and then Father O would interpret what he had said in Japanese. Thus, I could lose myself in my private thoughts for quite a while. It wasn't that there were no children's voices or birds chirping, but they seemed rather distant and far-off.

"What kind of work do you do now?" I asked Mr. Gajowniczek.

Father O interpreted, "Until 1965, Mr. Gajowniczek worked in welfare facilities at the city hall. But he says his health was never very good after he came back from the war. He was often sick. And he hurt his back. These problems seem to have healed with time, but now he's retired. That's what it means to get old."

Mr. Gajowniczek maintained a formal posture. He listened with a genial smile to my questions coming from Father O. "After returning home, it seems Mr. Gajowniczek never developed any special work or hobby."

That's it! I finally understood that I had been unsettled because this quietness that had been unnerving me was completely the opposite of what I had expected.

"What happened to your children?" I asked through Father O.

Right away, Mrs. Gajowniczek, who until then had sat right next to Mr. Gajowniczek quietly listening to her husband talk, spoke up.

"We had two boys, but they're both dead."

It took my breath away; I couldn't believe my ears. Mr. Gajowniczek continued the story.

"During the war, my family was in Warsaw. The older boy Bogdan was eighteen, and the younger boy Juliusz was fifteen.

"As you know, the Warsaw Uprising happened on August 2, 1944, and with everyone attacking the Germans, Bogdan also joined in the war effort. Afterward, Mother and the two boys escaped to Rawa Mazowiecka.

"On January 16, 1945, the Soviet air force bombed Rawa Mazowiecka. That very day, the missus had to go to Częstochowa. But her car was stopped by the German army at Tomaszow Mazowiecki, where she was held for a week. The missus was now so worried about things at home that she decided to give up on Częstochowa and immediately return home. And that was where she learned that the boys had died." At that moment, Mrs. Gajowniczek silently left her seat.

After some time, she returned from an adjoining room with two old framed photographs.

Bogdan was a handsome eighteen-year-old, with his hunting cap and wearing something like a parka with a soft leather collar. He was one of the patriots who joined in the citizens uprising. You could see the medal of the Blessed Mother that Mr. Gajowniczek had received from Gawlina,[10] who is called the Bishop of Poland's Army, and which he had given to his son, who never took it off.

Juliusz's picture was not taken when he was fifteen years old. It was a picture that preserved the vestiges of a sweet little boy of about ten with a crew-cut. He was wearing a white-collared uniform that looked a lot like a Japanese student uniform. As always, he had a Bible stuck in his pocket. It is inconceivable that at the time of the Warsaw Uprising he and his brother could emerge unscathed were it not for the protection of the Blessed Mother—so said the man who is his father.

Pulling myself together, I noticed fresh tears in Mrs. Gajowniczek's eyes. Not to be deterred, I fearlessly plowed on with my questions.

---

10. Most Reverend Józef Gawlina (1892–1964), Bishop of Poland's Army.

"When you first met up with your husband after the war, what did you say to him?"

Her husband valiantly tried to smile. But his smile was contorted, and all he could do was twist his handkerchief in his hands.

"When Gajowniczek came home, I was at my sister's place in Rawa Mazowiecka. I just said to him, 'Do you know what has happened to us?' My husband was just silent. I could see he immediately understood it all from my greeting. We didn't say a word, but crying, made a visit to our sons' graves."

What was this?! This . . . this unrelenting wretched life . . . is this what Father Kolbe got in return for the cost of his life?! "Did you not think, when you found out you had lost your sons in spite of Father Kolbe's great sacrifice for you, that maybe this world is not worth living in?"

I continued with my questions, and Mr. Gajowniczek answered quietly, "There was indeed a time when I thought it would have been better had it been I, rather than my sons, who died."

Mrs. Gajowniczek seemed unable to bear it anymore, and left her seat. I too was at my limit. I don't know why, but I just followed her out of the room. When I reached the front hall, I could see Mrs. Gajowniczek standing by an open bedroom window. Without a second thought, I went right into the bedroom. And then from behind I put my arms around her shoulders, and when she turned to face me, tears flowed down from my eyes too, as though the dam had burst.

Chapter 7

First Doubts

Section One

Ever since the day when I learned that Mr. Gajowniczek, whose life had been saved by Father Kolbe, had lost both his children, I felt as though I was standing in the midst of clouds gathering before the storm. It wasn't that the sun was not shining, but like the sunshine on the winter solstice, I could hardly feel any of its warmth.

So, that's what we can expect from the world—I muttered to myself, like an immature twenty-year-old. Father Kolbe endured two weeks without even water and finally was tortured to death, and what did it all lead to? He couldn't even assure the happiness of a single household. It was just too much for me.

The world is filled with stories where people's good intentions and love finally bear fruit. The kind of stories we find in television dramas and novels are so heartwarming. But is it really a good thing to have our hearts warmed so? Isn't it just a kind of fraud? That sort of thing doesn't really cleanse our hearts or give us hope.

At least, Father Kolbe's death teaches us that the world is not such a simple place that it can be saved by people's good intentions. He wagered with his life—but in the end he lost.

From the night following my visit to Auschwitz and to Mr. Gajowniczek, I felt as though I had fallen into Hell. Is this world such a wretched place? If so, then from now on I must change and make up my mind to live with that knowledge. But there wasn't any need for me to "change and make up my mind." If I hadn't actually experienced how cruel a world this is when I was young, there are all sorts of ways in which it is true that I would never have become the "I" that I am today.

That night, I had a strange thought.

I wondered what might have happened had Father Kolbe not asked to take Mr. Gajowniczek's place.

Since he hadn't been picked, Father Kolbe would not have had to die. If I had been in that predicament and somehow survived to the end of the war, I have no doubt I'd be telling people over and over again about the day I escaped disaster, the day of my singular good fortune, my pure, good fortune. And my friends and acquaintances would be happy for me without the slightest sense that there might be anything wrong with me avoiding death while someone else had to die. I was thinking, what if Father Kolbe had just remained silent. The answer is quite clear. As a priest, he understood that at that moment he would be abandoning that man (Mr. Gajowniczek), even if no one else thought so, and he would spend the rest of his life thinking that that man's death was his responsibility. He realized that if he did that, he might physically survive, but as a priest he would already be spiritually dead.

I wonder if one human being in principle is capable of being so deeply connected to another? Doesn't it mean that there clearly is some lack of concern when you rejoice at escaping death even at the cost of another person having to die? For Father Kolbe, to survive at that price didn't seem at all a good thing. That's right. The priest died because of his "personal tastes." Now, I know people will angrily accuse me of impudence for saying so. But we all do—to put the matter more gently—choose our way of life on the basis of our likes. And most people's likes are capricious. Like water seeking its own level, they choose what they are good at, what is pleasant to them. And even "likes" sadly can be broken. And all that remains after one's "likes" have shifted is an empty life of inertia. To successfully live out one's life in this world, a person must stake his life on his "likes." When you do so, there may even be times when that life itself can no longer be lived.

Professor Gardavsky, the Czechoslovakian Marxist philosopher, wrote the following tough words in his work *God Is Not Yet Dead* as if he were explaining the life of Father Kolbe:

> But Jesus has another far-reaching view of what a miracle is: according to this, a miracle is not a trivial decision just like any other, an arbitrary act which benefits somebody; it is the radical answer to an urgent summons, an action which can only be accomplished if our whole personality—everything we are and possess—is brought into play; for this is the only way we can possibly make that crucial step which takes us beyond limits that have never been surpassed before.
>
> The miracle transcends everything that is trivial, banal, ordinary, natural, "normal." What happens is unique, entailing absolute self-realization. And so Jesus's miracles teach us more about the essence of an action which has a historical effect than we can learn from boring descriptions of the exploits of the heroes of the classical world.
>
> By performing his miracles, Jesus shows the skeptical members of his Jewish audience—people who have never taken the slightest risk, who would never in their wildest dreams have thought such a thing possible—that the "natural course of things" really can be radically interfered with, and that man is capable of performing miracles.
>
> Of course he does also show that this can only happen provided that certain requirements are fulfilled. He lists a whole series of prerequisites of this type on various occasions, though in the end they boil down to one basic idea: the "law" of *love*. This golden rule of Christianity has been misinterpreted by later periods, along with everything else. And, again along with everything else that was new in Jesus's message, it has frequently been misused by those in authority, to their

own advantage. In this falsified form, as an "all-embracing" love, all-forgiving, classless and abstract, it has been severely criticized, and rightly so. And yet love is one of those eternal themes where it is extremely important to understand what it originally meant in Jesus's own time. For it does not have even the minutest trace of sentimentality, it has nothing to do with bewitching our senses and our emotions, it does not contain any sort of moral instruction intended to teach us to put into practice certain absolute values within an abstract moral system, nor does it proclaim a feeble pacifism. In fact Jesus's mission has nothing to do with demanding specific and concrete virtues of us—chastity, poverty, and obedience, for example. He doesn't draw up a specific moral code. He doesn't prescribe certain duties regardless, without taking the circumstances into account: for instance, he doesn't think of marriage as indissoluble, and he doesn't say that wealth or poverty as such are necessarily a good thing. Any reference he does make to specific "virtues" is merely a repetition of Moses's instructions—and the Jews were already very familiar with these.

The heart of the matter is to be found elsewhere. Jesus is convinced that before we can come to a radical decision, before we can achieve a "miracle," we must be filled with love: we must be aware—steeped in the sort of profound knowledge that governs our whole being and is sometimes felt with total immediacy—that we only *exist* when we surpass ourselves: in our own eyes, in the eyes of our fellow-man, and in the eyes of God; and when we know that this act of transcendence challenges our minds, our strength of purpose, our passion—both in the active and passive sense—and demands that we should bring all our senses into play. That being so, we do not need any instructions about what concrete action we should take in any given circumstances: whether we should share out our riches or keep them for ourselves, whether we should desert our wives or stick to them, whether we should kill our rivals or let them off.

If we think out Jesus's concept of love to its radical conclusion, we will see that it always involves a confrontation with death. But if love is present in the form of a passionate desire for life on a more elevated level—and that is the essence of Jesus's appeal—death cannot win (not only physical death, but death in a thousand trivial shapes and forms). That is why love is both the most difficult state for us to achieve and the most elevated, its diametrical opposite being the fear of death. Surpassing this limit involves 'rising from the dead' or 'living as a man'. This means that everything is easy, even those things that are totally impossible. Once we have reached this point, they are miracles no longer, since everything seems perfectly natural. The only people who think of them as miraculous are those who have not made the decisive step.

So Jesus's preaching does not tell us to love everybody. He doesn't tell us what to do in every single situation. All he asks of us is that we should enter into the situation wholeheartedly. And his own actions show us that it really is possible: man is capable of performing miracles. Miracles are performed. They are the nodal points in the web of history, the junctures where something unique takes place, an incident which can never be repeated. And if we look at it this way, love turns out to be the radically subjective element of history.

Why be afraid of this type of miracle?

Why not wish for one instead?[1]

In this single passage, I found a clear answer to what had caused my doubts and anxieties that night. In a word, Father Kolbe did not die for the Gajowniczek family. The priest threw away his own life

---

1. Vítězslav Gardavsky, *God Is Not Yet Dead,* translated from the German by Vivienne Menkes, (New York: Penguin Books, 1973, pp. 47-9). Emphasis in both Sono and Gardavsky original.

for the sake of life.

My work in southern Poland was now finished, so I returned to Warsaw with Father O.

It seemed as though autumn had deepened more than the mere ten days I had spent here. The daylight was growing dimmer. As we were walking through town on the day of our departure, Father O seemed nostalgic and, stopping in his tracks, offered a friendly greeting to a young man.

He told me it was his nephew who writes poems, and he introduced me to him. In his jacket pocket, where one might expect to find a handkerchief, the poet sported a yellow leaf he had picked up somewhere.

Section Two

I entered bustling Rome. It was my second visit to Rome. The first time I came here was in 1962, but I didn't see much as I was suffering from that common ailment of writers—insomnia. This time, fortunately, was not so pointless. The only problem was I had no idea how to go about interviewing in a foreign country.

Poland was really just the background part of what I was after on this trip. I did not come here to write a biography of Father Kolbe. My real purpose was to see whether or not the miracles done in Father Kolbe's name really happened.

That night, I checked into my old, Italian-style hotel along the lively Via Veneto and immediately spread out the thick folder of reading material on my desk. Here in Italy, the Vatican's Congregation for the Causes of Saints of the Sacred Congregation of Rites was formally investigating two miracles submitted for the beatification of Maximilian Kolbe.

According to the report, one of them was the miraculous cure of Marquis Francis Luciani Ranier from thromboangiitis obliterans (Buerger's disease) in Rome; the other was the equally unbelievable recovery of Angelina Testoni from intestinal tuberculosis and tuber-cular peritonitis.

I faced certain linguistic challenges with the investigation being carried out in Italy, so a Japanese I will call Mr. S kindly agreed to interpret for me. I was told that all the records of these cases were preserved and under the supreme command of Father Antonio Ricciardi of Father Kolbe's Order of Friars Minor Conventual.

First thing the next morning, I was able to get through to Father Ricciardi and made an appointment for the afternoon of the following day. The reason I wanted to meet him right away and get my plans quickly set is—well, it is one of the bad habits of the Japanese—that they'd have to declare me a success if I got something done in Italy only two days after arrival. Compared to Poland, Rome is a dusty town. And to make matters worse, the Via Veneto was overflowing with American tourists. They say a lot of Japanese travel overseas, but it's nothing like the Americans. First off, I had to kill a day going through four or five letters for me that had arrived in Rome. When I got to my hotel in Rome, the man at the front desk handed them to me, saying things like, "My, how everyone loves you!" in a sing-song voice, but most of those letters were business letters from publishers and newspapers, and not a single one of those letters offered me their "love."

After writing my replies to those letters, I went out to the post office. I came well advised that it is best to post letters yourself since this was the kind of country where if you ask the hotel clerk to do it for you, he'd probably just forget to do so, without meaning you any ill-will.

It took a good hour just to mail four or five letters, and when I got back to the hotel after walking through those terrible exhaust fumes, I realized I was having another attack of my long-forgotten nasopharyngitis. In the midst of my misery, I recalled Winowska telling of an episode about how much Father Kolbe suffered when he was a student in this town in 1912.

Why would a young man find it so detestable to be given the opportunity to study in a foreign country? According to Winowska, it was because Father Kolbe was afraid of girls.

"I ask you, Mother, to pray for me *in a very special way*, because I need it greatly; down there in Rome, there are dangers, very serious dangers. I understand that some women accost even the religious, and yet it will indeed be necessary to go out in order to attend the courses."[2]

This letter was written just before he left for Rome. Father Kolbe was eighteen years old then.

But about a month later, Father Kolbe found that Rome was not such a decadent town and wrote again to his mother.

"Things are not so terrible as I thought when I wrote you. Would the Italian women really have nothing better to do than to accost us? Besides, we always go out in groups."[3]

I thought that this episode would probably be read in Japan as expressing Father Kolbe's childishness rather than his seriousness. I have heard that in monastic life, which is governed by the three vows of chastity, poverty and obedience, some do occasionally fall into this kind of scrupulosity we see in Father Kolbe. Scrupulosity is the name for believing that some trivial matter that actually is not sinful is a sin. It may be found in religious life when someone pursues holy purity to an extreme degree, but the danger of falling into this spiritual condition is certainly not limited to those in religious life. It is a spiritual condition common among the young, when they are very sensitive to all sorts of things and, overcome by fear about how best to protect themselves, desperately seek to avoid places where there might be even the slightest danger. There is no question that Father Kolbe caught this neurosis which serious youth often catch.

---

2. Winowska, *Our Lady's Fool* (Plumereau, trans.), p. 15. Emphasis in Winowska, but not in Sono's citation.

3. Winowska, *Our Lady's Fool* (Plumereau, trans.), p. 15.

The next morning, I went to the Conventual Franciscans at the appointed hour to see Father Ricciardi. Father Ricciardi listened to what I had to say, through the interpreter, and seemed amiable enough and suggested that I should go as soon as possible to see Ms. Testoni who lives in Sardinia. But the case of Marquis Ranier was a more difficult matter, since the Marquis himself had died in 1969. But, Father Ricciardi added, I'd prefer you not say anything about this publicly. I had no idea that the Marquis had died, but I was a bit annoyed to be told not to say anything about that.

"Could you introduce me to members of his family? If not members of the family, then perhaps at least other witnesses?" I asked Father Ricciardi. When I did, the priest shrugged his shoulders, pursed up his lips, and made a face that could either have been troubled or perplexed.

"There's just no way the witnesses will meet with ordinary people. The Marquis's wife, her daughter and her son-in-law, Dr. Battibocca, know the details involved very well, but they are all upper-class and are not likely to meet with a journalist." That struck me as a strange argument, but I remained silent and listened to Father Ricciardi. I'm not asking to be a friend of the Ranier family or get an invitation to dinner or anything like that. Even emperors and presidents will, in an appropriate place, meet with journalists. When I asked if he wouldn't ask them once again, Father Ricciardi made a face to show I was nothing but a nuisance. The reports concerning the witnesses to the miracles have all been sent to the Franciscans in Japan. If you want pictures, get them from them. That should be sufficient. At that point, the ways things had gone, I had to call it a day. It seems I might have stumbled on the least appealing aspect of Italy. But I really didn't feel like calling it a day. On the way back to the hotel, I came up with a way to resolve the situation. I realized that the Tokyo ordinary, Archbishop Seiichi Shirayanagi, was supposed to be in Rome for the synod. Thinking things might take a turn for the better if Archbishop Shirayanagi appealed to the Franciscans, I called the Japanese Embassy to the

Vatican and ascertained the location of Archbishop Shirayanagi's lodgings. Archibishop Shirayanagi was staying at the Paris Mission, but when I called I got an even better piece of news. The Apostolic Nuncio to Japan, Archbishop Wüstenberg[4] was in Rome on one of his occasional returns.

A path was cleared. Through the good offices of the two archbishops, I soon got an American Franciscan priest named Kos to make arrangements for me to see Father Ricciardi again.

This time, things were clearly different. I was able to meet the head of the Order of Friars Minor Conventual, and Father Ricciardi had made contact with the family of Marquis Ranier. Father Ricciardi offered me the very Italian kind of excuse that "you looked like a young lady in her teens, so I didn't believe you were a writer," but I have to add that I've got too many years on me to believe that malarkey.

Section Three

Actually, there was no need to go searching around Rome for people who had experienced a miracle in Father Maximilian Kolbe's name. According to Father Ricciardi's book, Father Kolbe's cousin Langer recovered miraculously from a case of pyelitis and Mrs. Teresa Jadam Maćkowska's thirteen-year-old daughter Sofia was healed in July of 1947 of her deafness. The young lad Gerardo Josef recovered from a kind of brain disease, and even Dr. Takashi Nagai, the author of *The Bells of Nagasaki*, testified that he was able to stop the flow of blood from the cut he got during the atomic bombing with some holy water from Lourdes he got from the Garden of the Immaculata in Nagasaki that Father Kolbe had established.

But Dr. Nagai was now deceased, and doctors who could back up the miraculous claims of the remaining Poles could not be found

---

4. Archbishop Bruno Wüstenberg (1912–1984).

in Poland under the prevailing social conditions there. Whether I liked it or not, it had become necessary to seek corroboration of those miracles that happened in the Free World.

Why was Father Ricciardi so bent on making sure I did not meet with the family of Marquis Ranier? Also, why did he try to muzzle me, ordering me not to leak to the outside world the fact that the Marquis had died? Judging from the circumstances, it would be quite normal to think that there was something fishy about the Marquis Ranier's miracle and he "didn't want anybody poking around his story."

The Marquis Ranier's testimony, presented to the Congregation for the Causes of Saints of the Sacred Congregation of Rites, is as follows:

I (Francesco Luciani Ranier, father was Loredano, mother was Raffaelina Crisostoni) was born on May 28 1898 in Montegranaro. I am Catholic, my occupation is agriculture, and I live at 104 Via Archimede Rome. I was miraculously cured of thromboangiitis obliterans (Buerger's disease).

Around 1948 I heard about the Venerable Maximilian Maria Kolbe. At that time, my legs were already getting bad, particularly the right leg, but Father Fiori, a family friend, knew about my illness and sent me a picture of Father Kolbe, encouraging me to leave matters to him for the intercession of Father Kolbe.

During the war from 1915 to 1918 and again during the Second World War, my health was good enough to be declared fit for military service. But when I was thirty-seven years old, I got an inflammation in both ears for which I received treatment, first from Professor Bonvelli and then from Professor Ferreri. There were times when I couldn't hear well, so I had to consult them about a hearing aid. I always wore this hearing aid for about the next year and a half, when I suddenly recovered my hearing at the same time my leg was amputated. Since this recovery just happened out of nowhere, this too surprised Professor Ferreri.

Now, about the incident of 1948. To be precise, it was the night before Christmas Eve. While I was walking, pain and stiffness descended on my calf and shank, and the pain got so bad I had to just stop in my tracks. Thereafter, the same thing happened over and over, just about every day, and it gradually got worse. I went for treatment at Professor Fadinelli's place, and he diagnosed it as a case of arthritis and ordered me to take a large quantity of a uricosuric agent (atophan). But the disease only got worse, and the medicine didn't have any effect at all. One night I felt an excruciating pain in both feet that worked its way up to my knees. The same thing happened the next day, so I came to Rome to consult a specialist. It was right around Christmas of 1949.

This time Professor Fadinelli (who is now deceased) found a small wound on the inside of my right foot, near the heel, and within a few days it started to get bigger and deeper. The wound hurt greatly and it got worse daily. Professor Fadinelli prescribed warm compresses, but they didn't help either. Along with the growth of the wound, my legs up to the knees were all swollen up. The right one in particular was in very bad shape. The condition continued from Christmas of 1949 until May of 1950.

I had become concerned about this disease, and asked the famous surgeon Professor Pieri who lives in Rome to take a look at it.

On that occasion, Professor Pieri said the following to Professor Fadinelli who was standing next to him, "It looks like you brought me a corpse. Had you called me two months earlier, I might have been able to do something."

Professor Pieri pointed out that my right foot was purple all the way up to my ankle, was cold and had lost all sensation, but I was already well aware of all that. As I mentioned earlier, both feet, especially the right one, had then swollen all the way up to the knees, but ever since catching this disease I never once had a fever.

At the Bastianelli clinic where they took me, Professor Pieri gave me a large injection deep into my right hip, but I have no idea what kind of injection it was. All I know was it was supposed to stimulate a sympathetic nerve.

Although the effect was not completely negative, the Professor sent me home saying there was nothing more he could do but amputate the leg. In truth, the wound now hurt so much I could hardly bear it, so I made up my mind to have the surgery and two days later was re-admitted to the hospital.

Just before the operation, I had an electrocardiogram and blood analysis on Professor Pieri's orders. I still have the results of the electrocardiogram, urinalysis, glycemia test, and the test for nitrogen count in the blood, and will submit them to this Court.

The amputation of the lower right leg was done at the Bastianelli clinic on June 9, 1950, by Professor Pieri. At the time of the operation, a mass of gangrene had progressed from the tip of my foot to my ankle. I believe it had all the symptoms of wet gangrene. I thought so because I was told if you touched the hard part it would froth up like soap and give off a terrible stench.

I underwent surgery twice. The first time was to remove the leg from just below the knee, but Professor Pieri noticed that the arteries had calcified and he immediately had to conduct another amputation above the knee. When they inspected the part that was first amputated, they were able to confirm that it was clearly calcified. The report of the examination was submitted by my son-in-law, Dr. Tommaso Battibocca. After the operation, I wasn't right in the head and couldn't even recognize members of my family. And my body temperature was over 102 degrees Fahrenheit for eight days.

Apparently, they declared that I had at best a week left in me. Well, that's where things stood, so my family and I wanted to leave the hospital and return to my hometown of Porto San Giorgio where I was born and where the family cemetery is. We went by car from Rome to Porto San Giorgio and I suffered quite a bit the whole way. (About a week before the surgery, I discovered that my fingers had gone numb and I had a strange painless itching on my left side. Those feelings all stopped after the surgery and it was around the same time that I got my hearing back.)

Eight days before the miraculous event. I was in a state of unconsciousness, but later I heard from family members that I had a high fever and was waving my arms around as if I were directing a concert and calling out deliriously in a loud voice. My ability to digest food and pass urine were significantly diminished, and it was all I could do to take in a small amount of liquid foods. Since my overall condition was deteriorating day by day, as was predicted at the hospital, my family was preparing for the worst. The day I arrived at the village, the village doctor (he's now deceased) Professor Giovanni Basili looked in on me in the evening when I arrived, and I was in such bad shape he said to my mother, "There's nothing more we can do for Checco (this was his nickname for Francesco). We must just accept it."

My fever came down, but after July 15 it was back up again, and I had a constant, stabbing pain in the amputated area. I had lost consciousness and was getting even weaker. Professor Basili and Professor Pieri gave me an injection and forced medicine down me. But both doctors had declared that my death was simply a matter of time. I heard that on the evening of August 4, both doctors had a conference at my house and concluded that the end was near, that I probably wouldn't make it through the night. I believe my son-in-law, Dr. Tommaso Battibocca, who happened to be there at the time, will speak about the events of that day. On August 5, my condition had not changed a bit. I heard later that I was no longer able to pass urine. Even though I was half-unconscious, I felt pain from the amputated area and I don't believe I was able to sleep on my own.

About ten o'clock in the evening on August 5, for the first time was I able to get a good night's sleep and I didn't wake up once until eight o'clock the next morning. I had not been given any sedative or soporific.

When I opened my eyes at eight o'clock on the morning of August 6, just when everyone was expecting my death, my condition was completely different. I was fully conscious, had no fever, had immediately recovered my ability to urinate, had a ferocious appetite, and the pain in the amputated area was gone. On the same day, I was able to sit up in bed, stand up to take care of my business, and was able to eat boiled spaghetti, with a large fish, fruit and wine—in short, a real feast. My family members were astounded at my sudden recovery and rushed off to tell Professor Basili and Professor Pieri. Those two came on the morning of August 6 and separately examined me and confirmed that I had gotten better. Both doctors were atheists, and while Professor Basili said it was just a recovery, Professor Pieri turned to my mother and said, "It seems your son's recovery is a miracle. It sure wasn't anything we did."

I clearly remember those words. After my right leg was amputated, I received a picture of Father Kolbe from Father Fiori who encouraged me to pray to him, and thereafter I prayed constantly to him. When my condition got so bad I wasn't able to pray, my wife prayed for me. But I didn't say anything about this to the two doctors because I knew they were atheists.

Here an inconsistency is pointed out by Marquis Ranier concerning the statement regarding when he first received the picture of

Father Kolbe. The picture certainly arrived after the amputation of his leg. Therefore, the Marquis corrected the statement to note that he did receive the picture in 1950. Such points suggest that the Marquis's memory may not be trustworthy. With a skeptical mind, I looked forward to the day when I would meet Marquis Ranier's family.

Chapter 8

Those Present at the Resurrection

Section One

It was a rainy day when I finally was able to visit the family of Marquis Ranier.

I wore a down-to-earth pongee. I had heard a bit about Italy being the kind of country where they pay a lot of attention to what you wear and what your accessories are, so after considering lots of different modes of presenting myself, I decided this one would be best.

That day, just as I was about to set out in the rain with Father Ricciardi, who was something like the general director of the office in charge of investigating the cause of Father Kolbe for beatification, the American Father Kos, a friar who would be our driver, and a Japanese named Mr. S who would be my interpreter, I met a strange man in the dark garage of the Conventual Franciscans.

It was the famous bearded friar Zeno Zebrowski who works on behalf of those in the Tokyo ghetto called "Ant's Town." I had often heard about this person, but until then I never had the chance to meet him. Brother Zeno had first come to Japan with Father Kolbe, and while Father Kolbe returned to Poland, was killed at Auschwitz, and the war ended, Brother Zeno had all along remained in Japan.

Brother Zeno was now back in Italy in order to attend the beatification ceremony for Father Kolbe. The interpreter Mr. S first told me all this background and then introduced me to Brother Zeno. Brother Zeno never stopped smiling, but I got the sense that he looked upon the whole world as if through a thin curtain. It is said that the Third Person of the Holy Trinity, the Holy Spirit, gives the clergy more or less the foreign language skills they need for the propagation of the faith, but one gets the impression that the powers of the Holy Spirit didn't reach Brother Zeno. I guess this brother found something more important to do with the time set aside for learning languages. Old Brother Zeno came with a younger friar at his side. I had met this man in Poland at Niepokalanów. At the time, he was wearing a jumper, and I thought he looked like a Japanese wholesale grocer. He was also proficient in Japanese, so he, Father O and I—the three of us—had a grand old time chatting away in Japanese together.

We set off in the rain, and finally stopped the car in a residential street in a sepia-colored quiet little town. Crystal clear drops of rain were falling from the trees that lined the street.

Before us was a typical Italian style apartment that from the outside looked like an ordinary square box, but the entire second floor was the quiet and graceful home of Dr. Battibocca, the son-in-law of Marquis Ranier. This was where the Marquis's widow had come to live after his death.

Father Ricciardi was on such intimate terms with the Marquis Ranier's family that it seemed like a family reunion.

Coming out of the house to greet us was the late Marquis's daughter, Mrs. Maria Louisa Luciani Battibocca.

The lady appeared to be in her mid-forties. She seemed to be of good upbringing and had run her house in similarly good fashion and had reached middle age without losing her shape. Wearing her checkered skirt and sweater, she showed good taste in clothes.

In good time, her mother the widow Ranier appeared. This was the Madame Marquis whom Father Ricciardi made out to be someone just too important to meet with me and who, I was thinking, must be quite a proud woman, but she turned out to be a very simple person of gentle elegance. Had these two women showed up with a taste for garish adornment, I think, conversely, I might have doubted that they really were "members of the house of the Marquis."

A bit later, Dr. Battibocca came into the living room, the son-in-law of the Marquis, one of the doctors who was always beside the patient and whose testimony about the miracle was given considerable weight. He had that characteristic sensitive look of those who, standing above things like citizenship and race, dedicate themselves to intellectual work, and the deep creases at the corners of his mouth reminded me of "self-restraint"—or "prudence," or something like that. I had read part of Dr. Battibocca's testimony at the beatification inquiry with considerable interest.

"I am Dr. Tommaso Battibocca, the son of Venanzio and Ceccaroni Cambi Voglia Adele, and I was born on October 4, 1921, in Camerino. I am a surgeon and I live at 295 Via degli Scipioni in Rome. I present my testimony to this court with no small degree of indecision and hesitancy since I am by nature cautious in all things and because of my role as a doctor and a relative of the person concerned."

The person now standing before my eyes did indeed seem the kind of person who was cautious enough that such apprehensions as he expressed at the outset of his testimony to the court of inquiry would come easily from his mouth.

Dr. Battibocca submitted a short medical report to the Church, and its substance is as follows:

1. I know Frances Luciani Ranier as I am his son-in-law and have looked after him since the onset of the earliest symptoms of his illness (pain and intermittent lameness).

2. As the symptoms worsened, a suspicion of arterite obliterante (blockage of the arteries) arose around the spring of 1950. We ran an oscillometer test many times, I don't recall exactly how many, but certainly after the appearance of the ulcer on the heel. I do not recall the exact results, but I am certain that there was no detectable vibration at the time immediately prior to the operation.

3. We continued with blood and urine tests, but were not able to discern anything unusual.

4. The first examination was done by Professor Pontano, on my advice. The Professor thought he had a kind of rheumatism and also told him to stop smoking. In terms of his smoking habit, I remember that the local doctor in Porto San Giorgio, Dr. Giovanni Basili, had earlier suggested in a friendly way that the Marquis try to give up smoking. His regular, primary care physician was Dr. Fadinelli, and this doctor was with the patient constantly after Professor Pontano's examination. Professor Pontano began to think it was a case of arterite obliterante (blockage of the arteries) after the appearance of the ulcer on his heel. I remember he was examined by Professor Pieri.

After Professor Pieri's examination, he was admitted to the Bastianelli clinic, and I don't recall what medicine he was given there, but he was given a sympathetic nerve injection. There was some discussion about a simpatectomia (amputation of the sympathetic nerve) but I recall that we did not go through with it.

5. Professor Pieri thought it was necessary to have surgery, and Dr. Fadinelli concurred. I myself as a doctor and a relative of the patient agreed with the opinion of the doctors in charge.

6. The small ulcer on the heel gradually grew larger, spreading underneath the foot and to the big toe. Zyanose had spread through all but one-third of his calf. We had hoped to save the knee joint but the surgeon, Professor Pieri, did not think that possible and so two-thirds of the leg was amputated.

7. After the operation at the Bastianelli clinic, Professor Fulgoni also examined the patient. I recall that this professor conveyed to me personally the unfortunate diagnosis of thromboangiitis obliterans (Buerger's disease). Professor Fulgoni's diagnosis implied that the situation was hopeless.

8. Dr. Fadinelli and Professor Pieri's medical assistance continued, but this assistance was really good for nothing but the patient's spirit.

The injury suffered before the amputation of the lower right leg, which was a blockage to the circulation, spread to the lower left leg and then even the upper left leg. I recall that, before the amputation of the lower right leg, we were not successful in discerning a pulse in the aorta in his neck. Still, during that time prior to the amputation (June 9 1950), there were no symptoms in the patient of brain ischemia (localized anemia).

On the advice of the doctors in charge, I took a section of the arteries from the amputated lower leg to the Santo Spirito Hospital in Rome so it could be subjected to Professor Bignami's histology exam. The exam results were positive for arteriosclerosis.

9. Whether at the hospital, or at the house where he wanted to return with his family, or even later at the summer home in Porto San Giorgio where his family really took him so he could have his wish to die there, the deterioration in his condition after the amputation was clear and showed the following symptoms: speech impediment, loss of memory, coordinated impediments in thinking, injury to mobility functioning (so bad that the patient couldn't sign his own name), dementia, intense pain after amputation. And as companion symptoms to these, there was a loss of appetite and nausea to the point that he suffered from poor nutrition.

I recall that at Port San Giorgio the patient received the constant attentions of Dr. Basili, not so much as a doctor but as a friend. The only form of treatment available to the patient after the operation was a cocktail of analgesics and morphine.

I do not remember the exact date, but on one night in early August of 1950, these symptoms of the patient took a serious turn for the worst. I happened to be there at the time and was urged by my wife's mother to do something since things had reached a more dangerous stage than we had yet seen. I explained to my mother-in-law, in order to cheer her up in any way possible, that it would be dangerous to give the patient another injection since his mind had remained clear despite all the morphine treatments he had been given for so long. So, he was not given another injection.

In spite of his condition, the patient soon dropped off to sleep and slept uninterrupted until the next morning. Even though he had been given daily injections of analgesics, that had never happened even once prior to that day.

When he opened his eyes the next morning, all the symptoms had disappeared—the brain ischemia (localized anemia), and the damage to his circulation in the lower and upper left leg.

He regained his health and, except for an increase in weight that took place afterward, he was as normal as he is today.

Dr. Tommaso Battibocca

M. Magliocchetti *(deputy appointed judge)*

Nicholas Ferraro, S. RR. C. *(in charge of faith and morals)*

V. Frazzano *(secretary)*

Section Two

With Father Kos as my English interpreter, I started asking questions of the members of the Ranier family. To summarize what the family members told me, the Marquis was a landlord so he did not have a particular job that one could call his own. He had a warm personality, and his real pleasure was stamp collecting. Other than that, he did a little hunting. He was also very skilled with his hands, and built models of the Christ child in the stable, churches and the like.

The widow Ranier told me, "Until he got that picture from Father Fiori, he knew nothing about Father Kolbe."

It was inconceivable that they were lying about anything, but gradually I began to lose my patience with it all. I had come here to listen to what the members of the Ranier family had to say, but Father Ricciardi, who had come with us, would take my questions from the sidelines and answer them with his own views. I had no interest in the replies of anyone but the Ranier family. I decided I would only take notes on what I heard from Father Kos after he interpreted my questions into Italian and immediately rendered their Italian answers into English. As a result, I soon found out that it was the testimony of Dr. Battibocca's wife, the daughter, at the Church tribunal that was the most coherent and informative of the details of the situation. The missus described the events of that night as follows:

In July 1950 I was married, but I went to Port San Giorgio to take care of my father and stayed there about twenty days. That was when I first heard about Father Maximilian Kolbe. My mother told me that a friar gave her a picture of Father Kolbe and told her to pray to this priest for the complete recovery of my dad.

While I was staying in Porto San Giorgio, my mother prayed intensely to Father Kolbe. And at times she even invited me to join her in praying by my father's bedside in a loud voice.

From August 4 to August 5 my father, who at that time was in critically bad shape, complained of terrible pain. The patient was constantly begging us for a morphine shot, saying he could no longer tolerate the pain, so my mother went and woke up my husband, Dr. Tommaso Battibocca, and brought him. My husband said he would give him another shot of morphine if the pain could not be relieved any other way, but in reality he was trying to get the patient to sleep without giving him another injection. It was late in the night when suddenly my father became quiet and fell asleep. We were afraid this was a sign that he was about to die, so we stayed nearby to keep an eye on him a while longer. Since he fell ill, my father had never been that quiet or slept that long. After some time, my husband and I went back to our rooms, but my mother stayed at his side throughout the night.

Around eight or nine o'clock in the morning, when my father opened his eyes, we were already awake. When we saw how peaceful he was, we were quite surprised. Father seemed completely normal and, while I don't remember what he ate, he soon had a meal and said he wanted to get out of bed, so we moved him to a sofa. Mother was convinced that this miraculous recovery was thanks to the intercession of Father Kolbe, and father himself was in complete agreement. I myself around that time prayed in this way, "Father Kolbe who saved the father of another family, please save my father, too." Just like that, he soon recovered completely so that on September 20 he was able to travel by car 180 kilometers round trip from Porto San Giorgio to Camerino to be godfather at my daughter Anna's baptism.

I knew that in her testimony, the wife of Dr. Battibocca had written, "I know the difference between a blessing and a miracle. And in my father's case, I can only think it was a miracle." But I asked the missus anyway, "When you saw a miracle, something ordinary people never get to see, what were your thoughts at that very moment?"

Her answer was short and clear. And I felt I could understand her Italian reply even without Father Kos's interpretation.

"It was as if I were watching the Resurrection of Christ!" According to Dr. Battibocca's testimony, the Marquis Ranier's condition after the "miraculous recovery" was as follows:

Without a doubt, the progression of the illness from then on had passed a turning point, and what was even stranger was that the brain damage had disappeared. In short, all the patient's functions had returned to normal and showed signs of having entered a period of recovery. This was evident in the fact that he spoke like a healthy man and ate normally. I do not recall whether a recovery in the amputated area happened in conjunction with this general recovery. One of the two decayed bone parts later came out on its own, but the other was taken out in surgery in Rome some months later.

Dr. Basili came once or twice a day because this unexpected recovery had to be verified, but he never said a word about the illness. Not one of the doctors believed it was a miraculous recovery. My mother-in-law had him seen in Rome by Dr. Fadinelli and, if my memory serves me correctly, the doctor was surprised that in spite of this clear recovery we couldn't feel a pulse in his carotid artery. Of course, at present everything related to his pulse has returned to normal.

Dr. Battibocca provided this testimony in 1964, and the Marquis Ranier died on October 12, 1969, from heart disease. The Marquis had lived on for nineteen years after the miracle. The night before he died, the Marquis Ranier felt ill and told his family there was some documents he needed to sign, but it had to be postponed. At the onset of his suffering, he was taken to the hospital, but before anything could be done he breathed his last.

I asked them,

"During those nineteen years, did he have a quiet life?" "Yes, it was quite peaceful. He would tell everyone he met that he had already died once and was only alive now thanks to a miracle."

At that point the Battibocca couple's two daughters appeared and greeted us. One was a high school student, the other a college student, and both had the manners of someone brought up in comfortable circumstances. The younger one brought out one of those model churches and telling me it was her late grandfather's work, gave it to me. It was so intricately made that one would never imagine it was the work of an amateur, and when the widow said that he would sell such a piece of craftsmanship and donate the money he got to the poor, there was little I could do but nod my head as if to say "of course he did." If I were from a rich family, I think it would suffice to just donate some of my money to the poor without going to all the trouble of making some kind of toy and selling it in a bazaar—that's what most Japanese probably would have thought about all this. I suppose the Marquis wanted to offer his own work to God and then give the money he raised thereby to the poor.

About then, I decided it was time for me to leave the Battibocca house.

Section Three

I met up with a Japanese in Rome. And I shamelessly began to bad-mouth Fr. Ricciardi out of resentment at his efforts to obstruct my work.

"So they say that was a miracle, but was it really?"

I replied, "Well, I really won't know until I get back to Japan and ask a Japanese doctor to explain it all to me in Japanese."

"When I hear stuff like it was a miracle, I expect a whole new leg to have popped up from the stump where they cut off his leg."

"Oh, that would have been perfect!"

I laughed so hard that tears ran down my cheeks.

"Why do you suppose that priest told you not to tell anyone that the man who had experienced a miracle had died?"

"I have no idea."

There was simply no need for it. It was natural enough to take what had happened to Marquis Ranier as the kind of unusual thing that people call "a miracle." If someone had told me that "another leg popped out right before our eyes" then maybe I would have been bored to death.

But I didn't need my friend to say anything, as I was already starting to harbor all sorts of doubts of my own. Why did Father Ricciardi, who had told me he was "too busy, too busy" with the preparations for the beatification ceremony, make it a point to accompany me that day to the Battibocca house? If to interpret for me, it was enough to have Father Kos's company. In addition, there were points where Father Ricciardi clearly tried to control the statements family members made at the Battibocca house. It was Mr. S whom I had asked to interpret who noticed it. Mr. S told me that, when the doctor's wife or the Marquis's widow started to say something in reply to my questions, the priest would say, "here's how you should answer," and he would interpret the reply himself.

In that case, was there some kind of a scheme to fabricate a miracle? There were thirteen witnesses to the Marquis's miracle, and of them eight were relatives: the Marquis, his wife, the Marquis's daughter, her husband, the Marquis's son, his brother-in-law, his son-in-law's younger brother, the older sister of the spouse of the Marquis's younger sister. The ninth witness, Mrs. Amelia Tocco, wasn't even present on the day of the miracle. The tenth witness was Father Angelus Fiori, the Conventual Franciscan friar who brought the picture of Father Kolbe to the Ranier house. The eleventh witness was a doctor named Josephus Cesareo, but this person testified that he never examined the Marquis; he only exchanged opinions with Dr. Battibocca and members of the family about the Marquis's illness. The twelfth witness, Dr. Jacobus Stella, was the Marquis's primary physician after March 2, 1959. Which means he could have no direct knowledge of the Marquis's condition at the time the miracle happened. The thirteenth witness was Fr. Laurentius M. Lucacelli, who said that while he was a frequent visitor to the Marquis Ranier family he had no idea whether the Marquis's illness was all that serious or whether there was a miraculous recovery.

Putting it all together, one could say that it was Dr. Battibocca and he alone among all the witnesses who held the key to this scientific affair. If his wife and mother-in-law talked him into it, saying something like, "no question that was a miracle. Don't you agree? Tell them that's what it was!" then it would be only human nature if in order to meet the expectations of those who loved him he found himself compelled to say it seemed somehow miraculous. The reason that Father Ricciardi said, "even if you meet with other witnesses, it won't help," made perfect sense. If those like Dr. Basili, Professor Pieri, Dr. Fadinelli, and Professor Fulgoni had refused to take the witness stand, then the other witnesses would have lost their authority. If I hadn't heard that Marquis Ranier spoke with great delight about his memories of his miraculous recovery to his family but in contrast avoided talking about the affair with outsiders, I would probably have believed that the drama of the Marquis's house was done, if not with malicious intent, then from an intolerable, well-intentioned good will with the whole thing being orchestrated behind the scenes by Father Ricciardi.

It seems that the Battibocca family tried to get admission tickets to the October 17 beatification ceremony through the Church but to no avail.

"When I asked for tickets, I did not tell anyone about my father-in-law's story."

That's what Dr. Battibocca told me at the time.

"As if I were watching the Resurrection of Christ!"

These words of Mrs. Battibocca were about the only thing I felt were true. I had become rather gloomy about the flimsy results of the first miracle.

"Do you know how to say 'a chatterbox' in Italian?" a friend of mine asked me.

"I don't know. My Italian is limited to a few words from cooking."

"It's *chiacchierone*. You kind of get the sense from the sound of the word, no?"

"That's really true. It makes me think of *The Chatterbox Ricciardi's Gallant Battle*,"[1] I laughed in reply.

"So, where did the second miracle happen?"

"In a place called Sassari on the island of Sardinia."

"Can you get there by airplane?"

I had no idea.

"I believe you have to land at a place called Alghero."

"When do you leave?"

"In two or three days."

In contrast to my visit to the Ranier house, this was clearly a blessed trip. In a short hour, the airplane flew over the Mediterranean, which seemed to smile back up at us, and while I was still gazing at the bright inlet, the plane danced out of the sky and landed at the Alghero airport. It took about thirty or forty minutes by bus to reach the town of Sassari. By Japanese standards, one could hardly describe this region as well-off. Olive gardens spread out over the hot, dry, barren land. Here and there I could see villages, with houses that looked like square boxes and the windows without eaves— they looked just like a woman's face after she has removed her false eyelashes. This was an unmistakably Spanish influence, and whether you called them olive gardens or just dry, gray dirt, I think I would have believed it had someone told me I was in Andalusia (a region of Spain).

The bus dropped me off in front of the offices of a travel agent in the town's central piazza, and my translator Mr. S and I hired a taxi and went off looking for the Conventual Franciscans. On my way here, I had tried to take note from the bus window of the places we passed, but there were so many domes and churches with crosses that it wasn't possible to know which was the Franciscans and which was not.

---

1. There may be a pun here. "Gallant Battle" (*funsen*) is a homonym for another word that means "erupting fountain." Although written as "The Gallant Battle," this imaginary book title might be heard as "The Chatterbox Ricciardi Overflows."

Finally, just past four o'clock, it was time for siestas to end. Mr. S and I had been kept waiting in a semi-underground reception room that was much larger than it needed to be, but I had no doubt that things would turn out fine since I had given them a letter of introduction from Father Ricciardi. Be that as it may, I still didn't know anything of the character of this person called Signorina Testoni that I was to meet. Certainly Signorina Testoni was no longer young. I had the feeling she would be one of those devout "ladies" in her fifties, someone that from a Japanese sensibility we would say was no longer a player. What if she launched right into a triumphant speech about how she was favored with the grace of a miracle, and then brought out her friends and chimed in with them about enjoying God's special favors—Father Kolbe's special favors? Would I be able to listen to that with a straight face?

Just as we were starting to enjoy the Sardinia breezes that wafted in through a window in the upper reaches of this room that felt like a hothouse, a young priest came in. He appeared to have seen Father Ricciardi's letter of introduction which I had sent and which laid out the nature of our business and through an interpretation that wasn't much of an interpretation, I understood him to say that he had already put in a call to Signorina Testoni so it would be fine if we visited her anytime from tomorrow on and she would probably introduce us to other witnesses as appropriate. He seemed to feel the more important matter was our lodging and asked if we had made reservations at a hotel. We had come without making any such arrangements. In that case, the priest said, we must immediately set out and find a hotel for you, and he crammed our luggage into his own Fiat.

At several of the hotels on the main street, Father was turned away. Finally, he turned down a side street that was barely wide enough to allow the Fiat through and, winding his way down it, stopped the car in front of a slightly dirty entrance that made me nervously question whether this place might actually be a legitimate hotel.

As we climbed up past the first and second floors, I couldn't figure out what they were used for. At any rate, the receptionist was on the third floor and the fourth and fifth floors were used for guest rooms. Don't even ask about an elevator. The priest himself carried my bags up for me, huffing and puffing up the stairs. We stopped to catch our breath, and lo and behold, there was a skinny fiftyish man and a fortyish woman double his size, with gigantic bust and hips, standing before us. I didn't know if they were husband and wife or what. Fortunately, they had a room available and when we entered to check it out, we saw that it was quite nice and tidy.

The Venetian blinds had been tightly closed for siesta, but when we opened them up we saw that the walls were violet and the flooring was a tile mosaic in bright celadon green and dark red. As I gazed out over the balcony, the red Spanish tiled roofs seemed lined up in rows with a look that was bright, healthy, and a bit stolid.

I got Mr. S to call and make preparations for my plan to meet with some people tomorrow, and this must have left Father, in the face of this typical Japanese meticulousness, thinking, "I told you I'd taken care of things and yet you still don't believe me." When you don't understand the local language, you really can get away with a lot. After a short nap, we were about to leave the hotel when that gigantic lady reappeared to ask if we didn't want any dinner. When we told her that we didn't, as we wanted to take a look around the town on our first night here, she folded her arms and harrumphed a bit. She was clearly sizing up our age, occupation and other considerations. After walking around the town a while, Mr. S and I went into a café, even though it was still a bit early for dinner in Italy. Inside there was a black and white TV, and several men who clearly had come here because of it were drinking beer. Following the Italian custom of taking a lighter dinner than lunch, I just ordered fried fish. They brought me a chunk of large-pored butter-less bread on a plate.

"Are you Japanese?" The fellow at the next table asked me in English.

"I'm originally from Sassari, but I've been living in San Francisco for a long time."

"What occupation are you engaged in?" I asked politely.

"I'm a stevedore foreman."

He had a charming smile. Even though he was Italian, he seemed to only want to speak in English. I turned to my translator Mr. S and smiling said to him,

"This fellow might be a Mafiosa. If he's the boss of stevedores on a San Francisco wharf, he'd have to be, right?"

The island of Sicily is Mafia headquarters. It's rumored that many in the Mafia work in things related to harbors. And one can't rule out the possibility of a Mafiosa from Sardinia.

The fish was soft and not very flavorful. The oil it was fried in had the aroma of olive oil. If I had to have fried food here, I wish it could have been squid tempura.

The "Mafia" fellow never said another word. When we left the café, some children came frolicking down the narrow, winding cobblestone street, screaming at the top of their lungs. As I looked up above that narrow road, a star appeared in the sky. Just when I thought it was a simple star, I saw the lights of an airplane and had a good laugh.

Chapter 9

The Semi-Underground Room

Section One

Signorina Angelina Testoni, who had experienced the miracle, lived at 31 Via Manno in Sassari.

What kind of place is Via Manno? Sassari is such a small town that everywhere is pretty close to the town center. Having said that, I think one could say that if Via Manno could be compared to Tokyo, it would be like the area from the Imperial Palace to Asakusa.[1] The best way to describe it is that my translator Mr. S and I only had to take a short stroll down the winding alley in front of our hotel, cross one bright piazza, then walk through a few blocks that had been rezoned as a "rather lively backstreet area," and there we were in Via Manno. As soon as I laid eyes on Signorina Testoni's shop I completely forgot that I was in Italy, or in a small town in Sardinia, on an island out in the middle of the Mediterranean Sea. That was because she ran a dress shop, the kind of place where we women all feel at home.

There was a show window on the left side of the shop displaying women's accessories and sweaters and jumpsuits for children and such. With an awkward sense of nostalgia, I noticed that these items had a certain kind of rural, unstylish quality about them. Whether it was the combination of colors or the designs, nothing seemed to come together quite right. Still, this wasn't Rome filled with its old statues and such; everything here fit well with the nature of Sardinia, which made things untamed seem quite attractive.

---

1. In other words, near the center of the town, but a bit seedy.

Since the shop was filled with customers, Mr. S and I stood for a while near the entrance and looked around the shop. It was obvious that the customers were housewives from the neighborhood. One was looking for a button, another found a fastener and a two-centimeter-wide gold ribbon—now what was she going to use that for? One had come to buy a pair of stockings, but there didn't seem to be a single customer shopping for anything more expensive than stockings. The ribbon lady took her ribbon to the counter where she had them measure out thirty centimeters and cut it for her.

Four people worked in the shop. There were two men—a middle-aged sourpuss and a sixteen or seventeen year old who looked like a young deer, and two housewives wearing black smocks that seemed like their uniforms. The housewives were no longer young. They looked to me to be in their fifties or sixties. Neither had colored her hair. All one could say is that they looked nicely cut from behind.

Finally, when the customers had finished their business, Mr. S entered the shop and introduced us. I knew from photographs that the younger of the housewives was Signorina Testoni, so I very naturally approached her and made my introduction and was introduced to her family. The two men were relatives, and the older housewife was her older sister Elena. The Testoni sisters were of short stature, with the older one no taller than my eye level.

"We can't really talk here" is what I guess Signorina Testoni said, as we were led across the street to the Testoni sisters' residence.

The building where the ladies lived really was as close as the end of your nose. Again I was reminded what a strange place Italy is—why don't they decorate the entry and exterior of their apartments? We entered dark stairs that seemed like the entrance to a warehouse and, climbing them, we encountered a heavy door that opened to reveal finally their cheery living quarters.

It was a very large living room. I was startled. I had heard that Signorina Testoni was a very poor seamstress, but she didn't seem to lack for anything here. Then another person appeared, an even fatter, even older granny. She was dragging a huge double chin, but there was something quite charming about her. This was her oldest sister Maria.

I sat down on the sofa facing these three old ladies. As they all sat in a row, these old ladies seemed even more charming. The oldest, Maria, had lived in Venice but returned to Sassari twelve years earlier and was now the manager of the dress shop. While Mr. S explained the purpose of my visit, I looked around the room. There was a chandelier suspended from the ceiling and a marble table right in front of us. An artificial rose was on display in a ceramic vase on the shelves. If that was the extent of it, one might call it a somewhat affected décor, but the wooden mask on the wall that appeared to be an African handicraft gave the room a warm atmosphere. Signorina Testoni noticed me looking at the mask and told me, through the interpreter Mr. S, "that is a souvenir my nephew bought me from Africa." She didn't miss much. In no time she was out of that black smock and had on a modest, navy blue and white dress. She looked very much the warm and gentle elementary school teacher. What I found most interesting was that as I watched these three laughing old ladies, I started to feel that I was sitting across from three little girls.

I started right off firing away. I said that it was written in the reports on the miracle that were submitted in connection with the investigation into Father Kolbe's beatification process that Signorina Testoni's life when she experienced this miracle was rather harsh, but I didn't get that sense from what I was seeing. Signorina Testoni's appeared comfortable and tolerant of the question, and through Mr. S's interpretation she told me that her life had improved after recovering miraculously from her illness twenty-two years earlier, but at that time her life really was very difficult.

"Signorina Testoni says she will show us the house where she lived when she was poor," Mr. S added.

Signorina Angelina Testoni was born here in Sassari on January 10, 1913. Her father was in the transport business and moved cargo with his horse cart. Her mother was nimble with her fingers and did sewing work. Angelina only completed four of the five years of compulsory education, and she put to good effect her skillful hands, which she had inherited from her mother and went right to work as a seamstress. In 1932, Angelina joined Catholic Action (a group that was active in assisting priests) and taught the catechism to children. In 1936 she became a Third Order Franciscan.

In 1942 Angelina began to feel a pain in her abdomen. Sometimes she would go for two months without an outbreak, but the symptoms were periodic, and over time the intervals became shorter and shorter. Perhaps it was because she was poor, but she put up with this condition for a year and a half. Soon the pain was accompanied by vomiting, and to lighten her suffering she would force herself to vomit. Her account of these things really conveyed the wretched life of a poor young seamstress. The pain began to spread from the lower abdomen throughout the whole abdomen, and by then she was getting no reprieve from the pain. Constipation and diarrhea attacked her in turn.

Angelina first saw a doctor two years later. This was Dr. Michele Piga. After taking X-rays, she was diagnosed with colonitis, but the medicine had no effect. And in 1945 she began to show symptoms of tuberculosis.

It seems that Angelina did not have any bitter memories of the things that happened during the war. Maybe it was because Sassari was spared from air raids, but when I reflected on the fact that she made a special point of telling me that she had her "tessarano" ration cards and could buy butter, bread, oil, rice and such, it seemed as though she was trying to say that the war couldn't do anything more to her than what she was already suffering. She admitted that the tuberculosis was the result of a weakened immune system from her poor diet. Certainly, it is hard to say how much more important her personal illness was to her in comparison with her war experience. Early in 1946, she got a diagnosis that it had entered her lungs, so she entered a seaside sanatorium. But Angelina suffered more from the chronic pain in the abdomen than from the tuberculosis. They had a place at the university hospital that was doing something called sun-ray treatment, so she went there on her own to consult them and was told that she had peritonitis. Around that time, every night her temperature would go up to around a hundred-five degrees Fahrenheit.

On June 3, 1946, she moved to the university hospital and there she received the sun-ray and calcium treatments that she had hoped for. But these failed to have the desired effect, so two months later she checked out of the hospital.

Her tuberculosis was not getting any better. She was re-admitted to the Sassari tuberculosis sanatorium, and on the second X-ray, they found shadows not only in her left lung but also in her right lung. On August 5 Angelina once again entered the sanatorium at Bonorva. And there she received treatment for her tuberculosis until November 10.

She had not been released from the hospital because her condition had improved. She was still vomiting and the vomit retained the shape of food. After leaving the hospital, she received iodine therapy.

Around nine o'clock on the first Sunday of August 1948, Angelina started vomiting feces. The vomiting continued for twenty-four hours at intervals of a few minutes to fifteen minutes. Her sister Elena, her brother Salvatore, and her friend Maria Manca stayed by her side, but they could do nothing to alleviate her suffering but watch.

The next morning she was brought the Holy Eucharist, first by Bishop Jau and later by Father Benvenuto Cannas, but because of the nausea she couldn't receive it. From that day until the day of her miraculous recovery, Angelina's condition was such that if she ate anything, she would just vomit it up.

According to the official report of the incident submitted to the Church, Angelina Testoni said the following:

> In light of my state of health, the Conventual Franciscan Father Agostino Picchedda had already for many years encouraged me to pray to the Servant of God Father Maximilian Kolbe for his intercession, but now with things having gotten so far, he insisted on the need to double up my prayers and even said he'd like to see a miracle with his own eyes. For some time now, I had already kept a picture of Father Kolbe near my pillow, and prayed to him from time to time, but this was also just in obedience to my confessor, Father Picchedda.
>
> Around noon on July 24, 1949, Father took the picture out from under my pillow and put it on my aching abdomen and blessed it.
>
> A bit after midday, the pain in my lower abdomen began to go away and I thought I could eat something without any problem. That night I slept well for the first time. The next day I ate several times, and my family competed with one another to grant whatever I wished. At first for several days I had to be careful so I ate things like lean white fish, but after a week I was able to eat whatever I wanted. Three or four days later I was able to get out of bed. On August 9 I was able to help with cooking for the first time, and on the fifteenth, I went to church for the Mass of the Feast of the Assumption. Ever since then, I've been quite healthy.

Putting together what I heard from her brother Salvatore Testoni, who had come to meet me, and her sister Elena, Angelina back then was very skinny and, not having eaten a thing for over a week, was in a terribly weak condition. At that time, Angelina was under the care of Dr. Pirisino who had given her a shot of spasmalgina (an anticonvulsant pain reliever) a week earlier because Signorina Testoni had complained of pain. The drug was in a container, and the one who actually gave the injection was Mrs. Rosa Gilda Piras, a public health nurse. Dr. Pirisino no longer went to see her, but not because Angelina was a patient who had little money; rather, it was because he had diagnosed her as a hopeless cause. Her sister Elena remembered clearly the day when Angelina had her first violent bout of vomiting. It was in early August on the Feast of Our Lady of the Snows[2] when around nine at night a Eucharistic procession passed outside her window that Angelina was first attacked by a bout of vomiting. Her older sister Elena dumped the vomit in a small vacant plot behind their poor apartment. It would have been better had she dumped it down the toilet but she could hardly think straight as she was so upset by how things were going and she just threw the contents of the wash basin out on the ground. Then, Pietrina Lai, a tenant on the second floor, gave her a tongue-lashing over the stench it caused. From then on, her younger sister never got any better, and in fact Angelina's condition deteriorated so much that her neighbors were saying things like "if you take your eyes off her for one second, she could die." Even Angelina's older sister knew full well that her sister had a premonition of death. According to her brother Salvatore, Angelina requested the sacrament of Extreme Unction (the ritual conducted for those at death's door that involves prayers for their recovery from illness and the salvation of their soul) from Father Picchedda, but Father told her, "you don't need such things as you will recover." Elena's eyes were transfixed the moment Father Picchedda placed the picture on her sister's abdomen around noon on July 24. The night before, Dr. Pirisino had come and he had told Elena that Angelina had only about five or six hours left to live. But

---

2. The original describes this as the Feast of Our Lady The Good Walker ("Yoki ayumi no seibo"). I've found no evidence of such a designation of Our Lady. Sassari does have arci-gremio (a gremio of porters is an ancient guild of arts and crafts) of Our Lady of Mercy of the city of Sassari. But that festive day is in October. The Feast of Our Lady of the Snows is August 5, so that is the translation I have adopted here.

Elena felt that Angelia got better the moment they prayerfully placed the picture on her stomach. She could tell from her facial expression that her anguish had stopped. Still, Father Picchedda who was standing right next to her never let on. Angelina herself thought that her regaining health might have just been temporary, and nobody was ready to declare then and there this shocking recovery a miracle.

Father Picchedda is now deceased, but in the official report, he said the following:

"As I recall, the patient was in a hopeless condition right when the disease was at its most dangerous point, but I encouraged her to seek the intercession of Father Maximilian Kolbe and she followed my advice, reciting the prayer that was printed on the picture. Around then, I dropped in on her every day, but one day while I was visiting, I noticed that she was doing much better. She was still in bed, but she announced to me that she was feeling good."

Once she recovered, Angelina was as good as she ever was. In 1950 she returned to her work as a catechista. Soon she and her sister opened the shop, and business was good, and the sun started to shine again on the Testoni family.

Now that I had an overview of the affair, I announced that I would like to meet with her friends who were present at her sick bed. Father Picchedda, who was certain she would die, was now himself dead, and Dr. Pirisino had moved to Perugia, but I was happy to find out that the others who had been there in 1949 were almost all still here in Sassari. Even Angelina herself never stepped foot outside Sardinia until after she recovered from her illness. That was just how life was for ordinary people back then.

While Elena was setting up appointments for me with those people, I made another request. I wanted to see the church that Angelina attended at the time and the house she lived in back when she was poor.

They told me it would be best to head straight for the church. The young man whom I had seen earlier in the shop would be my guide. In the meantime, they would make all the arrangements to have the house open for me on my return.

Mr. S and I had as our destination the Church of San Giuseppe. It was a bit of a distance, but I was happy to stroll around a foreign town in the crisp air on such a fine autumn day. I was told that in Italy young ladies are regularly pestered by the stares men give them, but I found only high school girls staring at a middle-aged woman like me. Well, maybe it's just because nobody has anything better to do in a backward place like Sardinia.

Entering the church, I saw it was built of soft, pink marble, and I immediately thought of Signorina Testoni's cheeks. There I found out that this church was erected in 1884 according to the design of Francesco Agnesa. The cupola above the altar depicts the shepherds worshiping the infant Jesus.

I wondered why Signorina Testoni never got married. When she fell ill, she was in her late twenties. Had she reached that age without any experience of love? Or was it that she was distressed by either poverty or a weak constitution? In any event, this is where Angelina Testoni brought all her sufferings and turned them into prayer.

I genuflected before the altar, and at that moment I suddenly remembered the dandruff scattered around the collar and shoulders of that black uniform smock of hers. For some reason, it made me feel close to Angelina. They say cleanliness is best, but I cannot help but have warm feelings for someone with dandruff all over them.

In front of the statue of Mary in the side altar, there were a lot of candles burning like mad. They expressed the devotion or the ardent calls for salvation of those who come here to pray. From where I was sitting, I unintentionally heard the low whispers from the confessionals. It's usually considered bad form to sit so near that you can hear what they are saying inside, but I didn't give it another thought since I can't understand a word of Italian. As I was looking on, thinking there must be someone inside even though you can't see them, out came a woman who looked to be in the early stages of middle age. She looked at a young girl who was waiting there and with a few quick words she pressed the young girl to go on in. Since the two faces bore a resemblance, I saw right away that they were mother and daughter. A man started cleaning the church, raising quite a racket with his electric vacuum, so I took that as my cue to leave.

Signorina Testoni had asked us to come back to the shop when we were finished at the church, so we were walking back behind the boy who was our guide when, at the rather bustling intersection near the shop, we spotted the sisters Elena and Angelina coming toward us. The house the sisters used to live in was about three buildings from that intersection. The lay of the land was interesting—the road went uphill from the intersection in the direction of the house that the Testoni family had rented. Since a house itself could not be on a slant, the Testoni family's rental house, the third one from the corner, was, one could say, beneath the upward-inclining road, seemingly buried half-underground. On the south side of the narrow road was a rather new, five- or six-floor building whose first floor was a supermarket. I asked what used to be there and was told that there used to be a building of about the same height. Since houses crowded in on left and right, that is on the east and west sides, I don't think this semi-underground residence got any sunlight at all.

Angelina had the key to the front door, so we were able to enter this abandoned flat.

Its width was, at best, about what we Japanese would call one and a half or two *ken*.[3] I felt as though I was standing here for the first time in the midst of the European type of poverty. This rental space was, well, a 1DK.[4] It was little more than a long, narrow dark space, like an eel's bed,[5] of about eight *tsubo*,[6] with a room in the back with

---

3. One *ken* is 1.82 meters.

4. A 1DK (one room, with a dine-in kitchen) is a small Japanese apartment, quite common among Tokyo residents when Sono was writing.

5. "an eel's bed" [*unagi no nedoko*] is an idiomatic Japanese expression for a long, narrow house. *Unagi* does not convey quite the negative connotation in Japanese as its English equivalent eel might, however, as *unagi* is considered a delicacy in Japanese cuisine.

6. One *tsubo* is 3.3 square meters.

a toilet and sink.

The Testoni sisters used the narrow space in the front for their "shop." There was still a mannequin, and it had marks all over its skin. And the only thing that separated the shop from their sleeping quarters in the rear was a curtain. There would have been a sewing machine and a cutting board somewhere, and since Westerners don't sleep on the floor, there would have had to be beds for the two sisters. And since these houses lack *oshiire,*[7] they would have needed a chest of drawers for their clothes.

Where would they have put their dining table? At any rate, there was no room for anything like a bathtub in this house. In Western Europe they also have public bathhouses where they rent out private rooms for bathing, so maybe they used something like that. I was intrigued that there was a Chinese-style card stuck on the wall that had Ten Shu Toku Yū ("The Lord Can Help") written in red characters.

I stood for a while in that dark space. Many legs walked past on the main street right outside. The street was above us so all you could see of the passersby was their legs. Buses and cars rumbled by, raising a terrible racket. Since the road ran uphill out front, they revved up their engines as they went by. I wondered if in 1949 there were fewer cars on the road than now. I really didn't want to believe that material circumstances have a determinant influence on Man's spirit—that is, that the spirit is not so independent after all—but it seemed to me that this room was a place that gave an example of precisely that. I really wonder if it had been me who had to live in such a place, and ill to boot—well, I just don't think I would have been able to have any goodwill for others, or any hope for this world.

Earlier, when we were back in the Testoni family living room, I had asked her a question in a very roundabout way. What I wanted to know was what Signorina Testoni was thinking on that crucial evening when she was in an extremely critical condition but still fully

---

7. Large built-in closets, standard in Japanese homes. (See note 16 above.)

in possession of her mind. "I didn't think about wanting to live or wanting to die. I just thought that things would turn out as God wills," she said.

I really liked that answer. It is the perfect reply, to be as indifferent as the oceans under all circumstances. Those who cannot reply like this launch all sorts of petty schemes and present an unbecoming image of themselves kicking and struggling to make things go their way. Yet, even so, I cannot stop myself from feeling a rather vulgar response, that it wouldn't be an entirely bad thing to live in this sort of house and if one fell ill from poverty to even accept death "as God wills." No, putting things like that only invites misunderstanding. It is just that while I do believe that I have a considerably better life than Signorina Angelina Testoni had in 1949, somewhere at the bottom of my heart, I think that if this life I lead at present had to end, well then it would just be over, and that too would have its good side. What I mean is that if I die, I would indeed lose the pleasures that I enjoy now, but at the same time, I would be freed from all those annoying little things that I carry around with me all the time. And that's how I started to feel that since this world cannot be called entirely good, it didn't matter to me whether I lived or died.

Signorina Testoni's idea of "as God wills" did not come from my own sloppy way of feeling, but was a more positive attitude, coming from one who really supports the will of God. Well, anyway these were my thoughts as I walked out of the gloomy room.

Section Three

That night was a quiet one.

The bed covers were thin so I burrowed deep into the bed with my nightgown still on. That fat hotel lady had said there would be hot water after five in the evening, but no matter how many times I turned the shower handles in the fourth floor bathroom, all I got was cold water.

I re-read Dr. Pietro Pirisino's deposition given to the Church in an effort to finally understand what the actual nature of Signorina Testoni's illness was.

> I am Pietro Pirisino, the son of Giacomo and Di Virra Maddalena, both deceased. I was born on December 28, 1913, in Monti, Sassari. I am a married man, a Catholic, a military doctor, and currently am the vice-director of the military hospital in Perugia.
>
> Until about three years ago, I had never heard the name of the Servant of God, Father Maximilian Maria Kolbe. About three years ago, Father Ricciardi of Rome came to my hospital and asked me to certify Signorina Angelina Testoni's miraculous recovery, and it was from him that I first heard about Mr. Kolbe. I had no interest in a special personal devotion to Mr. Kolbe.

I was interested to find that old chatterbox Father Ricciardi appearing here, pushing himself onto Dr. Pirisino with his characteristic, cheerful coercion. But note that the doctor offered nothing but a very cold reply about the miracle.

> I have no clear memory of the period when the so-called recovery took place. Nor do I know if there was any kind of a report or such made about the recovery. The only thing I am certain of is that about three years ago I wrote a simple certificate of acknowledgement from a doctor's perspective of the facts in response to a request by a petitioner for beatification.

From what I know, they took X-rays in the radiology department of the Sassari Civil Hospital.[8] I believe the doctor in charge has left behind the related documents, as is customary. But whether you can still get copies of those documents as they were, I do not know.

I really get the sense here that this Professor Pirisino was bringing up all sorts of unnecessary things to avoid the real issue at hand. Although the patient was on the verge of death, it was only the public health nurse who gave the injection of the painkillers; the doctor himself didn't show up even to examine the patient. It was much later when the doctor finally showed up, and even then only when he must have thought she had gone ahead and died; he must have thought it strange that he hadn't been asked to bring a death certificate with him. Then, with Signorina Angelina right there sitting up just as fit as a fiddle, Professor, didn't you think there was something wrong with your cold attitude?

"When I took over the treatment of Signorina Testoni, her parents were already deceased. She was living with her only sister and this sister, as far as I know, was healthy, and I know that she also had a healthy brother. So with that information, I cannot say whether it was a genetic disease."

With that, the long and boring deposition finally came to an end. He might as well have said nothing at all.

The next report was that of Dr. Salvatore Palmas. I expect to meet this Dr. Palmas, but this seems to be a good opportunity to gain an overview of the entire situation.

Expert Opinion Based on Medical Examination
I examined Signorina Angelina Testoni in November 1965 at the request of the Investigative Committee of the Church . . .

---

8. Ospedale Civile di Sassari.

1. Signorina Testoni has high blood pressure (180 milimeters) and beneath her left collarbone there is an infiltration of the lung, and on the right there is a mark left from pleurisy. In my examination of the abdomen, objective observations found nothing abnormal. The result of the x-ray examination of the digestive organs showed evidence of treatment for inflammation of the ileum. One could see a large, forty-centimeter-long crease running horizontally along the ileum. It was large in diameter and there was no evidence of adhesions. At present, there is no concern about contracting the disease again. And there are no symptoms of a relapse.

As the responsible physician, I replied to this point in an article, "Was Testoni's Recovery a Special One?" in the journal *Societá del Promotore della Fede*. It is true that the patient recovered through some extraordinary means. Whether we consider tuberculosis as the cause, or whether we assume a partial enteritis, both were completely cured.

In addition to that of Dr. Palmas, there was another medical testimony from a Dr. Giovanni Budroni, but he was asked the same questions and gave pretty much the same answers. But the answer he gave to the questions from the *Societá del Promotore della Fede* was written down with a good bit of detail:

"The patient's recovery was a special one. One reason was the speed of the recovery; another fact is that in ordinary cases there is first a constriction and then healing. But in this case, the diseased parts remained in an enlarged state and were healed."

And attached to this was "The Report from the Technical Council Concerning the Miraculous Cure of Angelina Testoni":

On October 29, 1965, Dr. Palmas and Dr. Budroni were invited by His Excellency Auxiliary Bishop G. A. Spanedda to the chancery at Number 35 Via Nizza in Sassari, where they were asked by the Bishop, Father Deolora, the diocesan secretary, and Mr. G. Spanedda, diocesan counselor, to undertake the responsibility for this matter. His Excellency and the venerable Dr. Osvaldo Zacchi placed the two doctors under oath, and then entrusted them to diagnose, in keeping with the strictures of canon law, whether Maria Angelina Testoni, who was born in Sassari on January 10, 1913, experienced, in the same place, a relapse after her complete recovery.

Here is their report of the results of their examination of Signorina Testoni that took place in the Central Hospital on November 17, 1965 (with her medical history and current condition omitted).

Testimony in reply to the questions asked.
1. The result of our investigation into her past illnesses is as follows:

a. It is possible to diagnose through X-ray that there was tuberculosis.

b. The existence of tuberculosis is determined by characteristics such as pain not being intense, a gradual deterioration, and a slow loss of weight.

c. Found a cloud on the chest X-ray. When streptomycin treatment was employed, there was a bit of improvement in a short time. The finding of the same disease in different hospitals by two famous doctors of the day is proof. The question of enteritis may be considered from the following matters. Dr. Crohn says enteritis is commonly caught between the ages of twelve and thirty, but the patient's age is outside that scope. In the early stages of this disease, there is diarrhea, fever, and pain in the abdominal area and the general worsening of the symptoms is exactly how it happened in the case of Signorina Testoni who contracted this disease. It moves from an acute outbreak to a chronic condition; it is characteristic of this disease to seem to disappear temporarily after the acute outbreak but then to come back much worse.

d. Was the inflammation of the abdomen tubercular? It might just as well have been regarded as Crohn's Disease. One theory holds that this disease arises from an allergic reaction. Others say that it is an ailment of small external wounds, blood vessels and nerves, that hyper-sensitivity in the small intestine is symptomatic, and that it breaks out when the lymph glands are weakened. What we think is that Koch's tubercle bacillus had an influence through weakened intestinal walls while passing through the intestines.

e. Why is this disease thought to be responsible? In the period from 1946 to 1949, Crohn's Disease was not yet well-known. (It gradually appeared in documents around the world between 1946 and 1960). The Crohn Theory became well-known after 1950 . . .

f. The peritonitis is thought to be a complication of the original tuberculosis combined with the Crohn's Disease which she contracted next.

g. As a result of the treatment, two things come to mind. If it is tuberculosis, it will not disappear without the use of antibiotics. Second, they used sun-ray therapy. If we consider it a usual case of Crohn's Disease, they did not fail to use medicine that has some effect.

Conclusion

Various things have come to light, so we are able to offer the following comments. When Signorina Testoni first contracted her illness, her condition was complicated. After she got Crohn's Disease, she had abdominal tuberculosis. The technical medical names for these diseases are intestinal tuberculosis, tuberculous colitis, ileitis. To repeat, this disease is a tuberculous or a tubercular type of ailment. The patient's recovery was not normal. Whether considered as tuberculous or as a normal ileitis, the process of recovery cannot be considered a normal one.

May 5, 1966
Sassari
Salvatore Palmas

When I realized that the very next day I was to meet those people brought together by the "day of the miracle," I closed the report, filled with a sense of new hope.

Chapter 10

This Humble Life

Section One

First thing in the morning, I hired a car and took off from Sassari for the forty-minute drive to the town of Alghero, where the blue ocean spread out before me, lifting my spirits to the heavens.

I felt that Japan had grown a bit distant from me. The Italian newspapers reported that a Chinese plane had crashed in Mongolian territory and that for several days afterward all flights in Chinese air space were suspended, and preparations for China's National Day were canceled—or so my interpreter Mr. S told me. Unlike Rome, Sardinia was not a place where one could easily buy an English newspaper. I understood that something had happened in the Beijing government, but for a non-political person like me, talk about China felt distant, trivial, and forced as I gazed at the deep ocean blue that seemed to color all of Sardinia.

But later, looking back, I realized that I was able to get accurate news more quickly in that remote Sardinian countryside than people back in Japan were. This may come off a bit too personal, but my husband Miura Shumon had gone to Singapore just before all the trouble started.

He had already read in a Chinese-language newspaper that preparations for National Day were stopped after September 12 and because of that the author of the article surmised that National Day itself would probably be canceled. At the same time, the Singapore newspaper also carried a report from Tokyo that a special correspondent from Japan met with a V.I.P. in Beijing and was dismissed with a sneer and the comment, "such a thing is not possible."

Miura happened to meet a political scientist named Mr. P while he was in Singapore. Mr. P said to him, "The report from the Japanese special correspondent is very valuable. Japan always writes up for the Beijing regime topics that it cannot yet publicize itself and also presents those events as Beijing wants them to be seen."

Of course, *there was talk* that Lin Biao's party was on the plane that crashed, but one of Japan's leading newspapers printed a story in November, about two months after the incident, that still implied that the theory of the fall of Lin Biao was just propaganda put out by the countries of the Free World and they only recognized Lin Biao's fall from power after another two months had passed—in January 1972—and even then, they insisted that he was still alive.

So you see, I was able to get the world's news in Sardinia with what might be called a healthy degree of slowness and a healthy degree of clarity.

My purpose in going to Alghero was to meet with Sister Giuseppina Serra, a member of the Daughters of Charity of St. Vincent de Paul who work in the Civil Hospital. I had tried to make an appointment beforehand through Mr. S, but for some reason or other I couldn't get through on the phone. I couldn't believe it wasn't possible to reach a hospital by phone, but to say that everything at such places has to run like clockwork would be thought inhuman in these Latin countries, and at any rate, I thought, if there were just one place I had to see, it would be interesting to just go right over and visit the Civil Hospital of Alghero.

It wasn't much different from the new style of hospitals in Japan. I went half thinking that I wouldn't be able to meet Sister Serra, but I was told she was right then at her duties as head nurse of the internal medicine department. We rode the elevator to the fifth floor and came out into an excessively large hall with a small gathering spot for employees on the right side, and there, after being bombarded with foreign words I didn't understand, we made our way to her bright office at the end of the floor.

Sister Serra was a woman just entering her mid-fifties. At first glance, I must say that she did not strike me as the type that exudes kindness and affection. She even gave off a bit of that cold feeling of one who is bony and sharp-minded, whose eyes would never betray the slightest sign of sentimentality. For some reason, I thought, "I'll bet she was top of her class in elementary school." At that very moment, a skinny, earnest, bony-faced young Sister Serra appeared clearly before my eyes.

The real Sister Serra was wearing a square, yellowish veil and, while she may have been the head nurse, she was the perfect image of a nun.

The room we found ourselves in was about five square meters, with white walls and a new red door. The floor was red tiled, and it made the bare mountains one could see through the windows appear to have stripes. Being such a bundle of curiosity, I just stood there staring at these things. Sister Serra politely offered us a seat, and suddenly coming to my senses I muttered something under my breath. Probably it was something like "well, such a dirty room." Because the next thing I knew, they brought out a dry cloth and wiped the surface of the chairs for us. They were attentive to every last detail.

She had been working as a nurse for twenty-five years already, and came to the Civil Hospital six years ago. This meant that at the time when Signorina Testoni was sick, Sister Serra was at the hospital in Sassari. In the beatification hearings, Sister Serra testified as follows:

"Signorina Testoni was admitted to the Sassari University Hospital twice. The second time was from April to June of 1948, when she was placed in the pathology wing where Dr. Demuro was the physician in charge. I know very well what went on back then, because I worked in that wing as a sister.

"Signorina Testoni was diagnosed with tubercular peritonitis and treated mainly with strong doses of streptomycin. The records show that when she left the hospital, we saw a superficial improvement in her health but that her abdominal ailment was not cured. While she was in the hospital, I myself often ascertained the illness in her lower abdomen. Her abdomen was swollen, stretched out in a ball, and wherever one pressed it hurt."

When Sister Serra heard the reason for our visit, she told us about the Signorina Testoni she recalled from her days in the hospital.

Angelina Testoni was at the time but a thirty-five-year-old woman of short stature and flaxen hair. She was quiet and sensible, and her only pleasure was receiving the Eucharist that the Franciscan priests brought to her. It was probably through the Eucharist that she first had an actual, very personal experience of God as the Comforter of her soul.

Angelina Testoni had what people call the papers that low-income people use to exempt them from medical expenses. No matter what country they live in, poor people everywhere know the same bitter taste of misery. But according to Sister Serra, Signorina Testoni was able to get expensive drugs that had been imported from America. And they knew she was seriously ill when even those drugs did not bring about a quick recovery.

That is not to say that Angelina Testoni's time in the hospital was nothing but unremitting suffering. This small, reverent, poor woman always had her face turned toward God—that is to say, toward the Light. Whenever her health improved even a bit, she took up her favorite pastime of sewing. She sewed dresses for girls who were to make their First Communion, and Sister Serra distributed them to girls in her hometown. But Angelina never took any money for this work. According to Sister Serra, there were even some girls in the hospital who had made their preparations for First Communion and those children were able to wear these special, one-time-only dresses (with their long hemlines that often look just like bridal gowns) that symbolize they are receiving the life of Christ for the first time on that special day.

Hers was not a happy discharge from the hospital. She had not completely recovered. This was right about when Angelina told me,

"Dr. Demuro said I may have to put up with some pain for the rest of my life, but that the disease itself is cured, but I just don't feel that is right." Dr. Demuro, the head of the hospital, seemed to feel we had given her "enough consolation." But in actuality, Signorina Testoni's condition simply continued to deteriorate from then on. It was about a year afterward when she, abandoned by the doctors, recovered from a near-death condition overnight.

Sister Serra did not see Angelina once during the interval. Then, in 1950, Sister Serra ran into a very energetic Angelina Testoni one day when she came on a visit to the hospital. She couldn't believe her eyes. It wasn't as though she expected her to have died, but someone in that condition with that disease might enjoy a temporary improvement, but it was beyond comprehension that such a person could have made a complete recovery like that.

That was when Angelina first reported to Sister Serra that she had made a miraculous recovery. She probably thought that Sister Serra was an ideal person to tell such an unbelievable thing to. And as someone who would neither take such news in an excessively sentimental way nor divulge this honor to others, Sister Serra truly would seem to be a good confidant. Signorina Testoni told Sister Serra that she was cured almost the instant she put the picture of Father Kolbe on her stomach and prayed to him.

"Did you think her story was unbelievable?" I asked Sister Serra.

"If it were some other disease, one might recover. And given the condition she was in, there might have been some improvement, but a complete recovery was simply not possible. Still, someone in that critical a condition, well, even now I don't see how it is possible."

"Is Signorina Testoni famous around here because of her miracle?"

I was indulging in the very Japanese way of thinking that perhaps she was trying to become the "lady of the hour."

Sister Serra said with a rather stern expression, "I don't think many people in Sardinia know about it. Maybe people in Sassari know a bit about it. I don't even know if the newspapers wrote on it, because I never read the newspapers."

"What kind of life do nuns around here have? Is the convent located nearby?" I asked Sister Serra.

"No, we live in the hospital. We each have our own room on the fifth floor. The sisters who are nurses are divided into two groups: one takes the first shift from 7:00 am to 2:00 pm and the other takes the second shift from 4:30 pm to 8:00 pm."

Sister Serra told me that this hospital now had ninety beds with a staff of twenty men and women.

"Also, there is a priest assigned to the hospital. Would you like to see the chapel?"

I replied that I most certainly would. We took the elevator to the fifth floor where we were admitted to the rather large chapel. There was a dark crucifix on the altar with an image of Christ that looked exactly as if he had been burned black. Sister Serra and we knelt before the altar in prayer for a few minutes and then finished and stood up together at the same time. This was an extremely ordinary public hospital. And, as such, I felt that in this place where a person's life or death hangs in the balance it was certainly necessary to have the presence of the One who is greater than human willpower.

No sooner were we out of the chapel when I ran into a large, cheerful nun. She was introduced to me as the Mother Superior. The hand I shook was a warm one. When I said I wanted to take Sister Serra's picture, Mother Superior herself led us out to a terrace that was filled with the strong Sardinia sun.

"Won't this be a good place?"

In truth, it was a bit too beautiful there. The blue ocean spread out just a kilometer or so in front of us, as if it would swallow us up, the houses with their white walls and red roofs—an incomparable beauty surrounded us. Dark green olive gardens wove together the houses, and the hues of color seemed to offer a visual lesson that inevitably a dark sadness awaits when the life of Man shines too brightly.

Sister Serra looked as though she was not too fond of having her picture taken. Maybe it was just that the strong sunlight was in her face, but she was frowning a bit. Just when my translator Mr. S was about to take the picture, Mother Superior made a sign to stop. She pointed out that Sister Serra's veil was crooked. As her hands nimbly straightened out the veil, I could see her maternal nature. It was a special moment. This from a woman who didn't have children of her own. I am always struck by how the life of a nun is able to gain something that transcends the ordinary life of lay people. And there two young nuns, so young that they still retained vestiges of their girlhood, appeared before my eyes, and we had our commemorative picture taken together.

Sister Serra saw Mr. S and me off to the first floor lobby. Just as I was thinking that the bus station was rather far away and we would probably have to walk the whole way, a man who looked to be of good character pulled up and greeted Sister Serra. I watched the scene, thinking that a good sister in any country will find some men who recognize their dignity, when Sister Serra asked him whether he would give us a ride in his car to the bus terminal.

When we parted, I had intended to casually shake hands and say, "sayonara," but we spontaneously and naturally hugged. I realized that I probably would never meet these two again. Yet, here with the sun and sea that were overflowing with the sense of life that bursts out in Alghero, I found something welling up inside me when I thought of the ordinary greatness of this cool, really quite expressionless, solitary nun who had just plugged on with her monotonous but important work as a nurse for twenty-five years.

Section Two

My meeting with Mrs. Rosa Gilda Piras that afternoon was back at the Testoni family shop. According to the report put out by the Church, she was born in 1903, so she would now be close to seventy years old, but she still possessed a sturdy physique that testified to how long she had worked as a nurse. She mentioned that she was on her way to another appointment, and had on a black dress with black stockings and was wearing gloves. She certainly made an impression of being in full uniform. She was a blond, although the better part of her hair had gone white, and with her heavy cheeks she looked very much the sturdy woman.

What was particularly beautiful were her hands, which I casually glimpsed when she took off her gloves. They were large, big-boned but even now supple, as if they spoke of the special grace bestowed only on those who work hard for many years.

"I was at the time a nurse assigned to Dr. Piga. That doctor mainly gave injections as a way to recover physical strength, and it may have only been a little help, it wasn't enough to induce a recovery for Signorina Testoni. The doctor said he had nothing else to offer, so he merely offered allopathic treatment.

"I should have mentioned this first, but earlier the patient was seen at the Sassari University Hospital and was admitted there, and I made a personal request to Professor Marginesu, who is now long dead, and he treated her with streptomycin. I believe her condition improved a bit after that.

"But she still had abdominal pain, along with the frequent diarrhea and constipation. I myself examined her distended belly, so swollen it seemed it might burst.

"I don't recall the exact date, but one morning as I was making my usual rounds to check in on the patients, her family members told me that she had vomited something, something that looked like feces. I asked them not to dispose of what she vomited as we would examine all vomit and bowel discharge. This was what her condition was like every day in that final week before she got better. There was nothing we could do for her but give her injections of camphor and painkillers. I was the one who gave her the injections. On one particularly bad night, as I was returning from her place, I even wondered if I would see her alive the following morning. I remember it was so bad that I even started thinking how difficult it would be to offer any words of consolation to that poor miserable family if Angelina died and left behind her only sister Elena. Yes, it was that bad. It was to the point that I could hardly find her pulse. I suppose a layman would say she no longer had a pulse. I went the next day, with a heavy heart, to her home. As soon as I arrived, there was Angelina looking so healthy you couldn't have believed what she was like just the night before.

"They said she had just finished a meal and still wanted to eat more. I was concerned and said,

'Don't you think you better go easy on the food?'

'Oh no, I'm fine,' she told me with a cheerful look."

I asked again, "Had the doctors given up on her by then?" "Well, I guess in the end it was kind of like that. But it certainly wasn't that he coldly kicked her aside. When her condition took a turn for the worse and she went home, Captain Pirisino, M.D. of the Army Medical Corps took care of her for free."

"A military doctor, you say?" I was surprised.

"From time to time a military doctor will see civilians for a proper fee. But in Angelina's case, there was no charge. It was because Angelina was a good woman and sewed clothes for the wife of the military doctor, so Doctor Pirisino couldn't begin to think of taking money from her for his services."

I learned that back then Mrs. Piras was what they called a public health nurse. If you translated her title precisely from the Italian, she was a "home visiting public health assistant." She also belonged to the Sardinia Malaria Society.

It was obvious that Mrs. Piras was headed somewhere and I didn't think I should detain her any longer. I shook her large, solid hand, thanked her, and took my leave. With a laugh like the Sardinia sun, Mrs. Piras walked off. My, was she big. She had such a powerful stride. As I watched her walk away, I reflected that it was that powerful stride of hers that had carried her through so much of life.

Around dusk, Mrs. Albertina Pinna came with her husband to the Testoni family dining room. She was quite charming with her big, passionate eyes and her cute, up-turned nose. It seemed to me that the reason her black hair looked the color of a wet bird's wings was that she probably dyed it. Somehow her high, sweet, chatty voice made her seem more plump than she really was. Her husband Mr. Pinna was now working in an Italian automobile club, but one could see from his large, strong build and white, open-collar shirt and light brown suit that he had been in the military in his younger days. From the moment the couple had arrived, I had the impression that two revelers from an Italian street festival had invaded the room. Without a word of greeting, the couple just started chatting away with the extremely quiet Testoni sisters and just kept at it, like a couple of birds chirping away.

"When did you first meet Signorina Testoni?"

I tried to ask, but the missus just started talking away, without waiting for the interpreter. Her husband seemed to scold her a bit, saying something like "How about waiting to talk until after she's finished her question?" and with an embarrassed smile, Mr. S, my interpreter, told me what she had said.

Mrs. Pinna had been a friend of Angelina Testoni since they were children.

In any event, back in 1942, Albertina and Angelina were both seamstresses. For Albertina, these were glorious years, a time of many dreams. Just the year before, she was engaged to a handsome military man and every day when work was over, she would wait for him and they would go out together, forgetting completely about the shop. That handsome military man was now her husband. He was from Naples, but the army had assigned him to Sassari, and that's where he met Albertina and got engaged to her. For him, too, it was a pleasant time when he would go to the shop every evening to see her after he finished his military duties for the day.

Albertina had fallen head over heels for him. While they were working, she talked non-stop to Angelina about how sweet he was.

And Angelina was always ready with a friendly ear, regardless of how difficult it may have been for her to hear such things. Back then, it was fashionable to wear skirts down to the knees, so when her fiancé came to get her, Albertina went out, full of gaiety with her romantic long skirt swooshing about her. You could read these events on the happy face of this middle-aged housewife as if she were speaking of just yesterday.

In 1942, Angelina Testoni was already nineteen years old. That was the year when she fell ill. I felt the contrast between them was significant: on the one hand, we have a cheerful young lady who had gotten engaged to a handsome soldier, and on the other hand, a poor unmarried young lady who was starting to feel symptoms of a serious illness.

"What kind of person was Signorina Testoni back in those days?" I asked her.

No sooner had the words left my mouth, while the interpreter was still speaking, when Mr. Pinna himself—who had just cautioned his wife to not speak until the question was asked—started talking as if not to be bested by his wife. They said something to each other, without a care in the world about us, and then the husband turned to Mr. S and Mrs. Pinna turned to me (as if she had forgotten that I don't speak Italian) and suddenly the Testoni living room was filled with an energetic non-stop duet of Mr. and Mrs. Pinna who didn't allow anyone else a chance to get a word in edgewise. They were basically saying in unison,

"Allegra, Affelio, Gentile, Bravissima, Buona."

And the way they were both punctuating each term with full-body gestures, I had no choice but to believe them.

The night before the miracle, the couple remained next to the dying Angelina until one o'clock in the morning. Rather than say she was dying, it would be more accurate to say that Albertina thought Angelina Testoni was already all but dead. When Albertina told me that "she was more over there than over here," this was her way of saying she was one step closer to Heaven than she was on this Earth.

The next day, Albertina went by herself to the Testoni home. Angelina seemed unbelievably healthy, and the word "how?" just popped out of Albertina's mouth.

"I think I've recovered."

Albertina Pinna thought that just maybe the recovery had something to do with the holy picture of the day before, but she didn't say anything about it. None of those gathered there said anything about that.

According to Mrs. Pinna, Angelina recovered "*piano, piano*" (little by little).

"That very day, she took a little *brodo*."

Her husband chimed in, "yes, that's right, that's right." I was told that *brodo* is a clear simple broth.

Even in Italy where they put off dinner until quite late in the evening the time to prepare dinner eventually comes. But the conversation between this couple and the Testoni sisters showed no sign of coming to an end, so Mr. S and I decided this would be a good time to bring things to a close, and we took our leave. Once we got out to where we could no longer hear the plump chatterbox Mrs. Pinna, even the bustling streets of Sassari's business district seemed eerily quiet to us.

Section Three

New residential developments had reached the outskirts of Sassari, as they seem to everywhere. I recognized them immediately as the equivalent of the cluster of high-rise housing we know as "manshon" in Japan. Of course, in this country they don't make the fine distinction we do in Japanese between a "manshon" and an "apāto." But in Sassari, they were no taller than the old historic buildings, and the spectacle these apartments presented, all lined up with flowers on every veranda and with their large doors and windows, presented the new face of a Sassari whose nationality couldn't be determined. It seemed to me that this Sante Angeli Orphanage had been built on this sloping hillside back when this whole area was vacant land. Of course, because I arrived at night, I couldn't get a good look at the whole compound. As I went from the gate toward the buildings, I went downhill, and along the way was a Shrine to Our Lady of Lourdes and at her feet many candles were burning.

My interpreter Mr. S and I were shown to a parlor to the immediate right of the front hall. There was an old piano and a large potted plant with beautiful leaves set on a russet and white tile floor. An old crucifix and sacred painting hung on the wall. In no time, Mrs. Michelina Caruta came from down the end of the corridor. She wore her hair in a tight bun and her eyes were large and sharp. With her charcoal gray sweater and her black skirt, she clearly gave the impression of having consciously rejected the world filled with all its affectations.

When she heard what I had come for, she mentioned that she had been contacted by Signorina Testoni, but she had a brisk way of speaking that betrayed a sense of moderation or caution. She had been working in this orphanage ever since she took up residence in it in 1946. The forty-eight children here were looked after by eight women of the "Sisters of the Company of the Cross"[1] and their eight assistants. It was a large institute that used to hold eighty people, taking in children from four to twelve years of age. The reason children were sent here was the same as in Japan: their parents had fallen ill or there were other family circumstances.

Of course, Michelina Caruta took up this kind of work only after her husband died. Her four children (two boys and two girls) had all been married off by then. In short, she was at a point in her life when she was wondering how to spend the rest of her life, and she opted for a path of service to others.

---

1. The Sisters of the Company of the Cross is an order of religious women founded by St. Angela of the Cross in Seville in 1875.

While listening to her story, I was struck by how a particularly strong religious way of life had permeated everyday life in Italy. I suppose I need to explain what I mean by "a religious way of life." To someone like me, who is not a specialist in these things, it just means having a goal that transcends one's own life. But I don't think that Mrs. Caruta simply woke up one morning and decided on this way of life.

"Signorina Testoni and I had a mutual friend who had entered the convent, you see. And we heard about many of her patients from that Sister because, well, she really liked taking care of the sick."

It seemed that was also what brought her to Signorina Testoni's place.

"Also, around here it is the custom that when people get sick everybody with any connection to them rushes over to take care of them."

So, it seems her point was that what she did for Signorina Testoni was nothing special, just a natural thing to do. I found in her words the particular warmth of life on this island that still retained the traditional social mores of old Italy.

And that's how Mrs. Caruta came to check in on Signorina Testoni very frequently around the time when she recovered. Sometimes she looked in on her two or three times a day.

"I first met Signorina Testoni through that Sister, but by the time I met her she was already seriously ill. From that time on, she and I grew extremely close. I became a frequent visitor at her home because, well, in the first place, the Testoni family was extremely poor, but at the same time, I was drawn to them because they are all such fine people.

"Around that time, Signorina Testoni was suffering from an extremely acute pain in her lower abdomen and from diarrhea and vomiting, but there were moments of respite and at such times she would rise from her bed to take care of urgent business. Of course, when her nausea was bad, she wouldn't eat anything so as not to induce vomiting but would only drink a bit of orange juice. Signorina

Testoni told me she felt there was no longer anything anyone could do for her, that since her intestines were all tied up in a knot, there was no way she could recover.

"I too prayed for Signorina Testoni's full recovery. Then, one night after dinner, I went to her house to check in on her, and there I was really surprised to find this woman, whom the night before I thought was at death's door sitting up in a chair. Signorina Testoni told me that she was feeling fine and had taken some clear soup. The next day she told me, 'I washed the dishes!' I warned her not to overdo it, as she was still sick.

"Some days later—I don't clearly recall the exact day—Signorina Testoni told me that she felt she had experienced a miracle through the intercession of Father Maximilian Kolbe, but she didn't tell me how that miracle had happened."

Both of these women chatted quite naturally about these events, perhaps because they were in shock from the immensity of it all, but they didn't act as though it was a big deal or anything. But that someone who thought they had seen a miracle would act so restrained, so reverent, so quiet about it just ran counter to everything I had expected. If it had been me who had seen a miracle, I think I would have broadcast that fact to anyone I could find.

"What kind of person is Signorina Testoni?" I asked Mrs. Caruta.

"She's a really fine person. Very dedicated to her work. A very careful person," Mrs. Caruta replied.

"This is a fine place to work," I told Mrs. Caruta. "What time do the children go to bed?"

"Usually, at 8:30. When there is a good television program on, it can be 9:00, and during summer, when it is hot, they can stay up until 10:00."

We heard the thundering feet of the children outside the reception room, as if they were racing past us toward a recreation room. We made our apologies and, as we were leaving the orphanage, she added as if she just had recalled it:

"There was someone who kept coming to see the kids for eighteen years, even longer than Signorina Testoni. Of course, that person is now deceased."

Suddenly, I had the wild thought that, if one could make a lot of friends in that place, it wouldn't be so sad to die. That night the stars were especially beautiful.

Chapter 11

The Via Turritana

Section One

One morning we went to see Gemma Piaggi in her apartment. We heard she was eighty years old, so we expected her to be a granny with a wool blanket over her knees even in the summer, but boy, were we wrong! Unlike the diminutive Signorina Testoni who was our guide, this woman was a majestic Amazon.

It was an ancient apartment with high ceilings, located in the center of town. We were led to a parlor that was decorated with many knick-knacks that seemed to hold the secret memories of an entire family. A bowl of wax fruit was set before a large mirror. There was a ceramic ballerina doll with its head slightly cocked.

Signorina Piaggi was wearing a black sweater over a black outfit. She had a simple and natural style about her. I was just wondering how she could afford to live in such a grand apartment as a single woman when I was offered a seat, so I sat down.

It seemed that Signorina Piaggi was yet another of those in this small town of Sassari with close personal ties to the Testoni family. They were not particularly intimate, but they did have a warm relationship. I felt acutely how in this small country town, families and houses had certain bonds connecting them to each other.

"I wasn't there on the day of the miracle," Signorina Piaggi announced.

"Nonetheless, when Angelina wasn't feeling so well, I would occasionally drop in to wash the dishes or do her laundry for her. You see, she really was in terrible shape. Angelina told me she thought she might die, and I thought she just might be right. None of the medications they tried had any effect.

"So, when I dropped in on her one day, I couldn't believe my eyes! There I saw Angelina, who all along had been on death's doorstep, just perky and fine."

Her simple and direct way of speaking hit me with a greater sense of reality than the medical reports.

"What is your everyday life like?"

I asked this, because I had become more interested in this strong old woman's way of living than in talk about Signorina Testoni's miracle.

"During the day, I do cleaning and other stuff around the house, and in the evening I have people come to chat with me. So, I entertain guests then."

"Have you lived your whole life here, alone?"

"Oh yes. But this is not my house. This is where I work. You see, I'm the caretaker of this place."

When my interpreter Mr. S had conveyed all this to me, I began to see that the owners had given this apartment, as a retirement home, to their loyal housekeeper after she had worked many years in their home. "Would you like to see my room?" "Oh yes. Please show us."

I jumped to my feet, filled with curiosity.

The room all the way at the back was her private room. Compared to the master bedroom, it was certainly small and intimate, but as the caretaker's room, it was quite impressive. It was decorated with framed pictures of her nephews' babies.

"Which church do you attend?" I asked her rather casually. I think Mr. S rendered my question accurately. But the reply came back to me a little bit out of focus, in an interesting way. "I used to go every day, you know. But these days, well, my legs aren't so good anymore, so I can't get there more than two or three times a week."

Signorina Testoni had been our guide to her, but for the moment she was out of sight, perhaps still back in the entry hall parlor. So I took the opportunity to engage in a bit of "behind her back" gossip.

"Why has Signorina Testoni not gotten married? Do you know, Signorina Piaggi?"

As soon as Mr. S put the question to her in Italian, this stately old grandmother's face broke out in a cheerful smile. Mr. S listened with a troubled look to Signorina Piaggi's reply. And then he told me, "She says that while she's been a long and intimate friend of Signorina Testoni, she doesn't really know much about her innermost thoughts."

"Well, that's probably just about right." I felt I had probed a bit too far.

About ten minutes later, we left the Piaggi house. "Now, where were we going next?" I asked Mr. S. We had already become completely used to walking all around the streets of this little town of Sassari, almost like we were debt collectors.

"At four o'clock, we are supposed to meet someone called Maria Manca."

"Where?"

"Via Turritana."

I no longer felt the need to ask anything more like "is it close?" Everything in this town is close, you can walk anywhere you need to go. We decided, before returning to our hotel, to go to a small shop in the back streets that specialized in "stand and eat" seafood. There were two or three men with tattooed arms like seamen. The food was in deep bowls and large plates under a glass case. It was that pickled dish of fried fish and potato salad mixed together that they call "frutta del mare." They take seafood like squid and shellfish and pour vinegar and olive oil over it and garnish it with something like chives.

The proprietor gave us a plate and told us to take whatever we wanted. Thinking it was a rather strange way to serve food, I filled my plate a bit on the greedy side, whereupon the proprietor took my plate and roughly plopped it on a scale. That's when I realized that everything was the same price. I don't recall exactly how much

I paid, but in Japanese terms it was about as cheap as two hundred yen. I bought a bottle of orange juice, found an empty seat at the counter, and started eating.

To say it was as delicious as "the fruit of the sea" doesn't do it justice. It was the most delicious thing I'd eaten since coming to Italy. It was like tasting the sun and the sea embracing in a field of olive trees.

Section Two

Via Turritana.

Of all the streets in Sassari, this one stands out as a street with character. First, it is quite narrow. When even the small Italian cars pass through it, pedestrians stop and pay attention to the danger. That's the kind of place it is.

And it certainly is not a straight road. It twisted and turned so much that there was no view of the sky, and along that winding road were little shops that didn't seem to have much hope of attracting customers. A sewing machine agency, a barbershop, a grocer's shop . . . A heavy air of stagnation hung over all of them.

It seemed that the upper floors were used for residences. Of course, if you looked up, there were many windows tightly shut that looked just like wooden doors with peeling paint. If I were in Japan, I'd think they were warehouses. And children were racing up and down that narrow alley on roller skates.

The door we were looking for, Number 56, was closed and my interpreter Mr. S muttered to himself, "That's strange." For we had just confirmed that this colleague of Signorina Testoni named Maria Manca lived at Number 56.

Suddenly, I noticed right in front of us a fence about chest high around what looked like it could only be the entrance to a shed, and approaching it we spied a woman with a drawn face and poor coloring standing there, watching the passersby. Although she didn't look all that old, with her hair tied up in a loose bun and her disheveled clothing with missing hooks, she somehow struck me as an old hag. For a second I thought I had seen that face somewhere before, but I was mistaken. It was no doubt the face of a minor character in one of those Sophia Loren films I love so much that are set in the ghetto. Of course, in the movies, the ghettos reveal clearly how even in the midst of deprivation there is a poverty that is rich with the vitality of life. There will be some ghastly washing machine jutting out from a window, and both men and women will be yelling at each other. But this hag-in-the-making thirty-year-old woman didn't make a sound. The only thing that came out of her was, with a sad shake of her head in response to Mr. S's question, "where is Signorina Manca?" a mumbled, "haven't seen her around here for a long time, so maybe she's dead." Mr. S was taken aback, and when he persisted with his questioning another fat woman appeared and told us "Signorina Manca is on the second floor of those stairs next to that closed door over there."

I have no idea how or why, but those stairs seemed to have been built for the sole purpose of not being seen by anyone. Be that as it may, what was even stranger was that this thirty-year-old hag not only wouldn't tell us a thing about the Manca house that was right before her very eyes but that, far from being ashamed to give us false information, she was as untroubled by lying as her bun of hair was by the wind. With her elbows on the windowsill or perhaps this fence, watching people pass her by day after day until her elbows themselves wore thin, she struck me as a stereotype of the Latin nations. I once wrote that they seemed to drink deeply of life and be masters at firmly keeping watch over life, but I'm afraid I may have overrated them. This "lazy bum" (I have no right to call anyone such names. Actually, I too am a big fan of idly watching passersby, resting my chin in my hands so long that my elbows are worn down) is just spurred on by a petty sense of curiosity and won't see anything worth seeing.

But never mind all that, this Signorina Manca must be a pretty quiet person if she has people thinking she's moved away, even while she's been there all along.

The paint on the walls of the stairwell was peeling but you could still see it was a horrible bright blue that was anything but homey. We rang the doorbell and went in and there to our surprise was an old lady sitting in a small, warm sunroom. It seemed her legs were bad and she couldn't get up to greet us. There was a cane lying next to her.

Out from the back came Maria Manca. It seems the old woman with the bad legs was her older sister. Right behind the sunroom was her private room and that's where we were taken. A bed with a slightly dirty flower-patterned bedcover and a sewing machine that also served as a table. A large, scuffed-up wardrobe.

Just as we were about to sit down on the sofa, Mr. S and I hesitated. The middle of the sofa was occupied by a large doll. We hesitated because this doll was sitting on the sofa wearing a pure white outfit that was beautifully knit by hand, just like what a spoiled young human girl would wear, and we weren't sure we should "remove" "her" from the sofa.

Signorina Maria Manca noticed our plight and saying something like "oh, my, my," picked up the doll and hugged it, thereby clearing a seat for us.

Maria was born in 1907 so she was already over sixty years old. She had the kind of flamboyant looks and square jaw and shoulders that made one think in her younger days she was quite the strong, competitive young girl. Maria was, like Signorina Testoni, a seamstress. And she really looked the part. She was wearing a dress that she had probably made from left-over cuts of cloth from the same material and the same pattern but with different colors.

"Angelina and I lived in the same building ever since we were little."

"The night before she recovered, I went to see her around eight o'clock. And her older sister Elena asked me if I could stay with

Angelina for a while. She said their older brother Salvatore lives over on Via Lamberto and she was going over there to get him. I'm pretty sure Elena also thought Angelina would die any minute."

"While I was with Angelina, she suddenly became very nauseous. I remember rushing to get her a washbasin."

"After a while, Elena came back with Salvatore. So, at about eight-thirty I finally left the Testoni house. I really wanted to stay longer. But I had an order that had to be finished the next day. It was tough. You see, nobody expected Angelina to make it through another day."

"Well, when I went to check in on her the next morning, I was shocked. They said she was feeling perfectly fine! Of course, she was still asleep. She was skinny as a kid, looked just like a *candelina* (a little candle). Her elder sister could easily pick her up and carry her."

Then, suddenly, she turned the tables on me and started asking me the questions. What kind of books do you write? How old are you? Do you have any children?

In all the interviews I had done, she was the first person to show such an open interest in me. It put me at ease, and even Mr. S found it interesting as I answered her questions. Then I decided to return the favor with a few of my own.

"You never married, is that right? Even though you were probably quite an attractive, popular girl when you were young. Why didn't you?"

"Well, I did have a lot of boys after me. There was one in particular. But I never said anything to encourage him. So, after a while, he went away and got engaged to someone else."

"Wasn't that all for the better?"

"But back then, he said something about how I probably liked him. So, regrettably, I made a face as though it weren't true. And then, it was over."

I found it all heartwarming. Girls who are set on winning, no matter their nationality, all make the same faces.

"He got married and had two children. After quite a few years had passed, I ran into him by chance."

"Where?"

Mr. S asked. Maria told him, but I don't remember the names of places well. At any rate, it seems the two had a dramatic re-encounter somewhere outside Sassari.

"And then, he lost his wife to illness."

"Well, then, wasn't it the perfect chance to rekindle the romance?"

Maria Manca began to pout.

"Well, you see, by then it was too late, the feeling was gone." Had her man become a rooster without feathers?

"Do you still take in work?"

"My last job was in 1969. Now, I sit around doing nothing. What else can I do? The year after retiring I had surgery on my legs."

"Was your work profitable? How much did you make a month?"

"Around 1966–67, I pulled in as much as 15,000 lira a month. That's with three or four outfits. I did even better when I was young. A cloak would bring me 7,000 lira, but I couldn't expect to just make cloaks. I'd like to show you . . ."

With this, she disappeared into the back and returned, carrying a little doll, about ten centimeters tall. It was a French cancan doll, dressed from head to foot in pink. But it was much more refined than the cancan dancers that work the stages because its clothes—from gloves to underwear to stockings—were all knit from a high-quality, fine woolen thread.

"Isn't she cute? She now has a full ensemble of outfits to wear!"

Like a little girl, Maria kissed this little doll right on the lips.

"She still doesn't have any ornament for her hair."

"Then, did you also make the outfit for that large doll we saw when we came in?"

"Of course. That little one is my friend."

The cancan girl was a cheap little plastic doll. It seemed to me the kind of thing that one could pick up in Japan for one or two hundred yen. But when you put this most attractive kind of outfit on her, she seemed like a real queen. When I picked it up for a closer look, I almost let out a cry. The doll had a manicure! But it was a poor job, with the paint plastered all over her fingers.

"How nice to live with your big sister!" I said to the doll, while holding it close in my hands.

"Are you kidding? She doesn't understand anything at all about me!"

It seemed to me that the two were having their own Cold War.

"Will you be going to Rome for Fr. Kolbe's beatification?" I asked, trying to get the conversation back on track. Signorina Maria Manca shook her head. She then turned toward Mr. S with an unpleasant, stern expression on her face.

"She says that to go to Rome—that is, to join a pilgrimage group—she'd need about 50,000 lira. She says she'd go if she had an extra 30,000 lira on hand right now. She wants to know whether Miss Sono, if she truly is such a wealthy writer, if she would give me the money."

Mr S told me what she had asked with a pained expression. I couldn't tell if she was joking or not, but she didn't seem to be particularly brazen-faced about it.

"Well, it would have been better had she already signed on, provisionally, with a pilgrimage group to Rome," I said.

"I don't think she's going to do that. It seems what she really wants right now is a television set. Even a used television here is more expensive than a new set is in Japan."

Mr. S explained Maria's reply to me. Then it struck me—I hadn't seen a television since I arrived in this country—not in a hotel, not anywhere.

"I have one final question. Why didn't Signorina Testoni ever get married?"

When Signorina Manca heard Mr. S's interpretation of my question, she fixed a steady gaze on me, but I didn't sense a whit of enmity in her look.

"That girl, well, when she was young, she made a secret vow to

171

God that she would remain single her whole life, as an offering of her virginity to him."

I nodded and followed up with another question.

"But nobody is supposed to know about a secret vow to God. So, there must have been men who came forward with marriage proposals to Signorina Testoni . . ."

"There may have been at first. But eventually, they seemed to get the message. And then, guys interested in breaking that vow disappeared."

I strongly felt the difference between Italy and Japan.

It seemed to me that, well, these Italian men, who are reputed to make advances at any woman they see, at least did have a fear of God.

In ten minutes, I had taken my leave of Maria's older sister with the bad legs and was out the door. The woman from the house across the way was still leaning on the fence, people-watching. And the Via Turritana continued to wind along rather unsteadily in the sunlight, with a softness, a languor, and a lot of garbage, as if echoing the footsteps of those walking by, sunk deep into the pavement and their own gloomy lives.

Section Three

Mr. S had made an appointment over the phone for me with Dr. Salvatore Palmas, Chief of the Department of Internal Medicine of the Civil Hospital. Dr. Palmas was our last interview before returning to Rome. I will probably never forget this island of Sardinia as long as I live. But as the temperature in the shade was getting cooler every day, I had a bit of an inexplicable feeling that I was being chased off the island.

The office of the Chief of Internal Medicine was a room that did not allow in any light from outside. Dr. Palmas was a burly, fifty-year old doctor. He wore a white coat, and on the wall behind his head was a crucifix. The top of his desk wasn't what you could call a disaster, but the way it was covered with medicine bottles was just what you'd expect of a doctor anywhere. What struck me, however, was that when his assistant came in with some documents, I felt the solid marble floor in this room shake. Well, so even stone buildings can shake a bit, I thought, allowing myself to be distracted by such trivial things.

"Tell me the truth," I asked the doctor, "do you think the case of Signorina Testoni is a miracle?"

"I really can't say one way or the other, but I certainly can't rule out a miracle," the doctor answered.

My interpreter Mr. S seemed to have great difficulty when medical jargon came up. But we did our best to keep the conversation going and somehow surmount that difficulty.

At present, Dr. Palmas seemed to think that Signorina Testoni's disease was Crohn's Disease. Crohn's Disease is a type of ileitis. Between 1946 and 1949, Crohn's Disease was not clearly accepted in the medical profession. Between 1947 and 1960, the disease started to appear here and there in medical documents around the world. And Signorina Testoni's miraculous recovery from that disease happened on July 24, 1949.

As I noted above, Dr. Palmas was not Signorina Testoni's primary physician at the time. He merely gave Signorina Testoni a medical examination in 1965 as part of his participation in the Church's investigation.

The doctor said that had it been diagnosed as Crohn's Disease she might have been cured by surgically removing the affected part of the small intestine. But the technology of the day made such a surgery difficult. And there were very few cases where the patient recovered from the disease without that kind of treatment. Yet, he concluded that one cannot rule out the possibility that the doctors who were treating her then had made a mistaken diagnosis.

I asked Dr. Palmas, "In Italy, do many people, even today, believe in miracles?"

"I think the majority probably do not believe in them. Even I am not willing to declare this a miracle. But, considering the times, it is true that it was very hard to recover from that disease back in those days. In that sense, it is surely correct to say that something happened then that was extremely unlikely. And also, the part that healed normally should have atrophied, but in Signorina Testoni's case, it didn't. Certainly that at least was strange."

On our way out, while Dr. Palmas was seeing us to the front door, he pointed to a dark part of the hallway and said, "On the other side of that wall is the chapel." Just as was the case with the hospital in Alghero where Sister Serra worked, a hospital must always have a place of prayer.

Returning to the hotel, I began to pack my things.

Since I didn't bring anything from Japan that I could offer as a souvenir, I went out to buy chocolates for the Testoni sisters.

Not once did I get any sense from those two old sisters of anything like propaganda. The only feeling I got from them was a sense of being given a long life, and to live that life modestly by working hard at their trade, as befits a citizen.

I chose some chocolates that came in a beautiful ceramic container. That way, even after the sisters had eaten the chocolates they'd still have the container, which they might put up on their dining room shelves and tell their guests about the visitor from Japan who had come to see them.

Carrying the package, I made my way to the Testoni sisters' shop. It was crowded with customers, so I decided to wait until two or three had made their purchases, just like the first time I came here.

And, when we tried to take our leave, the entire Testoni family came out from behind the counter. We would be able to meet again soon. The Testoni sisters would surely be coming to Saint Peter's in the Vatican for the October 17 beatification, so we would see each other again there. The Testoni sisters took the chocolates with joy and in return told me to take some stockings on my way out. I bent over and hugged Angelina and said goodbye. Such wonderful people!

When I got back to my room, it was time to say goodbye to that chubby lady proprietor.

"Are you going so soon?" she said, as she came to the top of the stairs with her skinny husband to see us off. With her hands on her hips and belly that looked like a small mountain, she told me, "Next time, come with your husband!" I have a special memory of this woman. One night at dinner she asked me, "Do you like your spaghetti with tomato sauce or just with butter?" and—even though I really don't understand Italian, I replied, "just with butter." My interpreter Mr. S marveled that I understood her question. I do have a knack for showing off a certain linguistic genius when it comes to my food.

I wasn't able to enjoy a real bath there, but that was only a minor flaw in a gem; it really was a quiet, welcoming hotel.

I doubt if I'll ever be able to return to Sardinia. The Via Manno, the Via Turritana, the piazza. The hot sun and the cool shade under the trees. The ordinary lives of the people here, with their extraordinary goodwill. Can we really say that no matter where you go people are all the same? The autumn sea, and the white houses. These people who have no connection to Father Kolbe revere his name, his life, and his death. How can I explain that?

I almost forgot. I have a confession to make. The truth is, I don't really believe there is an eternal life. I also don't think it is possible to meet one's death filled with the joy of gaining eternal life.

Mostly I think that when you die everything disappears. If that is true, then what about God? I do think that I have seen God in this world. I'm not saying I had a special experience. Nor am I saying my faith is all that deep. The difficulties of this horrific world, the particular charms of mankind, the mystery that exists deep within a single person's life that has both goodwill and malice—in such as this, I have experienced a rich life that I cannot explain without God!

If we return to nothing when we die, then what about eternal life?! Some will surely ask this. But in a different way, I do believe in eternal life. Like that thread that Signorina Testoni was able to pull from Father Kolbe.

Father Kolbe did not have his own children. So, he wasn't able to pass on his life biologically to others. But he kept on drawing the hearts and minds of many young friars. Even in the concentration camp, when he had been deprived of every outward manifestation of respect as a human being and his actual life was dwindling away to the point of extinction, this priest was still able to make a deep impression even on his enemies.

Perhaps that is what eternal life is—passing on to someone else the essential brilliance of a certain spirit. Even if we don't have the sense of a heavily supernatural eternal life, such as when we speak of participating in the life of Christ, it is certainly possible in this way to transmit a certain eternal life. It was in this way that Father Kolbe, even after his death, was able to continue to convey to us this life/love. Through his intercession on behalf of this truly quiet, composed, gentle woman who lives on the island of Sardinia, Father Kolbe once again raises the question for the whole world to consider: what is Man?

Similarly, Angelina Testoni was a woman who tried to live a simple and modest life, just like one who enters a monastery. Note that I never once heard her say that it was a miracle! All she would say is that "all I know is that I prayed for the intercession of Father Kolbe, and then I suddenly got better." My plane left Sardinia bathed in the light from the afternoon's setting sun. I was told that the Testoni's pilgrimage group would cross this ocean by boat, alighting at Naples and, after sightseeing on the Isle of Capri and a pilgrimage to Assisi, enter Rome in time for the day of the Beatification ceremony.

It was night by the time I got back to Rome. It was good to be back in the din and bustle of that city.

I thought, if there were time, I'd like to go see that military doctor in Perugia who was Signorina Testoni's primary care physician, but Father Ricciardi who was essential for making the connection appeared to be among those who were extremely busy with preparations for the Beatification ceremony, and in the end I couldn't get hold of him.

In the meantime, my ticket for the day of the ceremonies had arrived at my hotel. I recalled Father Ricciardi telling me, "if you come in kimono, we'll see to it that you receive the Holy Eucharist from the Pope himself," so I slipped my kimono out from the bottom of my suitcase and sent it out to be ironed. The ticket I was given seemed to be for a special seating area for those who would receive the Holy Eucharist from the Pope's own hands.

From time to time, Auschwitz would still haunt me. Each time, I would suffer a bit of insomnia. On those days, there was nothing I could do but have a small bottle of wine sent up to my room late at night. When I go out drinking in public, I never get really drunk because even a little alcohol makes my face flush red.

When I sat there imagining how *in reality* Father Kolbe had to face his end struggling with thirst and not a drop to drink, I couldn't bear it. I was able to lighten my horrors by getting stinking drunk and thus avoid having to face the reality, and then I could finally find my sleep like a foolish dog.

Chapter 12

The Sound of Downhill Footsteps

Section One

On October 17, 1971, at a little past nine o'clock in the morning, I went over to St. Peter's.

The beatification ceremony wasn't until nine-thirty, but I thought I should leave a bit early to get my seat, since the previous day Rome had been overflowing with clerics and others involved in the ceremony who had come from Poland and all over. There was already a tremendous crowd. Some estimated that one hundred thousand people had come. I had never before seen so many different races gathered together in one piazza. There were a lot of lay pilgrims, but if I may put it in a rather disrespectful way, it really seemed like a convention of clerics. I had never realized before how priests—they were all equally priests—could have such a range of different styles about them. There was one priest who looked just like Don Camillo leaping out of the pages of the novel.[1] You could find many who affected an elite, English aristocratic style about themselves; but there were also a good many hippie padres wearing civilian clothes. If there were priests with brimmed hats and the hems of their soutanes flowing in the wind, there were also army chaplains in uniform. It really was like a convention of priests. I found it all too fascinating and, holding my breath, spent a few minutes just taking in the spectacle.

But then, already feeling the crowd that had filled the piazza

---

1. Don Camillo Tarocci is the main character in Giovannino Guareschi's fictional stories (based on the real life Father Don Camillo Valota).

pressing in all around me, I hurried on to St. Peter's. By that time, there was only one passageway roped off, and you couldn't see a thing beyond the throngs of people that lined it. There were gentlemen in tails with medals completely covering their jackets who guided us to our seats. These were not ordinary guides. My interpreter Mr. S told me that only those men from long-distinguished families were allowed to perform this service in these seats of honor.

I was led all the way up to a seat near the altar, and there I spotted the Testoni sisters and Mrs. Gajowniczek. I greeted the Testoni sisters, and then handed Mrs. Gajowniczek a photograph I had brought for her. It was one of the many I had taken of Mr. and Mrs. Gajowniczek when I met them in Poland.

Several rows up from the Testoni sisters I saw Brother Zeno. Somebody told me that immediately in front of me was the Polish Ambassador to the Vatican[2] and his wife. The space immediately behind me was standing room only. When Mr. S, the interpreter, asked a young lady standing in the first row of those behind us how long she'd been there he was told since seven o'clock in the morning.

From my seat I could see over on my left those broadcasting the event live on television, and the papal altar with Bernini's famous baldacchino, which I had secretly named "the twisted poles," and to its left, the statue of St. Veronica. Alongside the papal altar were seats for the archbishops and the red-capped cardinals, but from where I was sitting, I could only make out a section of it. Then I was struck by the great disconnect I found between the life of Father Kolbe, which I had discovered on my trip to a faraway land, and the overbearing pomp and circumstance that here and now was sweeping us all up into it.

---

2. The identity of this "Polish ambassador" is unclear. The ambassador from the Polish government in exile (in London), Kazimierz Papée had been dismissed from his post by Pope John XXIII but still lived in Rome until his death in 1979, but his wife Leonia had died in 1961, ten years before the beatification. The People's Republic of Poland did not have a Concordat with the Holy See, but on 25 January 1971, Prime Minister Piotr Jaroszewicz had indicated a desire to normalize relations with the Holy See.

By and large, people want to convert historical truth into something useful. I wrote earlier that insofar as Father Kolbe's saving of Mr. Gajowniczek could not bring happiness to that one house, his actions were really ineffective. When considered in an extremely superficial way, that is true. But that night, a passage from [Viktor] Frankl's *The Doctor and the Soul* came back to me. It is where a prisoner from the concentration camp reflects:

All of us prisoners knew quite clearly that there would be no happiness on this earth that we could expect in the future to compensate for what we had experienced while locked up in here. So, if we had a mind to settle accounts with happiness, we only had one method left, which was to 'run for the barbed wire' (which carried a high voltage charge), that is, all we could do was commit suicide. The reason we didn't do that is that in some way, shape or form, we felt a deep sense of duty. For example, I felt a duty to my mother to preserve my life. We really loved each other. That's why my life had meaning, no matter what else happened. But I faced the danger of death every day, every hour. So, my death and the sufferings I endured had to have some kind of meaning.

That's when I decided to make a deal with Heaven. If it was my fate to die, then my death would be the price for my mother to have a long life. And if I had to endure suffering to the day I died, then my mother would be able to die without suffering. Only from this standpoint of sacrifice was I able to endure this life filled with unremitting suffering. I was only able to live once my life had meaning. So, I concluded that if suffering and death have meaning, then I could suffer my sufferings and die my death."[3]

3. Passage quoted from Viktor Frankl, *Ai to shi* (Aerztliche Seelsorge), the Japanese translation by Shimoyama Tokuji.

I can only think of Father Kolbe's death as an act that saved Mr. Gajowniczek. That's exactly why I feel such emptiness at the fact that he couldn't make it possible for the Gajowniczek sons to be reunited with their father.

But, as Frankl discussed through the experience of this prisoner, there is a deeper, hidden meaning that is more important. This is the internal world that is completely unknown to the "next guy" as they lay sleeping in their bunks, their lice-infested scarecrow bodies squished together like canned sardines. There is a solemn "internal world" in the mere number of prisoners at Auschwitz. One person will shed light on this internal world and establish its place in eternity, thereby finding life in the midst of death and nothingness. Another person, lacking that strength, will simply go to his death haunted by fear. Frankl writes about how there are people who never give up being human, no matter what circumstances they find themselves in. Father Kolbe was one of them. I shuddered when I thought that if I were given such an opportunity, I probably would not follow his example but die a coward's death. Although that didn't come as any particular revelation, even still it made me feel a bit melancholy.

I'm inclined to think that Man really can't suffer from social, abstract propositions. At least with my limited powers of imagination, I can't really understand the essence of a problem, any problem, until I've translated it into something that has a direct bearing on me. The only ones who understood the true meaning of what Father Kolbe did were Father Kolbe himself and God. It is likely that all these people gathered here today, like me, do not understand the meaning of his life. It just scares me to death to say that Father Kolbe "hoped where there was no hope." But, I must say that, when I think about it, I don't think I have any experience of a world "without hope." That fact also makes me feel depressed. For better or worse, I have lived a life of no particular commitment. Even if I think I have suffered about as much as most people, it hardly measures up to the extreme suffering involved in "to die my death." What an unremarkable life it's been!

I can hear the joyful cries of all the people. The papal retinue is approaching. Those people behind me who've been holding out since seven o'clock this morning are now screaming like mad. The clamor of thousands reaches to high heaven. And even though we were told photographs were forbidden, the flash of cameras pop all over the place.

This is the first time I've ever seen Paul VI this close up. This thin Pope with sunken cheeks was, nonetheless, a man who, according to Jean Guitton's acclaimed *Dialogue with Pope Paul VI* (in Yoshio Kobayashi's translation) had a young, poetic spirit:

> Guitton: "When I spoke earlier with you about French poets you said that from a Christian, no from a Catholic perspective, it was, perhaps, Verlaine who was the best of all French poets in terms of a sense of rhythm, harmony of verse and poetic composition and particularly for an inimitable, deep integrity as the most complete poet."

> The Holy Father: "That's right. It is because it is Verlaine (even to hear that name makes me, as a foreigner, feel nostalgic) brings out that which is most hidden in our souls, what we suffer most among ourselves, what is most quiet, most worrisome, and yet cheerful, that which is ineffable."

> Guitton: "What do you mean by that which is ineffable?"

> The Holy Father: "What cannot be expressed . . . simply put, that which cannot be said because it is beyond human language. In a word, the unity of worry and peace, worship and kindness, exaltation toward the divine and thirst for the Eucharistic bread and wine (what Verlaine calls the eternal Chalice). In short, the blessing of loving God with a pauper's heart."[4]

---

4. This quoted section does not appear in Anne and Christopher Fremantle's English translation, *The Pope Speaks: Dialogues of Paul VI with Jean Guitton* (New York: Meredith Press, 1967).

Coming back to my senses, I noticed they were singing a hymn in Polish. For my part, I prayed and reflected in Japanese. It was a special, quiet moment in the midst of the crowd.

Suddenly, the joyful cries of the people arose again. There, above the main altar with Bernini's Chair of St. Peter, in the golden space where one usually finds the dove that represents the Holy Spirit, they had set up a picture of Father Kolbe.

During the Mass, only two things implanted themselves deeply on my mind.

One was a gentleman—the Polish ambassador, I was told—decorated with medals and honors, receiving the Holy Eucharist with his wife.

Mr. S, my interpreter, muttered under his breath, "I thought Poland was a socialist country. Can the Ambassador be Catholic?" Before I had gone to Poland, I might have let slip a similar thought.

The other thing was the back of Mrs. Gajowniczek which was right in front of me. At first it was straight and facing front, but gradually the nape of her neck began to droop until her head was completely bowed.

Then, finally there was a slight trembling in her gray-speckled flaxen hair. The missus was crying right in the middle of Mass! How should this woman make sense of this man's fate? Mrs. Gajowniczek was the only one who could see Father Kolbe's death as truly her own death.

Then, we got around to reciting in various languages our prayer that all things would be decided by God's good will. We prayed in French, in English, in Polish, in German, in Spanish, in Portuguese and in Italian. But not in Japanese. We should understand that these languages reflected the Catholic countries that had the most influence in the Vatican, not the languages that had some special connection to Father Kolbe.

Finally, the Pope got into his palanquin and made his glorious exit. Those in the crowd who tried to follow him found their way blocked by the Swiss Guard, who crossed their lances and closed off the road.

I left with the Testoni sisters and went out into the piazza. Somehow, I just felt, "it's finished, it's finished."

Section Two

On my return to Japan, I spent a few days in India, collecting some materials for a new novel. I felt very energetic. I had to laugh when I remembered all the trivial things that happened on my trip. What do I mean by trivial? Here's an example:

While I was in Rome, they put together something like a public relations committee for foreign journalists, as part of the preparations for Father Kolbe's beatification. They decided there would be short speeches from the Polish Cardinal Wyszyński,[5] Father Stano of the Conventual Franciscans,[6] and me speaking of the time when Father Kolbe was in Japan. When giving a speech in the West, one must always, without exception, submit a written draft of what you will say in advance. So, one morning at eight o'clock, I set off for the Conventual Franciscans to submit the draft of my speech. Since I'd been staying in this same hotel for over a month, all the maids knew me by sight. My small room was directly across from the maids' station. Just as I was about to head out, at what was an unusually early hour in the morning for me, the maid who spoke a little English asked me, "where are you going?" I told her that I was going to the monastery to give them my draft, so it would be a good time to clean the room. No sooner had I spoken when from somewhere around this large, fat woman I saw the face of a somewhat older boy who was standing with her and he said something in Italian. Immediately, the maid burst out in laughter, and asked me in a teasing way,

5. Stefan Cardinal Wyszyński (1901–1981).

6. Gaetano M. Stano, OFMConv. b. 1909. Died between 2001 and 2009 in Rome.

"Do you know what he just said?" "No, I don't. What did he say?"

"He said, 'you better watch out for those friars.'" As she said this, the two of them just cackled away.

This had nothing to do with religion. It seemed to me that I had come in direct contact with what makes Italy, Italy. Maybe that's what people mean when they talk of what you can learn on the road.

Some days after I had returned to Japan, I discovered I wasn't as healthy as I had thought. I had come down with a case of cardiac neurosis. My pulse was irregular, I had shortness of breath, and to top it all, I caught a cold that turned into bronchitis.

For those who are new to cardiac neurosis, it might seem so frightening that they think they are about to die. But I was not worried, as my mother had suffered from the disease for many years. I knew I wasn't going to die from it, so I just rested whenever I felt short of breath. I thought maybe I shouldn't have drunk wine while I was in Italy, but things weren't that simple. I would become exhausted and fall asleep, whether it was day or night. But during that time, I reflected on the fact that there were in this world both "men who would, calmly and with full intent, spit in the face of God" and also men who, regardless of whether they felt like doing it or not, "would quietly, and on their own, carry out good works without fear, even if it cost them their life, all the while being trampled on by others."

When I was feeling a bit better, I would talk about these "awakened, richly human beings" with close friends of mine who like literature. I let slip that I was thinking of writing about the kind of person who coldly, calculatingly and deliberately commits evil.

"You'll never get Japanese to read that kind of thing," one of my friends said.

"Take Kawabata's novels, for example. They show the horror of an uncertain, disconnected mind. That's what makes them so Japanese. Even if someone could write into a novel one of those rich characters who are like stew on beef steak topped off with grated cheese, Japanese just aren't going to be interested in that kind of thing."

I let it go at that. Then, a few hours later, my pulse started acting irregular and I broke out in a fever.

I was sick with exhaustion and couldn't think it was anything other than being exposed to the poisonous air of Auschwitz, but after about three weeks, I got over it. Only then was I able to take a trip to Nagasaki where Father Kolbe had first become so clearly linked to Japan.

People who visit the famous Ōura Catholic Church in Nagasaki are more tempted to enter the rectory to the right of the church than the church itself. Archbishop Aijirō Yamaguchi of the Nagasaki Diocese lived with his sister in the front room on the second floor of that building. According to a short vita, Archbishop Yamaguchi was born in 1894. That means he received the gift of life in Urakami in the exact same year that Father Kolbe did.[7]

"My legs are no good, and neither is my memory," the archbishop said to me, with a sense of modesty. But in fact the archbishop's memory of those days, like when he first met Father Kolbe in the bishop's residence of Ōura Church, was quiet sharp.

Back in 1930, the young Father Yamaguchi was in residence at Ōura Church, serving as the rector of the Nagasaki Catholic Seminary, which was established in 1874. The archbishop spoke of those days with a certain reserve, saying that "I was the custodian of the students," and this led me at first to wonder whether the archbishop was a kind of dormitory superintendent or something.

According to Winowska's book, Father Kolbe and his group landed at Nagasaki on April 24 of that year.

One day, when a bearded foreign priest, another priest, and two brothers suddenly showed up at the bishop's residence here at the Ōura Church, it so happened that Father Yamaguchi had returned early to the residence as there was a funeral for a diocesan priest. Told

---

7. Archbishop Paul Aijirō Yamaguchi (1894–1976).

they had guests, Father Yamaguchi met the group of four visitors downstairs in the reception room. The four were Kolbe, Mirochna,[8] Zeno and Florian, two brothers and two priests.[9]

"So, those four were accepted as guests and temporarily lodged in a separate building up behind the bishop's residence. That building was built as a mission school but has been torn down and now there's not a trace left of it," Archbishop Yamaguchi said.

"Father Kolbe was a simple man, in the Franciscan style, and he never let on that he had tuberculosis. He went from here all over the city looking around, and it seems they had a residence ready for them in an empty house owned by the Amenomori Hospital just below the hill here."

Back in those days, Father Yamaguchi spent his days going over to teach in the Urakami Seminary in the mornings and when he returned to Ōura in the afternoon, he would check the diocesan accounts, entertain visiting priests, and the like. Father Yamaguchi's room was on the second floor of a building set quite a ways back from the current bishop's residence. The building was built halfway up the cliff, so Father Yamaguchi's room, which at that time was a corner room on the second floor, was an ideal spot to see people as they were coming down the hill. That's because, by being on the second floor, you could get a clear view of people coming down the steps on the hill.

---

8. Fr. Mieczysław Maria Mirochna (1908–1989). See below, Chapter 13.

9. Yamaguchi's "Furarion" might be a mistaken reference to Fr. Florian Koziura. By all accounts, it should refer to Hilary. The group of friars that accompanied Kolbe to Japan were Severinus (John Dagis), Hilary, Sigmund and Zeno (Sigmund and Hilary appearently were left behind in China, temporarily). It does not appear that Koziura ever went to Japan. In 1931 Koziura was superior of Niepokalanów, a position he held until Kolbe replaced him in 1936. The "Seven Samurai" of Nagasaki in 1930, as Fr. Ozaki Tōmei has tagged them, were: Kolbe, Severino, Sigmundo, Zeno, Hilario, Mirochna, and Damian. Cf. Ozaki, *Nagasaki no Korube shinpu* (Nagasaki: Seibo no Kishi Sha, 2010), pp. 59-60. Hilary ("Hilario") and Zeno landed with Kolbe in Nagasaki in 1930.

When Father Yamaguchi grew tired of study, he would wait eagerly for the sounds of footsteps passing by outside his window. At the slightest indication of someone passing by, even while sitting at his desk, his eyes would quickly look up in that direction. It was just as if he were looking for an excuse to avoid his studies.

Just then, Father Yamaguchi saw the figure of Father Kolbe coming down from his clapboard house up on top of the hill. Father Kolbe was on his way somewhere, but he certainly wasn't going outside the compound looking like that. Father Kolbe, as usual, entered the side door of the chapel and went into the sacristy to make a visit to the Eucharist.

Although Archbishop Yamaguchi did not spell it out, I felt I really could understand the scene there. He was saying, here's this foreign priest who was about the same age as me who came to Japan unable to speak the language (although Father Yamaguchi and Father Kolbe had studied in Rome for a long time and should have been able to get along fine in Italian) and set about assiduously doing his prayers and work. Perhaps Archbishop Yamaguchi in his younger days felt as if he had found another friend who was as serious and talented as he was.

"Anyway, he was someone with a great trust in Mary, the Immaculata. The old folks in Nagasaki used to greet priests with the expression, 'praise be to Christ!' but for Father Kolbe, the greeting was 'Maria!'"

When Archbishop Yamaguchi told me this story, I immediately thought that Father Kolbe's "Maria!" was something like saying "open sesame."

"As soon as he set up a printing press in the house owned by Amenomori Hospital, I was curious, so I went over there to take a look. They were living a terribly frugal life. For dinner, they had soup, but I heard it was just barley soup. They said they also had *zūshi*. This is a Nagasaki specialty of rice mixed with soup, but I think what they were eating was probably some kind of porridge made by re-heating cold rice. I can't imagine they could buy anything like meat. If they ever had meat, I suspect it came from a local ham

189

dealer named Uraoka who decided on his own to look after them. We too did what we could for them financially."

Winowska writes that, on May 24 of that year, Father Kolbe sent a telegram to Niepokalanów, the headquarters of the Knights of the Immaculata: "Today we are sending out our first issue. Have a printing establishment. Praise be to the Immaculate! Maximilian."[10] Putting it all together, we can see that it was around this time when Archbishop Yamaguchi visited the new printing press and saw the kind of poverty in which Father Kolbe and his group lived.

Archibishop Yamaguchi's room looked out over the sea and the town of Nagasaki. With the winter sunlight pouring into the room, I felt like I could see right then the figure of Father Kolbe coming down the steps from the top of the hill. Leaving through the gate, and slipping past the souvenir shops out front, I went down a fifty- or sixty-meter-long slope and found a large, irregular wooden building where the Amenomori Hospital used to have that house. Someone told me that now it was a dye-works or something.

Dr. Fukahori Yasurō of the Fukahori Pediatric Clinic in the Fukukawa-machi district of the city gave me his recollections of those times:

> I left Nagasaki Medical College in 1930 and was teaching in the pediatrics clinic.
>
> Back then, Bishop Hayasaka of Nagasaki had fallen ill and he was surrounded by professors in the department of internal medicine where he was being treated. I too joined them. The professors made their diagnosis. Afterward, I went every day to give him an injection. So it was from Bishop Hayasaka himself that I heard all about Father Kolbe.

---

10. This translation of Father Kolbe's telegram is taken from Therese Plumereau's translation of Maria Winowska, *Our Lady's Fool*, p. 115.

Father was really enduring a terrible life of poverty. When my father heard that, he offered me, saying, "I've got a son, so feel free to use him whenever and however you please."

That's all it took, and I was summoned a lot. Father Kolbe often had a fever. He would have the chills, shivers, and a high temperature. First, I thought he had malaria. But then I thought there was something wrong with his chest. So, I had X-rays taken and found chronic pulmonary tuberculosis, with both lungs filled with shadows. It also appeared there were cavities. Usually, this meant admission to a sanatorium and bed rest, but this patient insisted on doing everything his way. This is what you get with bad food, poor nutrition, hard work, walking about every day distributing magazines. Didn't he insist on doing the printing himself, even though he barely understood Japanese? When I told him, "you can't keep this up," he said, "I am fully aware that I am sick."

Nonetheless, I told him that he cannot work with his body in this shape. But, his fever went away in one day and he went right back to work. A few days later, I went to check up on him, and he wasn't there. This kind of thing repeated itself about every two or three months. Looking back now, it's a wonder that more than ten years later he hadn't died from tuberculosis. I think the bacilli were most likely still active. But we didn't take a culture, you know.

In any event, he was one tough guy. When I said to him, "You keep this up, and you won't live much longer," he replied, "I'm going to die soon enough, so I have to get some work done while I can."

But the poverty was horrible. He slept on a bed he made himself from boards. And for bedding, all he had was one blanket on top and one underneath. I went to examine him, you see. And there he was, sleeping in the overcoat that he wore when going outside. Well, I thought, he's got the chills, so you can imagine how cold he must feel. That time, we got him through the danger by gathering blankets from the other friars.

The food was also horrible. There was some fried rice in an aluminum container set out there, and they had used suet, so you can imagine how it stunk. The soup was just vegetable soup. There was a bit of oil in it, but nothing like a soup base to flavor it, just a greasy mess.

Even the journal was regarded with skepticism by none less than Bishop Hayasaka who said, "I wonder if anyone would ever read such a journal even if they could get it published."

I remember that I defended it, blurting out, "But everyone's gone nuts over it!"

But to myself I thought that with the crappy paper they're using, no one will read it except the true believers.

But I really have to hand it to him. Father Kolbe was a genius, but not the kind who acts cold and distant. Most impressive was his very strong self-control.

After listening to Dr. Fukahori's story, I asked him whether his medical exams were all done for free. "I never thought of taking any money," he told me. "Or you might say, in this case, I couldn't have."

Friar Cassiano Tetich[11] has an impressive physique, and even though he was seventy years old, he moved so well you forgot how old he was. I thought it was because the only job he had held since 1932 was as a cook. It seems this friar was now working in the "Misakae no En" in Konagai-chō that the Conventual Franciscans run.

He came to Japan in 1932 and shared in all the joys and sorrows of Father Kolbe until 1936 when Father Kolbe returned to Poland. Even now, Friar Cassiano's Japanese is not very good. He says it is because he's been in the kitchen the whole time and didn't have the free time to study the language. According to this friar, life in the Order of the Knights of the Immaculata was as follows:

---

11. Cassiano M. Tetich (1902-1988).

Morning: coffee and rolls. Except the coffee was made from barley and they put sugar and milk in it.

Noon: soup (made from potatoes and whole wheat) and a bit of cooked rice to go with it. Sometimes Friar Cassiano would go out and buy some fish for them. Occasionally they would have milk and cheese but never any butter.

Night: just rice and soup.

Back then, there were fifteen Poles in their community. They rose at five in the morning and, after thirty minutes of silent meditation, there was Mass. Then, they would recite the Divine Office and have breakfast. During the day they worked, and at night there was another thirty minutes of silent meditation. At that time, there would be readings from works such as the life of Saint Francis.

Brother Zeno, famous later for his role in Ants' Town,[12] was with them. According to Friar Cassiano, Brother Zeno was known as someone who could take care of anything. Brother Zeno would fix dinner and he also lent a hand with the laundry. Friar Cassiano said that in particular "at night we often would forget about the laundry."

"Why is that?" I asked, thinking it strange. "At night, it was dark so we couldn't tell whether it was clean or not," he replied with a straight face.[13] But then if you asked others, they would say that the soup Brother Zeno made was so horrible that no matter how much he pushed it, no one wanted another cup of it.

It was Father Kolbe's order that in the evening, after nine o'clock, they were to use their minds for their souls, and not for study. Friar Cassiano and his fellow friars recited the rosary while doing their work. The only chance they had to learn Japanese vocabulary was

---

12. "Ants' Town" (*ari no machi*) refers to a ghetto in Tokyo made famous for the social work of Catholic convert Kitahara Satoko (known as "Maria of Ants' Town) whom Brother Zeno enlisted in helping out the poor there in the early postwar period.

13. There is a pun here that doesn't translate well. Cassiano's first comment implies that the laundry "fell" from their consciousness (meaning, they would forget to do it); his reply says the laundry appeared to have fallen off the line outside (because it was dark) so they were not reminded to bring it in. I've taken some liberty with the translation to effect an analogous pun.

during meal times. Father Kolbe himself would never take a break until all the other friars had finished their work.

Back when he was in Poland, Friar Cassiano had sought his local pastor's permission to join the Order after having seen the magazine of the Knights of the Immaculata. The pastor wrote a letter to Father Kolbe and got a reply three days later. In the letter, he had written the time he should arrive at Niepokalanów, and to bring his own bedding if he had some, and if not, just come as he is. Right around that time, Friar Cassiano had lost two older sisters and a younger brother in the space of one year. Only his mother was left at home; his younger sister had gone off to work in the city. When Friar Cassiano said he wanted to enter the monastery, his mother's friends tried to put a stop to it.

"What will you do if you send your child off to such a place and he dies?"

This mother, who had just lost three children, was not in the least bit hesitant to now let her only remaining son go. She said something to Friar Cassiano to the effect that if God was going to take all my children, then I want to go with you to this monastery. Friar Cassiano was the thirty-fourth friar to enter Niepokalanów.

Friar Cassiano was returning to Misakae no En, so I gave him a ride partway back in my car. It was really pouring down rain. I really should have given him a ride all the way back to Misakae no En, but I was short on time then and had to drop him off in a town on the way. I worried he wouldn't be able to hail a cab. I felt very uncomfortable at the thought that I had deserted a friar in the pouring rain.

I have often seen his kind of "silent type" in the monasteries. At the school where I had been, there were sisters who had come before the war from the island of Malta and who were still working there. Coincidentally, they too were cooks. Since they too had never set foot outside the confines of the convent, they didn't know any Japanese except for a few words. These ladies spent decades just peeling potatoes and washing dishes, knowing nothing of Mt. Fuji, Kyoto or Nijūbashi.

When I thought about what their lives were like, I was unable to maintain my composure. Was everything that I had been looking for all my life actually so terribly shallow?

Through the rear window of the car, I saw Friar Cassiano standing in the rain. I was struck deep in my heart by the thought that Father Kolbe's great works were made possible in part by the likes of this big, quiet Polish man.

Chapter 13

Living Stars and Dead Stars

Section One

When I met Father Mieczysław Mirochna in Nagasaki, I felt I had finally arrived at the most difficult thing to understand about Father Kolbe. Father Mirochna came to Japan in 1930 and lived with Father Kolbe in Nagasaki until 1936. He is currently the priest in charge of the institute in Koganai town of Nagasaki prefecture that is dedicated to helping children with serious mental and physical handicaps called Misakae no En.

When Father Mirochna arrived in Japan, Father Kolbe was already starting his printing work in the house he had rented from Amenomori Hospital (there are certain discrepancies in Archbishop Yamaguchi's memory concerning Father Mirochna, but I'm going to just leave things as I heard them). The everyday life of Father Kolbe that Father Mirochna had joined was just as Friar Cassiano and Dr. Fukahori Yasurō had described it. But now I got a renewed appreciation for Father Kolbe's sharp eye as a cultural anthropologist. This was revealed by one seemingly insignificant fact. Before arriving in Japan, Father Mirochna had been told to be pretty much "ready for the worst." That is, the director of Niepokalanów had warned him that the weather, climate, customs, just about everything, was radically different from what he was used to. Because of that, when Father arrived in Japan, he was saved from feeling any great sense of disappointment.

Father Mirochna said, "All your own personal likes, hopes, and plans are gone and you must just be as the Immaculata wants you to be. Your own will and plan is to do whatever it takes to subordinate yourself to Maria. Then the Blessed Mother will give us work to do. We are nothing more than her instruments. Father commanded me not to get in the way of the Blessed Mother. That is the highest love one can have for the Blessed Mother, and thus, for God."

I must confess that at that moment I was shaking with fear. To try to explain here what the nature of that fear was is an extremely difficult thing to do. To put it in a nutshell, it was because all around us there are so many people whose way of thinking is completely different from this. They take Man as the measure of how to live as a human being rather than God. We are truly living in a period when Man is the undeniable lord of Man. So, what's wrong with that? The idea that for better or worse it is a man who makes the rules for his own life and it is up to that man whether he accepts them or not has permeated all corners of society. If you were to suggest anything like the fact that it is impossible for Man to self-regulate his own life, that alone would be enough to make people think you were a traitor to the human race.

How many times in the past have I come up against this iron wall of belief in one's self only to retreat, carrying with me this mysteriously inexpressible thought? These people say rather simple-minded things like "of course I turn to the gods when times are tough," and they offer up prayers to the innumerable pagan gods when a family member is sick or dying. And, if they are lucky, and the family member recovers from the illness or even if he dies they soon forget the fact that they themselves had prayed. In such cases, a god is merely something they use to fill the cracks in human psychology.

So we can see no one is as incapable of acknowledging the imperfections of this world as they are. It really seems as if they believe that "human nature" will be darn near perfect so long as everything is politically invented or socially constructed or economically well-distributed.

But it is not true. So long as Man remains framed by human goals, he remains at a standstill. Father Kolbe's goal was God. He tried to be the best person he could in order to reach God. Every person he met and every method was mobilized for that purpose.

While it is true I've read a few theological explanations of the devotion to the Blessed Mother Mary, to be quite honest, I must say I've never been able to understand anything about theological Mariology. This devotion to Mary seems from my perspective to be about mercy (*nasake*). It's like the words to one of those popular songs that start off by calling out, "Mom!" Now, I'm not one to look down on or disparage popular songs. I am just saying that popular songs about love for one's mother are not meant to be listened to rationally. And yet Father Kolbe listened with his intellect to a song about love for his Mother.

From the perspective of someone who lacks faith, this certainly would look like a world gone mad. They might say it is just a typical folk belief. Or they might put it down as a good example of how religion is an opiate. Since I too am wary of that, my attitude is always rather ambiguous.

But Irenaeus shows that the existence of Mary is certainly neither a folk belief nor a superstition. He has said that "Christ, 'who as mediator between God and Man, makes possible for Man to entrust himself to God and for God to accept Man by leading both to friendship and reconciliation by being endowed with the nature of both,' is the perfect mediator who possesses and unites both God and Man within himself. Mary's role is to give human nature to her Son who, as God, did not possess it and to make him a member of our family, our brother."

When viewed in her most basic circumstance, Mary reveals her overflowing humanity while at the same time carrying out her task more beautifully than any other human has. Mary, who had to stand there beneath the cross and watch her own Son die for the sins of mankind, reveals the image of Man who truly needs to be lifted up out of the depths of agony and to be connected to, united with, God.

Strangely enough, there is nothing written in the Bible about Mary's death.

In "The Letters to Paula and Eustochium,"[1] which is cited in *A Primer on Marianology*,[2] Mary's death is treated as follows:

"For many of us, it is difficult to determine whether the Blessed Mother was taken up to Heaven in bodily form or whether her body was left on earth. No one has any idea about when, how, or who might have taken her corpse or where they might have moved it or whether she was bodily resurrected. Nevertheless, some people declare that the Blessed Mother rose from the dead and now exists as one who has been granted eternal life in Heaven with Christ."[3]

Be that as it may, there is something even more surprising. Father Mirochna has noticed that forty years ago the Japanese had an unbelievable, blind attachment to their ancestors. This is the emotional basis from which all aspects of the Japanese people's religious faith are derived. The question of how best to plant Christianity in Japanese soil was the most pressing issue of the day for Father Kolbe and his companions. Reflecting on those times, Father Mirochna recalled a day when Bishop Yamaguchi came to Father Kolbe to inquire how best to convey the faith to the Japanese people. Of course, Father Kolbe replied, "You are the one to know that." But I think that perhaps the cool-headed, wise Bishop Yamaguchi already knew that Father Kolbe, who had just arrived in Japan, had probably found some sort of key to that question.

The truth is that Father Kolbe had already started his work. As soon as he went out proselytizing, Father Kolbe spoke to Buddhist monks. He did so because he wanted to learn Buddhist doctrine. But Father Kolbe did not do so in order to find points of disagreement and attack them. It was his belief that in any religion one could find

---

1. St Eustochium (aka Eustochia, 368-420) was the daughter of St. Paula. The "letters" are also known as a sermon by St. Jerome to Sts. Paula and Eustochium.

2. Antonio Evangelista, *Maria ron nyūmon, Chūō Shinsho series 8* (Tokyo: Chūō Shuppan Sha, 1971).

3. Epist. IX ad Paulam et Eustochium, II, PL, 30, 123-124; cited in Antonio Evangelista, *Maria ron nyūmon*, p. 357.

through the light of truth the same, unstoppable love for mankind. That is to say, in a sense, that Father Kolbe may not have taken the matter very seriously. He was of the mind that if you at least understand the essential relationship of Man to God, then you should also understand the confluences between religions.

"This is what we mean by the spirit of ecumenism (the movement toward unity among all Christians). Father Kolbe was already doing what the Second Vatican Council laid out in 1964," Father Mirochna said quietly. That's when I hit on the key point that unlocks the secret of Father Kolbe's faith.

According to Father Mirochna, what was characteristic of Father Kolbe's faith was the idea that one could achieve perfection most quickly by going through the Blessed Mother Mary. I must confess that, as I was conducting my interviews, there was a time when I considered that a rather vulgar way of thinking. It was because I had a fleeting thought that Father Kolbe's unparalleled respect for St. Therese of Lisieux and the Blessed Mother Mary was really just something like the love a man feels for the opposite sex.

But as I talked with Father Mirochna I came to see that I was completely mistaken about that. For Father Kolbe, respect for the Blessed Mother Mary was not emotional, but the effect of rational thinking. Mary was the highest masterpiece of God's created beings. Mary was the only perfect being in all creation. That is why it is said that if you ask for Mary's intercession in your prayers to God, He always hears and grants them. Such prayers, he said, are the most efficacious because when Mary stands before God she has the power of a mother. My first reaction to all this was an extremely common one: sure, it makes sense, you go to someone with connections and influence.

"When you show respect for Mary, you are not showing equal respect for Mary and God. You are showing respect for God through Mary. Mary is the way to Jesus. Nobody put Mary to work like Father Kolbe. He completely offered himself to Mary. When we do that, we belong entirely to Mary; she does as she pleases with us. 'We have no other way to gain eternal life than to unite ourselves with the Eternal One. But if the Eternal One has never been in our same human condition, how can we unite with Him?'"

Suddenly, I became aware of a certain coincidence. The deaths of Mary and Father Kolbe bear a striking resemblance. Both were, during their time, completely unheralded events. There may have been a few dozen eyewitnesses, but they had none of the solemnity that always accompanies what the world considers an important death. It is precisely because the social background of Mary's time and Father Kolbe's time were so different that twenty-five years after Father Kolbe's death the whole world knows the circumstances of his death. But they are alike insofar as the image we have of both Mary and Father Kolbe while they were still alive is one of complete tranquility. You could even say that Father Kolbe died as a martyr for the Blessed Mother whom he loved so well.

Section Two

I'd like to introduce some of Father Kolbe's letters that give a sense of what his life in Japan was like:

September 1, 1930, Nagasaki
Beloved brothers!

I know I must reply to your latest communication that was filled with letters of congratulation, but it is just not possible. All I can do is say to everyone "you are repaying God through His Immaculate Blessed Mother . . .

In truth, we are all without exception worthless servants, and we probably don't think much about the fact that if we are not careful we will waste God's grace.

I thank those who have consecrated themselves to the carrying out of the Blessed Mother's wishes. To carry out the Blessed Mother's wishes, not our own. I pray that we will accept martyrdom for our beloved Mother, that we will be humble instruments for the realization of all that the Blessed Mother wishes, that she will grant that we will never go against her plans, and that we will always desire that which I consider the most fundamental of virtues—humility! I pray that my energies will be exhausted in this work, that she will use me as freely as a broom, and that I will see the smile of our Immaculate Blessed Mother and the whole world subject to the Blessed Mother . . .

I want to say to the most important One who lies within. Don't forget from time to time to consider what will happen to them in ten years, in seventy-five years, a hundred years later, or even two hundred years, or even a thousand years from now!

October 20, 1930, Nagasaki
Beloved brothers!

Are you really so worried about things? I never torture myself so. The reason is that I know the Immaculate Blessed Mother is always thinking of us . . .

Here, bread, potatoes, milk and such are all considered luxuries and are expensive. So, we don't even drink milk. We also have to consider the binder, mimeograph, a machine for Chinese characters, and another printer.

November 12, 1930, Nagasaki
My dear Provincial,

Nomenclature is a rather difficult matter. I say this because there is a group of Bernardino Fathers in Japan and they say they are Franciscans, so people get them confused with us. In England, they call us "separated brethren," in France, they call us "Cordeliers," and in Austria, it's "friars minor." What shall we do in Japan? How about if we call ourselves "the Friars Minor of the Immaculata"? It would be just like "St. John of the Cross" or "St. Therese of the Infant Jesus." I believe it captures well the nature of our work.

P.S. When we are busiest with work, Father Alphonso is absent so I have exempted him from the rule that we retire at ten o'clock. Do I have your permission? . . . Truly, had I not dedicated myself to the spirit of the Immaculata and the spirit of holy poverty, I think I might have lost my faith over here.

November 28, 1930, Nagasaki
My Venerable Provincial. . .

P.S. A middle-aged Japanese priest came to our friary and said, "you people are the true Franciscans." He said so because a group of Bernardinos live not far from here and they are known in Japan as Franciscans. Let us give thanks to the Immaculata and St. Francis.

I've decided to take off our white collars. The reason is that I noticed that diocesan seminarians regularly wear them. So, we've lost a bit of our elegance, but more importantly, we are now more Franciscan. This is how we'll move forward.

December 11, 1930, Nagasaki
Maria! My beloved brothers! (this was a way of addressing seminarians).

I have work to do so I will be brief. The problem is a very simple one. Exhaust your strength in your work. Work until you drop. And be thought of as crazy by your brothers. Come join us here where you will use up your vigor, tire in the work of the Blessed Mother, be scorned, and then die.

Give my regards to everyone. We put out 25,000 copies of the December issue of *Seibo no Kishi*. We are beginning to get conversions from paganism. Today, we had a Japanese applicant named Satō Shigeo. You must not fear the opinions of people. Because we are not led by people. What I really want to tell you is: *sursum corda* (lift up your hearts)! Why? Because we only have one life to live. There won't be a second chance.

January 18, 1931, Nagasaki
Brothers! (at the Niepokalanów monastery)

I rejoice at the news from the Provincial that the majority of you have given a firm reply to our decision on how to understand the meaning of holy poverty. In the past, there were, even at Niepokalanów, some points that were unclear. For example, I have never owned the land of the Prince (this refers to Prince Lubecki who owned the land where Niepokalanów is; moved by Father Kolbe's zeal, he donated the land at no cost) in any real sense. This was the result of my prayer that things would work out as the Blessed Mother wished. My brothers at Grodno, please remember that (Grodno was where many who were opposed to Father Kolbe's works were). I fear Niepokalanów becoming so rich that it could support everyone in the diocese.

In reality, this work of our Blessed Mother was established with money donated for the purpose of spreading faith in our Blessed Mother. Thus, I have the responsibility to say that no matter how holy the purpose, to use that money, even one cent of it, in a manner other than what the Immaculata intended is unjust. The reason is that we cannot use donations for any purpose other than what they were intended for when they were given to us . . .

That is why the seminarians must be firmly instructed that their goal is not to become priests under the authority of the provincial. They must be prepared to subjugate the whole world to the Sacred Heart of Christ through the Blessed Mother. This subjugation must be done as quickly as possible, and it must be accomplished through the use of all of the most modern means . . . They must not be afraid of enduring anything for the Immaculata—whether it be starvation or freezing, or even if they lose their lives under the burning sun, even if they must leave their fatherland . . .

January 30, 1931, Nagasaki
Beloved and Respected Provincial,

I reply to your letter of January 7. Because we are so far apart, our letters are always crossing in the mail. When the typewriter arrives, I'll be able to make copies so I won't have to write the same things over and over. My health isn't so bad. I had a temperature and wasn't feeling right so they took an X-ray. As you know, I'm afraid of X-rays but my brothers pushed me to do it. So I'm writing this letter right away to humor them. I'm doing my best to keep an eye on my health.

February 2, 1931, Nagasaki
Maria! My dear Father Florian . . .

Today is the Feast of the Candles[4] . . . It is now nine o'clock at night. We've already had the evening talk, examination of conscience, and Confession. I am writing . . . even as I have a certain uneasiness in my heart . . .

You see, I'm not sure that it is the Blessed Mother's wish that I write letters from here. I do not know whether it is her wish that I stay focused only on Japan, or that I consider the whole world and not forget to establish societies of the Knights [of the Immaculata] everywhere and bring more knights into them.

---

4. Or, Candlemas; more commonly known today as "The Feast of the Presentation of the Lord" or "The Feast of Mary's Purification."

In the Provincial's latest letter, he touches on the second option, so if I enumerate it:

1. Poland's Niepokalanów will take responsibility for publishing the *Knights of the Immaculata* in other European languages, particularly in English, French, and Spanish. Half of humanity reads English, and even what the blacks (sic) do is published in Chinese. A lot of people use French, and Spanish is spoken in South America. The development of the *Knights of the Immaculata* in these languages will serve to shore up the base of the propagation of the faith. That's because with the American dollar, the English shilling, and the stable currencies of South America, it should be easy to establish a Knights society, the Knights of the Immaculata, and a Niepokalanów in the countries of China, Arabia, Siam, Annam, and those under the influence of Indian languages.

2. In order to facilitate this work, we must immediately increase the brothers to more than two hundred through the *Knights of the Immaculata*. The general principle is that the number of issues of the *Knights of the Immaculata* will increase in proportion to the growth in the number of brothers. We know that various new problems will arise as we confront this problem. I myself experienced this at Niepokalanów. All the members of the Province have complained that the number of brothers is so large. But if Niepokalanów failed, what on earth would happen to these brothers? Some have even suggested that it would be more economical to set them to work in the tailoring business.

3. This may seem a matter of laziness, but it is important for the propagation of the faith that those who wish to become novices learn to ride a bicycle. And I think it would be extremely beneficial for those brother monks who want to cooperate in the work of propagation to learn to ride as well. It's really an economic way to mobilize them . . .

February 15, 1931, Nagasaki

Maria! My Dear Father Florian,

I had thought to take my time getting back to you, but I'm not sure when that would be, so I decided I'd better write right away. I'm writing even as I skim through your letter.

The truth is I am not so seriously ill. It's just that I had a high fever and wasn't feeling my usual self. . . It looks as though there are many ways in which I need to be purified. But even more important perhaps is that for me when I will die and how I will die are not the same thing.

I do not exist for myself but belong entirely to the Blessed Mother, so when the Provincial wrote to me that there was important work waiting for me, I said "non recuso" (I do not refuse).

But perhaps . . . on the Day of the Final Judgment, you will all see how many people I have corrupted, how inconsistent and negligent I have been in my work. I will work at correcting these faults, through the help of the Immaculata. May all my faults not evade the eyes of others . . ."

March 4, 1931, Nagasaki

Maria! Beloved and Respected Provincial,

. . . Today, a small statue of the Immaculate arrived from Niepokalanów. The customs official who is not yet a believer repeatedly said, while inspecting it, "my, how beautiful." And then he asked, "who is it?" and "what does it mean?"

. . . often I feel that we should add the adjective "Immaculata" to our title of the "little brothers." It's not just about the name, but to convey something of greater significance . . .

When that times comes, the various names that divide the Franciscans will disappear—"Capuchins," "Conventuals," "Observantes," etc. Then we will only be one large family known as "the Little Brothers of the Immaculata," as we will all be working together, united under the banner of the Blessed Mother. Because the Immaculata belongs to all of us, just as the very first issue of the *Knights of the Immaculata* was born from a cooperation between us and the Capuchins, Conventuals, and Bernardinos . . .

April 23, 1931, The Niepokalanów of Japan
Maria! My dear Father Florian!

I wish to offer my congratulations to you, as we have established a Niepokalanów in Japan on your patron saint's feast day. May we always be most perfect instruments of the Immaculata, whether at home or abroad!

What is better than this? We have yet to discover anything more sublime, more noble, more useful for all the souls throughout the world, nor anything more sweet to the most Sacred Heart of Jesus. Therefore, let us pray only for this, and ask our Lord only for this.

Frater Maximilian Maria Kolbe
Frater Medodo Maria
Frater Mirochna Maria
Frater Zeno Maria
Frater Hilario Maria
Frater Mariano Shigeo (Japanese)

I got Father Iwanaga Shirō . . . to come all the way to Urakami, Nagasaki from Kure. He came with Father Nakashima Manri to talk to me about Father Kolbe.

"In any case, it was the height of militarism, you see," Father Iwanaga said quietly.

"There was a lot of resistance but he was a man of quiet determination, you know. At the seminary, he offered lecturers on Scholastic philosophy. I attended them. I believe he had about ten students. He lectured in Latin. He would explain the meaning of Latin words in Latin. I believe the friars all spoke Latin among themselves.

"Ah, but the poverty was terrible. If you went there on a feast day, they would bring out a Polish sausage that had been sent to them from Poland, but that was something special. Basically they lived on straw mats spread out on plank boards. It was so bad that some who had just come out of the Ōura Church would say they thought the church pews were a luxury in comparison."

Father Nakashima picked it up from there:

"Boy, the food was really bad. All they had was stuff people had donated to them. They gave me a large bowl of some kind of rice porridge and when I finally got it down, they pushed me to have more. I really thought one bowl of that was enough.

"The cloth they used to wipe the chalice (the cup used in the Mass) was filthy dirty. That didn't bother me, but I thought it was disrespectful to God, so I suggested they get a new one, but I don't know that they could. Oh yeah, then there was the time we went for a night swim at Iōjima. There is a secluded beach there with few houses around. So they went there to swim because they didn't have a bathtub at home. At first, they went skinny-dipping. Soon enough, they started swimming in foreign long-johns and a shirt. That really got the Japanese people's attention.

"You have to understand that they were pretty filthy. Everyone had some kind of skin disease. Some of it was from mosquito bites.

They had been given a mosquito net, but they wouldn't use it. It was important to offer it up, they said.

"The land where the Seibo no Kishi [Knights of the Immaculata] is located was then just a bamboo grove, and I was there when they bought it. Mr. Zeno was there, too. Father Kolbe at that point was not yet very good at Japanese. Yet, the price went down little by little from an original asking price of one *yen* fifty *sen* for one *tsubo* to ninety *sen*. That Father Kolbe sure drove a hard bargain.

"But I doubt Father Kolbe could have done this kind of thing if he wasn't mortal. It's really a question of whether Man will work for what comes after death, or not. Yet, in spite of that, while he was alive, Father Kolbe often said, 'don't be a slave to work.' He would say, 'treat work as an extension of contemplation.'

"In my opinion, today we often make a big mistake. It is in thinking that we must express our faith mainly through work. We think if we are working, then through our work we are forgiven. Father Kolbe didn't share that way of thinking. Even though he was such a hard worker himself. On the surface, he seemed so gentle and mild, but he was a man who really loved theoretical arguments. Still, he would first show people what he could do, and persuade his opponents with the results of his actions.

"Most important was to follow this order of things:

"First, above all, one must live as perfect a life as possible as a Christian.

"Second comes prayer. Third is sacrifice. And fourth is work. Father Kolbe put these four into practice. But today people have forgotten prayer and sacrifice. And they hardly ever give a thought to living as a Christian. They really seem to think that if they just do their jobs things will turn out okay. Father Kolbe was really amazing. Because he really saw through the times but, without letting his talent go to his head, he was able to practice this order perfectly.

I returned to Tokyo. What Father Nakajima said was still ringing in my ears. But there was still something left to do. I had to ask an expert in these matters whether the miracle was really a miracle. I explained to Dr. Matsumoto Shigeki of the Second Tokyo National Hospital the data I had collected in my investigation. The case of the Marquis Ranier was compromised by the fact of his death, so I limited myself to the Crohn's disease of Signorina Testoni and asked whether this might have been something like a miracle or not. Here is what Dr. Matsumoto said:

"To vomit up fecal matter means that a part of the intestines has become stopped up and the matter can neither move forward nor back. However, on rare occasions, the stoppage can go away naturally—sort of like popping a zit—and then things can get moving again.

"Did this Testoni person say she had diarrhea that night? I see, you didn't ask about that? Well, I think she probably had diarrhea. Once things moved on through, she would rapidly get better.

"You want to know whether or not it was a miracle? I am not a believer, but theoretically it wasn't anything like a miracle. It was simply that on the day she put a picture of that priest on her stomach and prayed, at the same time a natural change in her symptoms occurred. Whether it was a miracle or not seems to me to depend on how one wants to think about it."

We've truly come back to the starting point. Does everything that happens in this world of ours come from human power or not? And if it was not a miracle but merely a "coincidence" then what really is a "coincidence" and where does it come from?

"Where did they flee when they fled from Your face?" Max Picard opens his *The Flight from God* with these words of St. Augustine, thus revealing that all throughout history Man has been running from God. Especially, he keeps running on, avoiding the face of God, while trying to find perfection in himself. But is it really possible for Man to come home when he is his own prisoner, living only within himself? What happened to Father Kolbe and to Signorina Testoni were small things. No matter how dramatic they might seem, they were really just like small stars in the cosmos. But there is a line that can be drawn from them that can form a constellation. And that constellation whispers quietly and purely the will of God. Is Man nothing but stardust? If there are stars like Father Kolbe that are able to keep shining brightly because of the depth of their contemplation, are there also dead stars?

But perhaps one day God, he who is the Pursuer, may will to end it before those who are pursued. Perhaps one day he may stand still and pursue no longer. Those in flight, though, want to fling themselves farther and farther, but they cannot, for he no longer hunts them. Now he drives them round his own still center. He is in the center and they are in flight round him as the dead moons revolve about a living star. But as God is more living than any star, so are those who flee more dead than any moon. What a spectacle: God at the center and round about him the dead moons of them that flee ever drawn to him but knowing him no longer! This, too, might be the end of the Flight . . .

"There remains only God in his full radiance, his utter clarity; and over against him is the Flight into which all dimness and all ambiguity have been driven. The more the structure of the Flight expands and the more desperately it plunges onward, the more plainly stands before us the one who is alone: God."[5]

---

5. Max Picard, *The Flight from God*, translated from the German by Marianne Kuschnitz-ky and J.M. Cameron (Chicago: Henry Regnery Company, 1951), pp. 184, 185.

Professor Kevin Doak of Georgetown University specializes in the study of nationalism and democratic thought and culture in modern Japan, as well as in the literary, cultural, and philosophical expressions of public thought and ethics. He has served as co-editor of *The Journal of Japanese Studies* and on the executive board of the Society for Japanese Studies. His writings in Japanese have been prominently published in major Japanese newspapers and journals and cited by former Prime Minister Shinzo Abe in his book *Atarashii Kuni E* (2013). Professor Doak's current research focuses on issues related to politics and religion (especially Catholicism) in modern Japan—ranging from jurisprudence to literary works and theology. The winner of the 2014 First Terada Mari Japan Study Award, Doak is frequently interviewed in Japan's leading newspapers and journals.

CPSIA information can be obtained
at www.ICGtesting.com
Printed in the USA
LVHW082132270522
719943LV00021B/1600

9 781951 319809